"I've been a Vickie Fisher fan for a long, long time, so I wasn't at all surprised to find myself enjoying her snappy dialog, cheering every lovable character... and missing them when this exciting, entertaining novel ended. Better ink your "This book belongs to..." stamp, because you're not gonna want to let this one get very far from your 'keepers' shelf. *No Regrets* is one of the most enticing novels I've read in a long time."

—*Loree Lough, best-selling author of 115 award-winning books, including* 50 Hours.

"...an excited pace, always something coming around the next page."

—*Carol A. Silvis, author/speaker*

"...one of the strongest heroines, because she sticks to her moral code and religious beliefs in the face of her steaming hot love for Nick."

—*Connie C. Scharon, Amazon best-selling author of* Enchanted Lover

NO REGRETS

VICKIE FISHER

ANGEL OF HOPE

Year of the Book
135 Glen Avenue
Glen Rock, PA 17372

ISBN 13: 978-1-945670-49-7
ISBN 10: 1-945670-49-5

Cover artwork by Michelle Tangires

Cover design by Katie Connolly Creative

This book is a work of fiction. All characters except for the spiritual hero are fictitious. If you happen to see your name, then thank you for having such an awesome name, but the character is a figment of the author's imagination.

Scripture verses are taken from the King James, New International, and English Standard Versions of the Bible.

To learn more about the author check out her website at: vickiefisher.com.

Dedication

To my children Benjamin, Sarah, and Luke.
Never give up on your dreams, no matter how long it takes.
Believe in them. They can come true.

Connie Scharon
Miracles do happen.

Acknowledgments

This book has taken a village to get it to the finish line, and I would be remiss if I didn't acknowledge those who believed in me and *No Regrets*.

First and foremost I have to acknowledge God, for creating within me the love of writing. Without Your son Jesus, nothing would be worthwhile.

My children, Ben, Sarah, and Luke—I started this book so so long ago I'm sure you begged for this day, years ago. Thank you for supporting me in my dream. For always encouraging me, helping me with my spelling and grammar, and listening to me talk about my characters. And most important, never rolling your eyes when I said I was working on *No Regrets*. I love you dearly.

Connie Scharon, you have read every version of and there have been too many to count. Thank you for pushing me, believing in me, and not letting me keep this hidden in a drawer. Thank you for never giving up on me. You are an awesome friend.

To my editor and publisher, Demi Stevens, of Year of the Book. Wow, what can I say but thank you? With your guidance, this book is beyond my wildest dreams.

To Rick Wilson, thank you for reading my book even though it wasn't in your normal genre. Your input was invaluable.

To Susan Meier and Loree Lough, thank you both for answering my many questions along the way, for reading chapters and giving me directions on where to go. Thank you for your friendship.

To Debbie Herbert, thank you for your advice, for working with me and making this book so much better.

To all my beta-readers: Carol Silvis, Connie Scharon, Megan Davis, and anyone else who read parts of the book, thank you. What would I have done without you?

To Michelle Tangires, for drawing my awesome cover.

For Katie Connolly, of *Katie Connolly Creative*, for putting my cover idea into place, and for being patient with my many revisions. You are amazing.

For my mother, Kay Thompson, who instilled in me the love of books. I miss you.

Chapter 1

Nicholas McFadden scaled the six-foot privacy fence with ease. Glock in hand, he surveyed his surroundings and hit the ground running. Stone pavers wrapped around a covered pool in the center of the yard, and benches with built-in flower boxes curved around a fire pit to his left. A pergola arched above the outdoor kitchen. He jumped the two steps of the deck. The only blind spot was to his right.

Backing against the house, he cautiously moved along the wall before stepping out, gun ready to fire. *All clear.* Returning his weapon to the holster, he felt beneath the planter for the key. Nothing. *Had his boss been wrong about the hidden key? Or did Capri get here first?*

Nick pulled out his tools to pick the lock. His hands shook. His heart pounded. He tried to insert the metal in the lock and missed. He leaned his head against the glass pane of the French door. *Focus, man, focus. It's only another day on the job.*

Taking a deep breath, he calmed the adrenaline rushing through his body. Glancing over his shoulder, he laughed at himself. The short dash across the yard hadn't caused this. It was the anticipation of seeing her again. From the moment he had heard her name—Brittany Fitzpatrick—his heart had been racing.

Get a grip, McFadden, she's just a woman. No! Not just any woman. She was his angel. The only one to make him believe in love. *Love! Where had that come from?* He mentally smacked himself on the back of the head. Love was a word for fools. *More like lust at first sight.* He smiled. Lust, no doubt about it.

Get your head in the game, McFadden. You won't be any good to her if you're dead. Nick glanced around the yard. Nothing like standing here and making himself an easy target for Capri's goons.

He forced all thoughts of the past out of his mind. In less than a minute, he jimmied the lock and slipped in. *Brittany, Brittany, Brittany, why don't you have an alarm system?* You would think the granddaughter of a judge would have more sense.

He pocketed his sunglasses, locked the door, and looked around. Open floorplans made his job so much easier. Other than the closed doors, the kitchen island created the only blind spot between the back and front entrances. Gun drawn, he looked over the countertop. *No mystery guest.*

He ran his hand down the quartz countertop. Had she made breakfast here? Nick took a deep breath, filling his lungs with the same air she'd inhaled. There was a hint of vanilla and something soft and feminine. Not the same scent he remembered. He rolled his eyes. Had he really thought her house would smell like cocoa butter?

To his right was a small alcove. A cushioned bench curved its way beneath the bay window. A half-empty cup of coffee and a newspaper sat on the table. His eyes lingered on an open Bible. *Strange.*

Cautiously, he opened each door: pantry, bathroom, and garage. He barely glanced at the baby blue sectional sofa on his way to the front of the house. To the left of the front door was a closet, her study was to the right, and at the back of the room, a single French door led to her art studio. Down the hall was a bathroom between two bedrooms, each with French doors leading to the deck. He paused, hand on the doorknob of what was surely her room. His heart skipped a beat when he entered the master bedroom. One glance at the bed and visions of what almost happened between them flooded his memory. He backed out. Nick leaned against the wall, taking a deep breath, before speaking into the microphone hidden in his watch, "All clear," he whispered, and hurried to the safety of her study.

"Wish I could say the same," his partner Miles responded. "A few minutes after she left the Maryland Institute of Art, she picked up a tail."

"Man, why can't this ever be easy?"

"We're about ten minutes away from you."

"Okay, I'm ready for her."

"After the rough time you had in Mexico, I'm surprised you took this job."

"You know me..."

"Right. Always first in line if there's a pretty woman involved."

Nick harrumphed. *If you only knew.*

The sheer curtains in the study gave him a clear view of the street. Nick cursed under his breath.

"What?"

"Capri has his boys sitting a few houses down."

"You sure?"

"Of course, I'm sure. I'd know Tommy's old Camaro anywhere, and I bet George is with him. Who does Capri have trailing Brittany?"

"Anthony and Dino." Miles said a few choice words before continuing, "Guess your pal Vincent figured this would be a quick grab and go. If he'd known you were on the job, he would have sent his A-team, not his goof squad." Miles chuckled. "Can you imagine what Capri is going to do when he finds out you've taken her right out from under his nose?"

"I plan to be long gone before then. Tell me again why I'm here. Wouldn't it have been easier to pick her up from work?"

"Too many people at MICA. You know full well the Capris have no problem killing innocent bystanders. Plus, Carl and her grandfather think you'll have more than enough time to allow her to pack a bag..."

"What! Are they crazy?"

"Her normal routine is to go for a run about a half hour after getting home. That's your window to get her out of there. Any longer and they'll get tired of waiting and come in after her."

"Half an hour is more than enough time. She knows I'm here, doesn't she?"

"Her grandfather is taking care of telling her."

"Good. I hate surprises." Nick glanced around the study. Bookshelves lined the wall behind her desk and her artwork hung on the opposite side of the room. A painting of a woman kneeling in prayer with Jesus standing in front of her, His hand on her head, caught Nick's attention. Had she gotten religious? Two framed photographs sat on her desk. He picked up the family photograph and traced the outline of her face, whispering, "Brittany Fitzpatrick." *It's time to finish what we started.*

"Ever since Carl mentioned her in the briefing, I've had the feeling I've heard her name before. Do you remember her?"

Ignoring Miles' question, Nick said, "We'll be going out the back door. Make sure it's clear." Nick muted the microphone. No need to have Miles hear their reunion. He studied the photo. Age had not erased the sweet innocent look that haunted his dream. It had been years since their brief interlude. Ten years and plenty of unfinished business between them.

Beside Brittany stood her cousin, Carissa Hathaway. The two of them made a striking contrast—Carissa the green-eyed blonde, and Brittany the blue-eyed brunette—though their looks weren't what set them apart. Even in the picture, you could see the difference. The scheming Carissa, and the sweet...

No! He wouldn't let those innocent blues deceive him again. Brittany had the look of an angel, but he knew firsthand she could be every bit as cunning and conniving as Carissa. He put the photograph down. "This time, sweetheart," he said, watching her red Mustang pull into the driveway, "I'm prepared for you."

Was he? Then why was his heart pounding? He turned from the window, no time to wonder; in a few minutes, he would be face to face with his angel. Or his demon.

Stepping from her Mustang, Brittany glanced around. Ever since she'd left school, she had an eerie sensation of being watched. Although she hadn't seen anyone following her, she couldn't shake the feeling. She palmed the small canister of mace attached to her key ring. Roland Park was a safe neighborhood, but it didn't hurt to be cautious.

Brittany grabbed her briefcase, purse, and the stack of art folders then hurried up the walk. A gust of cold air blew her long hair into her face and threatened to rip the folders from her hands. Her tights felt frozen to her legs. She should have pulled into the garage. At least it would have protected her from the wind and prying eyes. She scrutinized the few cars parked down the street. *Stop being a paranoid baby.*

She fumbled with the front door key and heard the inside phone ring. Entering the house, she slammed the door shut with her butt, and quickly locked it. Dropping her briefcase by the door and the folders on the hall table with her keys, she rushed to the telephone.

"Hello," she said breathlessly. "Hello?" The only answer was a dial tone. She checked caller ID—her grandfather. She would call him back in a few minutes, after her nerves calmed.

What's wrong with you? She double-checked the lock before hanging her coat in the closet. Peeking out the glass panel beside the door, she glanced up and down the street. Nothing. As she turned from the door, the nape of her neck tingled. Maybe instead of a run, she ought to start grading these art projects. It would be much safer.

Eyeing the mace, she said a silent prayer. *Dear Heavenly Father. You've taught me to trust my instincts... so if you're trying to tell me something... now would be a good time!*

Picking the mace up along with everything but her purse, she took a deep breath. At the study, she pushed the door open with her foot. A few steps into the room, she heard a movement behind her. Panic spun her around; dropping everything but the mace, she sprayed wildly and lunged for the door which clicked shut behind her.

A man's arm came down around her, pinning her against him. His other hand grabbed hers as he fought for control of the canister. The spray hit her face. Brittany screamed. Her lungs were on fire. The canister dropped to the floor.

She gasped for breath, tears streaming down her face. She couldn't open her eyes. Her attacker held both her hands firmly in one of his. There was no escape. Suddenly she was lifted from the floor. Her legs kicked, but it was as if it didn't even faze him. She barely registered the opening of the study door, and then they were running. Fear like nothing she had ever felt gripped her. Where was he taking her? *Please God, not the bedroom!*

A quiet voice in her spirit whispered, *Be still.*

A calm settled over Brittany. God was with her. The attacker released his hold on her hands. As he put her down, she lunged away, hitting something hard, she reached out, feeling for a way out. She was in the bathroom; the door was to her right. Could she escape? His arm came back down around her, pinning her between him and the sink. She heard the faucet, and then felt his hands splashing water into her face. "Keep this up until the burn stops."

Confusion swirled through her. Why was her abductor being nice?

The man pulled her hair away from her face. "I'm sorry, angel."

Brittany's heart constricted, whether from fear or excitement, she couldn't tell. She recognized that voice. She forced her eyes open. Glancing into the mirror, she couldn't trust her vision. "Nick?"

He grinned. "Wasn't sure you would remember me. It's been a long time."

"Has it?" She tried to calm her pounding heart.

"Ten years, four months and..."

"You know how long it's been?" she sputtered in surprise.

Nick winked. "I never forget unfinished business."

The last time they were together, they had almost... Brittany watched color flush across her cheeks. His body pressed up behind her. She shut her eyes. His closeness made it impossible to think. She tried to move away, but his arms were around her, his hands holding hers.

Nick stepped back. He reached for the soap. "Wash the mace off your hands and face." He went to the second sink and did the same. "Do you always carry mace inside your house?"

"Why are you in my house?"

"I'm rescuing you."

Brittany cringed at the sight of her red face and swollen eyes then glanced at Nick's reflection in the mirror. "Looks like the only person I need rescuing from is you!"

"I'm sorry." Nick's hand brushed hers and a spark sped straight to her heart. He jerked his hand away, but his gaze held. Gingerly, he placed his hand on her elbow, guiding her out of the bathroom and back to the study. A few steps from the window, he stopped and pointed.

"See that car a few houses down? Inside it are Tommy and George, Vincent Capri's men."

Brittany involuntarily touched her shoulder. The bullet Vincent had meant for Nick had hit her instead. She thought after saving Nick, he would have forgiven her, but he hadn't. "What makes you think I need rescuing from someone sitting in a car?"

"They're waiting for you to go for your afternoon run. Once you do, they'll start to follow you, and when you turn the corner there are two others waiting to grab you." He glanced at his watch. "We only have about twenty minutes before they get restless and come looking for you."

"How do you know that?"

"Because I know how they think." He guided her back toward the door, "We have to go, before they get tired of waiting."

Brittany jerked her arm away. "What do they want with me?"

"Haven't you been listening to the news?"

She shook her head.

"The Capris were released from prison this morning."

"Impossible."

"Well they're out and the first thing on their agenda is revenge." Nick looked at Brittany. "They vowed to make your grandfather pay for their heavy sentencing."

"An idle threat."

Nick picked up the photograph of her parents from her desk. "Your parents were killed by a family member of someone your father sent to jail, and you talk about idle threats." Putting the picture back, he continued, "Capri's men are sitting right outside your door, and unless you want to hang around to see how idle that threat is, I'd advise we get out of here. We've wasted too much time already."

Backing away from him, she said, "How do I know you aren't with them? You break into my house and attack me."

"Whoa, *you* attacked *me*. I just defended myself."

"You were hiding behind the door. What did you expect me to do? Turn around and say, 'Hi Nick, nice to see you'?"

He laughed. "I wasn't hiding. You opened the door, as I was about to—" He touched her arm, "We need to get out of here."

She took a step back, hitting the wall. "I'm not going anywhere with you!"

"Why not?"

"The last time I saw you, you were making a drug deal with Vincent Capri and now I'm supposed to believe you just happened into my house to save me from him?"

He pointed to the bulletproof vest with PSA written across the front. "If this isn't proof enough that I'm with the good guys, then you probably won't believe this either." Reaching inside his bomber jacket, he pulled out a leather case. With one easy motion, he flipped it open, and handed her his Private Security Agency's badge. Brittany studied it front and back. She knew how easy it was to get a fake ID. But a vest?

"Happy?" Nick placed his hands on the wall beside her shoulders. Although he wasn't touching her, he had her pinned. She could barely breathe. The rich warmth of his expression was straight from her dream. He gently ran a finger down her cheek to her lips. She closed her eyes. This wasn't the Nick she had fallen in love with.

She smacked his hand away. "Don't touch me."

His arm came down on her shoulder. "Time's a wasting, and we need to go." He guided her down the hall. "I have orders to let you pack something. I recommend doing it quickly." Pausing at the door to her bedroom, he added, "I believe this is your room." His eyes ran the length of her, taking in her sweater dress, tights, and ankle boots. "That dress is very becoming, though you could do without the tights." A soft smile crossed his lips. "It's a shame to cover up..." He laughed. "Never mind. Unless you want to climb the fence in your dress, I would advise you change."

"Why would I be climbing the fence?"

"It's not like we can walk out the front door now, can we?"

"I'm not undressing with you in the room!"

"That's not what you said ten years ago."

"A lot has changed in ten years." She glared at him. "I'm not the same foolish child." Someone needed to tell her heart that. It felt like the same foolish heart.

Nick laughed. Sitting on her bed, he nodded toward the bathroom. "Change quickly. We have to go."

Grabbing her clothes, she entered the bathroom and slammed the door.

"Hope you grabbed something comfy. It's a long drive to your family's Colorado estate," he called out, loud enough for her to hear through the door.

Brittany quickly changed into black yoga pants, a long blue sweater, and white t-shirt. Coming from the bathroom, she asked, "There's no place safe between here and Colorado?"

She tried not to look at Nick lying on her bed. She had dreamed of this day, prayed for this day, but not like this. In her dream, he swept her off her feet, told her he loved her, and they lived happily ever after.

He checked his watch. "Five minutes to get out of here. I'll help you pack." He rose from the bed. "What's this?" he said, picking up a book from her nightstand. Brittany bolted across the room, grabbing for it. Nick laughed and held it over her head. "Hot book, huh? Let's see." He opened it at the bookmark and his mouth fell open. He scooped up the photo booth pictures taken the last day they had been together. "You still have these?"

"Obviously." She tried to grab them.

He held the photos over his head. "Any reason why you use them as your bookmark?"

"No!" How could she tell him in every book she read, her hero had his face? Not that she needed the pictures to remember what he looked like; the vision of him was branded forever into her heart.

"Interesting." Putting the photo strip into his jacket's inner pocket, he said, "We'll finish this later." Looking at his watch, he added, "Get your overnight bag. Now." The house phone rang. "Don't you have a cell phone?"

She started toward the ringing. "Of course I do, but I forgot to turn it back on when I left school. It's probably my grandfather again."

"You can call him from the car." Nick rolled his eyes. "He was just going to tell you about me." He rushed her out of the room and back into the study. A quick look out the window confirmed Capri's henchmen were still waiting. "Ironic, isn't it? Every time we meet, Vincent

Capri is involved. Just think if you hadn't blown my bust..."

"So, you haven't forgotten?"

"Forgotten! I almost had him red-handed, until you showed up."

Brittany put her hands on her hips. "How was I to know you weren't a lifeguard, but a D.E.A. agent?"

"What were you doing there anyway?"

"Instead of condemning me, you should be thankful. If not for me, you'd be dead." Brittany backed out of the study.

Nick punched the air. "Idiot."

"What!"

Nick pointed to his earpiece. Unmuting his microphone, Nick grabbed Brittany by the hand. "Let's go."

Brittany reached for her purse just as the front door shattered. Nick spun, pulling her behind him.

"McFad—"

Nick fired. The gunman fell backward, blood spattering everywhere.

Brittany threw her hands over her mouth, trying not to scream. Her purse fell to the floor. Nick's arm wrapped around her waist, half lifting her, and made a dash to the kitchen. "Get behind the island as fast as you can." They were almost there when the back door flew open. Nick shoved her behind the island and started firing.

Brittany cowered in fear. *Please God, help us.*

She jumped when Nick touched her arm. "Let's go, sweetheart."

"Is it over?"

"No, this is just the beginning." Nick paused at the back door. "Miles, where are you?"

"Chasing after Anthony. Not sure where Dino is."

Warily, Nick checked the backyard before taking Brittany by the hand and leading her from the house. Brittany froze as they started down the steps, panic rising at the sight of another dead man. She wanted to scream, but nothing came out.

"Brittany, look at me. Look at me." He lifted her face. "Don't look at him." He wrapped his arm around her, shielding her from the body. Pushing her in front of himself, he said. "Run for the fence."

She took off, Nick right on her heels. Before he could boost her over the fence, someone yelled, "Look out!"

Nick pushed her to the ground. She watched in horror as the man fired and another man fell through the covered pool. Nick gave the man a quick nod of thanks and she saw him raise three fingers. Were there more?

He helped her up and over the fence. No sooner had he cleared it, than another shot rang out. Nick threw his arm around Brittany, his body sheltering her as they hid behind a woodpile. Crouching in fear, Brittany never stopped praying. Somewhere above the pounding of her heart, she heard the faint sound of a siren. *Thank you, God, for sending help.*

"Let's go before Vincent calls in reinforcements."

Brittany tried to calm the hysteric sobs in her throat. "The police are coming. We'll be safe now."

"You're safer with me."

"Am I?"

"No time to argue." Nick grabbed her hand and started to run. She stumbled. "Need me to carry you?"

She shook her head. Not missing a stride, he wrapped his arm around her waist. She had no choice but to run with him.

"The car is just beyond this yard." He gave her a reassuring squeeze. "You'll be safe then."

She stared at the gun in his hand. Fear swirled through her. *Please God, protect us from all harm.*

Chapter 2

"Get in," Nick said, opening the passenger side of a black Porsche. As Brittany slid inside, he shut and locked her door. Sliding across the hood, Nick quickly jumped in the car. Brittany's hands were shaking as she tried to buckle her seatbelt. Nick moved her hand. "I got it," he said, and snapped the belt in place. Speaking into his watch he shouted, "Miles! Where are you?"

"I'll be behind you in a minute."

Nick looked in his rearview mirror. "What happened back there?"

"Anthony took a phone call then got out of the car and walked straight toward me. Someone tipped him off. Once he spotted me, he started running toward the house."

"Don't like it." Nick looked in the rearview again. "Stay a couple cars behind. I'll let you know when you can drop back." He muted the microphone. Brittany slouched in her seat, trembling. She jumped when Nick touched her shoulder. "Relax, you're safe now."

Her body shook uncontrollably, and she covered her face with her hands. "They tried to kill us." A moan broke free. "You shot him."

He stroked her hair, "Don't think about it."

"I'm going to be sick." She threw her hand over her mouth.

Nick pulled into a convenience store parking lot. Brittany jumped out, ran to a trashcan, and vomited. Nick stood guard, his hand behind his back gripping his gun. He was ready if anyone pulled into the parking lot.

She started sobbing. "I'm sorry."

Nick caressed her back. "It's okay." He relaxed slightly when Miles' black Corvette pulled in beside them.

Miles hopped out. "Looks like the four guys back at the house are the only ones Capri sent."

Nick watched the cars driving by. "We don't have much time before whoever tipped them off figures out she got away."

"I'm thinking about ten minutes, tops."

Nick nodded. "Time enough to get her something to drink and some mints to settle her stomach."

Miles returned a few minutes later and tossed a Red Bull at Nick. "Figured you might need this."

"Thanks." Nick placed the drink on the roof of the car.

"She okay?" Miles asked as he handed Nick the bag.

"She will be." Nick glanced inside.

Miles shrugged his shoulders, "I didn't know what she likes to drink so I picked up one of everything." He handed Brittany some napkins. "Thought you might need these."

"Thanks," she said without lifting her head.

Nick tossed a Gatorade to Miles, and handed Brittany a Coke.

"I don't..."

"It will help settle your stomach." He rubbed her back. "You think you're alright to get back on the road?"

Miles opened his car door, "I'll do a once around the block, before falling in behind you."

Nick nodded as he held the door open for Brittany. Inside the car, she looked in the bag by her feet. She tried to laugh, but it came out as a sob. "We won't get thirsty."

Nick placed the Red Bull in the cup holder. "Leave it to Miles." He backed out of the parking spot, and inched his way back into Baltimore traffic. Brittany looked at the car beside them then slouched in her seat. Nick patted her leg. "You can breathe. You're safe now."

She peeked around the seat to the street behind them.

"No one's following us."

"How do you know?" She glanced from him to the cars around them.

"I know." Nick laid his hand on her leg. "I promise you. You're in good hands."

With a shaking hand, she removed his hand from her leg. "Keep your hands on the wheel, please." The alarm rose in her voice. "Why aren't we heading to the airport?"

"Capri will be expecting you to show up there. Think about it, you'd make an easy target while we're waiting to board the plane."

"You know I have a private jet, don't you?"

Nick glanced at her in surprise. "You have a jet?"

Nick whistled and thought about it for a minute. He could have her to Colorado in a few hours, and then be back home before daybreak. He glanced at her from the corner of his eye. But then he would have to say goodbye before he even had a chance to say hello. Her safety was his main concern, not his selfishness. *Wasn't it?* He thought about it for a few minutes, going over it in his mind. Suddenly he said, "Not a good idea."

"Why not?"

"I'm sure Vincent knows you have a jet."

"You didn't. Why would he?"

"As I understand it, Carissa is still involved with Vito Capri. Do you think she could have told him about your plane?"

Brittany sighed. "Yes, they've even used it a few times."

"Then we keep driving."

"Can I use your cell phone?" She attempted to laugh, "Seems like I dropped everything in the rush to leave my house.

"Who do you want to call?"

"My grandfather."

"I don't think so."

"He'll be worried."

"If his phone is bugged, it's better for him to worry. I want a big head start on Capri before he knows you got away."

"Like he doesn't know already."

"If he did, we wouldn't have gotten away so easily."

"You call that easy?"

"Yes. We were lucky there were only four of them. If I know Vincent, he's home in his study toasting himself for the success of your capture."

"But I'm not captured." She glanced warily at him, "Am I?"

"Stop looking at me like I'm the big bad monster." He reached over the console laying his hand on her leg. "You never looked at me like that before."

Once again, she removed his hand. "Ten years is a long time. People change."

"Well, I promise you I haven't changed." He winked. "I'm still the charming guy you knew and loved back then." He grinned as her cheeks turned red. "As for Capri, he isn't going to be too happy when he finds out you're with me."

She wondered how safe she really was. Sure, he had saved her from Capri, but who would save her from him? She stared out the window. These feelings were nothing more than a rehash of old memories. She had to keep her head out of the clouds and focused on reality.

Nick weaved in and out of the Baltimore traffic. As they stopped for a red light, she looked at him suspiciously, "You said I'm not captured, yet I'm not allowed to use the phone. I'm locked in and going someplace against my will, so what do you call it?"

Nick laughed.

She slid closer to the door.

"You can trust me." He reached across, gently turning her face toward him. "My job is to get you safely to your grandfather's compound. Until we get there, you'll have to do things my way. You can start by trusting me." Nick gave her an injured look. "Sweetheart, you know I would never hurt you."

The light turned green and they started moving again. Brittany stared out the window. A couple walked arm in arm down the street. *Never hurt me!* Had he forgotten how devastated she had been when he laughed at her declaration of love? Or the pain she felt when moments after they had nearly made love he left her for another? Maybe he just didn't care, but why should he? To him, their relationship had been nothing more than "a nice interlude from life." *Some interlude.* Her heart had never gotten over Nick. Though others had tried, they could never completely wipe his memory from her heart. Their kisses had lacked the fire, their touch didn't send her to the brink of ecstasy. No, she hadn't forgotten Nick. Her dreams were full of him. Only in her dreams, Nick didn't walk away. Instead of saying, *"Love is a word for fools,"* he returned her love.

Looking at him from under her lashes, she wondered why he above all others could awaken this deep longing inside her. Was it his raw masculine strength that promised to protect her? Or the hint of danger that showed in his eyes? Whatever the reason, Nicholas McFadden had once again stirred the emotions she thought were dead. A fact she found disturbing.

What's wrong with you? Since when have you let a handsome face turn your head? She silently laughed. Handsome was an understatement. Age had only improved the man she once believed to be perfect. She visualized her hands releasing his dark wavy hair from its ponytail, traveling across the firm set of his jaw. His five o'clock shadow would feel rough against her hands when she held his face and gazed into his large brown eyes. She sighed. Gone was the cold blackness of danger. In its place, were eyes as warm and inviting as cocoa on a cold winter day.

Her gaze lowered to his muscular chest. A vest covered it now, but she remembered all too well the playground of black hair there. She shivered as she imagined her hands entangled in paradise.

His powerful hands barely held the wheel. The car responded to his slightest touch. Her eyes lingered on his hands and she thought of that touch, the feel of his body pressed against hers. She felt the heat rise as her eyes traveled down his stomach. She could feel the essence of his virility wrapping itself around her.

"Do us both a favor and drop those thoughts."

"What?"

"You have the same look in your eyes that almost got us in trouble ten years ago."

"Whatever thoughts you think I have, you're mistaken."

"Am I?"

"Yes!"

"We'll see." His seductive smile made her weak.

Brittany looked out the window. The setting sun brought with it a mixture of warmth and coldness, just like Nick. *Brittany, get ahold of yourself. These feelings are just a mixture of gratitude and old memories, nothing more. Nicholas McFadden is not your type.* Closing her eyes, she prayed. *Please God, you know the temptation this man is to me. Please, please, please give me the strength to fight this battle within me.*

Nick's cell phone rang, and Carl Miller's name came across the car's caller ID. "I sent you to keep her safe, not get her killed!" his anger flowed through the speakers.

"She is safe."

The second Brittany heard his voice, her voice choked up. "Uncle Carl—"

Nick glanced at Brittany in surprise. *Uncle?* He mouthed.

"Brittany, are you hurt?"

"No, just glad to hear your voice."

"I'm sorry you had to experience this ordeal, but I assure you, you are in good hands. I wouldn't have sent Nick after you if he wasn't the best."

"I know."

"Nick, we were expecting you at the airport."

"I think it's safer to drive. I'm sure Vincent knows about her plane."

"You're probably right. Are you in the Porsche?"

"Yes."

"Great. Be safe. Brittany, I'll see you at your grandparents' compound."

After Carl hung up, Nick said, "Carl is your uncle?"

"Not by blood. He's my grandfather's best friend, and was my mother's godfather, so he's like an uncle."

Nick unmuted his mic as he made a left-hand turn. "I'm heading up Falls Road, and taking the back roads over to Hampstead," he said to Miles. "You can head back to face Carl."

"Thanks. Why do I always get the hard part?"

Nick chuckled. "I'll call you later about a meeting place."

"Be safe."

"Always." Nick removed the earpiece and turned off the mic. He patted Brittany's leg. "It's just you and me for now."

For the next hour, the silence was only broken by the voice of the GPS. Westminster came into sight.

"I can't believe it's taken us two hours to get this far," Brittany said. "At this pace, we won't ever get out of Maryland."

"By now Capri knows you're gone. The first place he'll be looking for you is the Interstate and the airport. He won't be expecting us to be traveling backroads."

"Well, I think you even confused the GPS." She smiled. "I know you lost me a few times."

He laughed and patted the device on the dash. "Bessie knows where we're going."

"You named your GPS?"

He grinned. "Of course."

"So where is Bessie taking us?"

"To my cabin in Tennessee. If I get too tired, we'll stop for the night. Otherwise, we'll drive straight through."

"I know there's a shorter way to Colorado than through Tennessee."

"There is, but Vincent doesn't know about my cabin. He does know where your grandparents live, so it's safer to continue going the most indirect route." Abruptly, he swung into a convenience store with gas pumps and pulled up to the tanks. "After I get gas, we can go in and use the bathrooms and get something to eat. I know it's not fancy, but their food is good, and it's fast. The less we're in public, the safer you'll be. If that's okay with you?"

"I'm okay with that."

Brittany found it hard not to watch his every move. While the gas was pumping, he opened the trunk. When he closed it, his PSA vest was gone. Instead of going back to the pump, he came to her side of the car. He stood tall and straight, ready to pounce at the first sign of trouble. When the tank was full, Nick slid back inside.

He grinned, "Ready for some fine dining?" He pulled up to the side of the store. "Stay in the car until I come around to get you."

She saluted him. He chuckled.

Opening her door, he said, "Stay close to me."

"Thought we were safe here?"

"Never hurts to be cautious." He grinned, putting his arm around her shoulders. "This is how we used to walk together."

Brittany remembered all too well how they used to be. She didn't need a reminder of how perfect it felt with his hand around hers, his arms holding her close, the fire... She was grateful when they entered the store.

Inside, they ordered food before heading to the restrooms. Nick opened the door to the women's room. "Good, only a one-seater." Holding the door for her, he said. "Don't come out until I knock."

Sarcastically, Brittany said, "You trust me not to climb out the window?"

Nick laughed. "Sweetheart, you're in the middle of nowhere, no purse, no money." He glanced at her. "Man! And no coat. I'll give you mine when we leave here." He leaned down and whispered in her ear. "Need it myself right now to hide my gun."

She slammed the bathroom door in his face.

Back in the car together, Nick removed his jacket and tossed it behind the seat. She nibbled on her burger, but wasn't really hungry. She watched him devour his sandwich and fries. Leaning her head against the back of the seat, she continued to stare. He looked so much like the Nick of ten years ago; she wondered if one little kiss could chase the heartache away?

"It's a little hard to eat with those icy blues of yours melting all over me," Nick grinned as he looked into her eyes. The air charged with an electric current, momentarily pulling them back to a time when love was all that mattered.

The urge to pull her close, to feel her lips upon his was overwhelming. Nick closed his eyes, hoping to crush the feeling. Instead, memories of a starry night with her in his arms assailed him. The sweet fragrance of her perfume drifted around him. Without another thought, Nick drew her close. Taking her chin in his hand, his fingers gently caressed her lips. So soft and full, lips like strawberries waiting to be devoured.

Her heart pounded against his chest, or was it his? He couldn't tell. It was as if their hearts had somehow joined and were beating as one. Nick jerked away. Grabbing the door handle, he all but jumped out of the car and slammed the door shut. *McFadden, get a grip. This is a job and nothing more. A job!*

Taking a few deep breaths, he tried to still the hammering in his heart. Glancing inside at Brittany, he wondered why she made his heart act so peculiarly. He laughed to himself. Whatever it was, this time it wouldn't work. She had made a fool of him once, but not again. Those sparkling orbs of blue would not deceive him twice. Nick reached into his pocket for his cell phone, and walked a few feet away from the car.

Brittany's heart ached. What had stopped him from kissing her? She gingerly touched her lips. The nearness of his mouth had only confirmed what she already knew—feelings she once had for him were in full bloom. Nothing had changed. His pulling away reinforced his words ten years ago. "*Sweetheart, you have no place in my life. You're not what I'm looking for.*" How many times had she prayed for a second chance with Nick, a chance to prove him wrong? Now that chance had arrived, and she was nothing more than a job. The next few days were going to be long ones.

After a few minutes, he returned. The tension between them could be cut with a knife. Pulling from the parking lot, Nick pushed the button on the radio. The DJ was saying "...the resident of the house, Brittany Fitzpatrick, has yet to be located. An eyewitness saw her last getting into a black Porsche."

Nick's fist hit the steering wheel. "Someone at P.S.A. didn't do their job."

"What job?"

"Keeping things out of the news."

"What difference does it make? You already said Vincent would know by now."

Nick stared at her. "He will not only know you escaped, but that you had help. It won't take him long to figure out who's the owner of the Porsche."

"After all this time, I think he knows already."

"As long as he thought you were alone, he wouldn't be too worried. You're very predictable."

"I am not."

He raised an eyebrow. "Every morning at five you run six miles, except for Monday and Wednesday, when you run in the evenings, always the same route. Each day you leave for MICA where you teach art. You're home every day no later than four, leaving again to go to your Arts Center, returning home most evenings by nine. Shall I continue?"

"Why does P.S.A have a file on me?"

"Your grandfather has used us to protect your cute little butt from time to time, so occasionally they've updated your file." He gave her a sly look. "It really does pay to have friends, or should I say, a grandfather in high places."

"What is that supposed to mean?"

"Your little stunt with Capri isn't even mentioned."

"My stunt, what is that supposed to mean?"

"You don't find it strange that you helped a known drug dealer escape and there is no mention of it in your file?"

"Why would it be? My innocence was never in question."

Nick gripped the steering wheel. "Wasn't it?"

Brittany folded her arms across her chest. "I did save your life!"

"And I yours." His eyes were black. Gone was all the warmth of a few moments ago. "Maybe that's why Vincent chose you. He's ready for his payback."

"I think you've been in the spy business too long. I'm sure Vincent doesn't even remember me pushing him off the pier."

"Don't underestimate Vincent Capri."

"Is that a warning?"

"No, a fact. Vincent hates to lose."

"What did he lose? He got away with the drugs and a quarter million dollars. I think he would thank me, not kill me for my unwitting help."

"You're wrong. When you pushed Vincent, he dropped the briefcase full of cocaine into the ocean."

"Well, he still got the money, didn't he?"

"How do you know how much money it was?"

"Because I counted it."

Part of him wanted to believe her sarcasm. But from the moment he'd first heard her name, every ounce of his instincts had been on full alert. Ten years ago, he had fallen for her sweet innocence. When she looked at him with eyes that could have come directly from heaven, he wanted to believe every word she said, but he knew better. He'd learned the hard way. Brittany Fitzpatrick was capable of lying to get what she wanted.

Vincent's brothers had been released from prison because of their association with Brittany's cousin, Carissa. Judge Hathaway should have recused himself, but didn't. Their lawyer had claimed a mistrial. Carissa and Brittany always did everything together. He glanced across at Brittany. Was she involved with the Capris? Unnerved, Nick looked in the rearview mirror, but there was nothing. He'd been in this business long enough to know that just because you didn't see your opponent, didn't mean he wasn't around. He knew they were out there waiting. He could feel it. He could only hope the woman beside him wasn't part of some evil scheme.

"Here." Nick reached under his seat and pulled out a folder. "Here's something I find very interesting. Ten years ago, we were the same age. Now you're four years younger than me." He dropped the folder on her lap. "Care to explain?"

"I had a fake ID."

"I examined that ID. It looked real."

"It was real, all but the date."

"So, another deception."

"I never deceived you."

"Really? How do you figure hiding the fact that you had a boyfriend isn't deceptive?" He glared at her. "By the way, how is Theodore?"

"If you had let me explain then, you would have known I'd broken up with him."

"What, like three seconds after I left you two on the beach?"

He couldn't help but shiver at her icy stare.

"Unless you plan on stopping the car and letting me out, you have no choice but to finally listen to the truth."

"Of course, I'm not letting you out."

She took a deep breath. "Yes, that first night I met you, I had a boyfriend." She twisted her hands together. "But the next morning I broke up with him."

He glanced at her in disbelief. "Why?"

"Because I never would have fallen so in... been so captivated by you, if I had loved him."

"Then why did he show up claiming to be your boyfriend?"

"I wouldn't answer or return his calls, so he decided to come after me." She touched Nick's arm. "I tried to tell you, but you refused to listen."

Nick nodded. "I was so angry." He laid his hand on hers. "I'm sorry. If I hadn't—"

"There are no ifs." She twirled her hair around her finger. "Only what was." She turned her head and stared out the window.

The pain he'd heard in her voice echoed the pain in his heart. He gripped the steering wheel. If he hadn't been such a hot head. He shook his head. That still didn't explain why she never visited him in the hospital. If she had loved him like she claimed, where was she? He wasn't sure if he could handle the answer.

Chapter 3

Nick rubbed his hand over his face. His eyes felt heavy. He cracked the car window, letting in the cold night air. He glanced at Brittany sleeping. The moon cast a heavenly glow about her. If only he were the moon, his hands could dance through her silky, brown hair, his fingers could caress the softness of her delicate face. Then he would wrap his arms around her like moonbeams and drink in the beauty of her body next to his. He brushed a strand of hair from her face. His fingers slid down her cheek. She smiled the same soft, sensual curl of her lips that had lured him from the beginning. All this time, and she still had the power to stir his deepest desires.

He shook his head. Lack of sleep was playing with him, and the best thing he could do was stop at the next motel before his foolish heart convinced his brain to fall for her again. He frowned. He had believed the fairytale, until it came crashing down around him.

Her betrayal was nothing compared to the torment of believing she was dead. He shivered. The memory of Brittany jumping between him and Vincent Capri, and taking the bullet meant for him, still caused his heart to scream in anguish. The image of her falling off the pier and into the ocean was haunting. He had jumped in after her, only to have Vincent pepper the water with bullets. How had they survived? *Survived?* It echoed like a scream through him. For seven years, he believed he'd been unable to save her. Her tear-stained face had haunted him. Her declaration of love echoed through his mind.

He looked at her sleeping face, and his heart leapt with joy. She was alive and here with him now. His angel.

For a moment, a dark cloud blocked the moonlight, causing a shadow to cross her face—a vivid reminder of the darkness lurking within the light. He looked up. Was the moon trying to tell him she was his demon after all? The past held too many unanswered questions. The main one being, if she loved him, why hadn't she visited him in the hospital? Had she been working for the Capris and her love was just an act? From the moment he had discovered she wasn't dead, he had believed in her guilt, but now he longed to believe in her innocence. "My angel or my demon?" he whispered. He growled at the moon, "This is all your fault."

His headlights caught the side of a barn. Nick slowed down. Maybe they ought to hide there for the night. No! He vetoed that immediately; a Porsche was no place to sleep. How Brittany managed it was beyond him. Rounding the bend, he saw the neon sign of a motel.

Parking, he turned to Brittany. "Sweetheart." He touched her shoulder. "Wake up."

"Where are we?" she asked between yawns.

"A motel. I need some sleep."

Brittany stretched and looked around her. Half the lights on the sign were out. A piece of cardboard covered a broken window in the first of a long row of dark run-down cottages. She suppressed a scream when a rat scurried from the compost heap beside the office. "I'm not staying here!"

"Yes, you are."

"Give me the keys. I'll drive."

"No!"

"Then I'm sleeping in the car."

"Listen, princess. This isn't open for discussion." Getting out of the car, he said, "I need sleep."

"You wouldn't be so tired if you weren't zigzagging your way to wherever we are going."

Nick slammed the car door, ignoring her. He impatiently rang the bell on the motel door. After what seemed like forever, an old man opened it. "We'd like a cottage for the night."

The man squinted at Brittany sitting in the car. "A hundred bucks."

"A hundred!"

The man looked at the Porsche. "Take it or leave it."

Nick handed him the money. With a grin, the guy dumped a basket of keys on the counter and turned to leave. "Take your pick," he said, turning to go back to his bed.

"You don't want to know which one?"

"Don't know, don't care. Leave the key in the room when you're finished." He yawned.

Nick looked at the numbers and grabbed the last set. "Night."

The old man lifted a hand and mumbled, "Young lovers, waking me up all hours of the night." He hobbled back to his room chuckling. "And always willing to pay the price."

Nick drove to the last cottage. Nick opened her car door. "Let's go." Brittany dragged her feet, Nick grabbed her by the hand, and pulled her along.

"All the others full?" Brittany asked as Nick unlocked the door. "If I see one roach I'm leaving."

Nick flipped on the light. "Not a bug in sight. Lock up, I'll be back."

"Where are you going?"

"To hide the car."

"I'm not staying here alone."

"Let's get something straight, princess. I call the shots, not you. Lock up behind me. I'll be back in five minutes." He shut the door and reopened it. "I said lock it."

"You just shut it!"

"It only takes a second for someone to push the door open."

"Give me a break. No one knows where we are, and if they did, who in their right mind would rush to get into this dump?"

"Lock the door and don't open it to anyone but me. Is that understood?"

Brittany saluted him and shut the door in his face. She flipped the lock, expecting him to try it again, but he didn't. She walked to the double bed, with its well-worn, orange-fringed bedspread and pulled back the covers. Thank goodness, the sheets were clean. Her eyes scanned the room. One bed. How dare he presume she would sleep with him! Brittany pulled a blanket off the bed and threw it into the recliner.

Her eyes drifted to the phone. She lifted the receiver, and listened for the dial tone. Smiling to herself, she called her grandfather.

Nick hid the car behind the barn. Satisfied it could not be seen from the road, he ran across the field to the motel. A car pulled into the parking lot and he watched a young couple knock on the office door. Once he was sure they weren't Capri's goons, he made his way around to the back. No point in risking being seen. He pried open the bathroom window, and climbed in.

The bathroom door swung outward into the bedroom. As he entered the room, he sensed more than heard, someone on the other side of the door. He body slammed it into the wall, barely registering the soft groan, followed by a thump, as a Bible hit the floor. Nick surveyed the room, empty. Gun drawn, he cautiously peeked around the door. "Brittany! Are you alright?"

She glared at him.

"Why are you hiding around the bathroom door?" He looked at the Bible, and chuckled. "And what were you going to do with that?" He couldn't keep from laughing harder.

Brittany pushed away. "You frightened me!" She pointed to the door of the room, "Haven't you heard of the door?" She pushed past him and picked up the Bible. "Stop laughing, it's all I could find. The lamps are bolted down." Then she snickered, "I was hoping for someone shorter so I could hit them in the head."

Nick laughed involuntarily. "Maybe I need to call you David the giant killer."

"Don't quit your day job, because you aren't as funny as you think."

"I was being cautious," he said.

"You're too paranoid."

"You had to know it was me."

"Oh, really! Do you always sneak in windows like a common thief?"

"I am anything but common, and you are not the helpless damsel you pretend to be."

"I pretend to be nothing."

"Well, the fire is back in your eyes, so you must be alright." Walking over to the bed, he said, "I'm beat. I'm going to sleep."

Brittany watched him lay his jacket and gun on the bed. Slowly, he unbuttoned his shirt.

With each released button, the heat rose within her. As if he knew he was tormenting her, Nick slowly removed his shirt. She tried not to stare, but her eyes had a mind of their own. He looked better than in her dreams. Dark hair covered his lean, muscular chest and narrowed to a thin trail of hair leading to... she spun around as he dropped his pants.

He laughed. "No fair peeking."

Her face turned scarlet as her eyes met his in the vanity mirror. "I wasn't peeking. I was wondering where you think you're going to sleep?"

A gleam sparkled in his eyes, and he crawled under the covers. "Guess we share."

"I don't think so."

"Suit yourself." Nick placed his gun under the pillow. "There's always the chair." He looked at the blanket already there. He patted the bed beside him. "This bed is more comfortable, though. Sure you won't change your mind?" Nick relaxed back on the pillows, his arms resting behind his head, the sheet laid across his hips. Why did he have to be so sexy?

"Never!"

"That's not what you said ten years ago."

"Ten years ago I was young and stupid." She flounced past him, and dropped into the chair.

"Don't forget the light."

She jumped up, angrily flipping the switch. He waited until she was once again seated and said, "If you're going to sleep in the chair, move it away from the window."

"Why?"

"You're an easy target there."

Brittany shot from the chair jerking the curtain back. "No one's—"

Nick sprang across the room like a tiger. One graceful move and he pinned her to the floor beneath him. Her t-shirt pushed up over her stomach. His body burned through her clothes. Brittany barely dared to breathe. The hunger in his eyes made her quiver.

The feel of her bare flesh against him inflamed every nerve in his body. He longed to run his hands along her soft curves, to remove every piece of clothing standing between him and ecstasy. Closing his eyes, Nick fought the waves of desire. A tiny quiver from her threatened to ignite the fire stirring within him.

Nick lowered his face to hers. The cool waters of her eyes called to him to join her. His lips brushed across her forehead, down her cheek to her neck.

A soft moan escaped her lips. Brittany pushed him away. "Stop."

Nick whispered in her ear. "Why, are you still a virgin?"

She wiggled beneath him. "None of your business."

"Stop wiggling, otherwise I'll be finding out."

She froze. "Please get up."

He winked. "I like it here."

Her voice quivered. "I don't."

"Then tell your eyes that." But Nick helped her to her feet. Softly, he smacked her butt. "Stay away from the window."

He grabbed the chair and carried it to the other side of the bed. The muscles in his arms bulged under the weight, making the tiger tattoo on his shoulder look as if it actually had pounced. As he moved past her she gasped; bullet scars covered his back.

He turned. "What?"

She gently touched each scar. "Your back."

"Compliments of Vincent."

She wrapped her arms around his waist, leaning her head against his back. She gently kissed one of the scars.

He turned, taking her hands in his. "Do us both a favor and stop touching. Unless you're having second thoughts about joining me?"

"No!"

"Too bad," he said, crawling into bed. "It would be nice to finish what we started so long ago." He grinned. Then laying his head on the pillow, he added, "Oh well, there's always tomorrow." Within minutes, he was asleep.

Brittany watched him. His thick long lashes lay softly against his face. Oh, how she longed to kiss him, to lie beside him. She crawled out of her chair and knelt beside it praying. *Please God, deliver me from temptation.* Returning to her chair, she closed her eyes without another glance at Nick. The soft sound of his breathing lured her to sleep.

Her dreams drifted back to a starry night long ago where moonlight and the soft sound of the ocean had promised to turn reality into something better than any dream. Wrapped in the arms of the man she loved, Brittany listened to the sweet sound of the words she knew were a prelude to 'I love you.' Nick kissed her neck. *"You are my angel."* The warmth of his lips traveled straight through her. Nick's lips had moved down her neck. *"I like the way your body fits next to mine, as if we were made for one another."* For a fleeting instant, she wondered if they had gone too far. No. She wanted him more than she ever thought it was possible to want another person. Her hands caressed his chest...

"Let's go." Somewhere between sleep and wakening, the panic of dreams and reality collided. "Brittany, wake up." Opening her eyes, she saw Nick standing over her. Grabbing her hand, he lifted her from the chair. "Let's go, sweetheart."

Disoriented, Brittany pulled back and fell into the chair.

"We have to go. Somehow Vincent found us."

Nick pulled her toward the bathroom. "Wait! My shoes."

He grabbed them from beneath the chair, "Just slip them on. You don't have time to tie them." Taking her by the hand, he led her to the bathroom, and opened the window. "Climb out."

"How do you know Vincent found us?"

"I saw them from the window."

Jumping down beside her, he pushed her ahead of him. "Run to the woods."

Branches lashed at them as they ran through the overgrown trees. Brittany tripped on her shoe strings. Falling, she hit her knee on a rock.

Nick almost fell over her. Pulling himself up short, he whispered, "Are you okay?" She nodded, biting her lip to keep from crying. Quickly he knelt down and tied both shoes. "The car isn't much farther. Let's go."

Once out of the woods, they ran through an open field to the car behind the barn. Opening the door for her, he tossed her the keys. "If I'm not back in ten minutes, leave without me." He reached behind the seat and grabbed his rifle. "Lock the doors, and if you see anyone coming other than me, shoot them." He handed her his Glock. Brittany pulled her hand away.

"What if it's not Capri's men?"

"It's a little past three in the morning. Innocent people do not prowl around abandoned barns in the middle of the night. Take the gun." She stared at it. Grabbing her hand, he placed it in her palm. "I don't have time to argue. If you don't want to shoot them, then run them over with the car. Just don't let them get you." He started to shut the door.

Brittany blocked it. "Why can't we just leave?"

"I need to make sure no one saw us running away."

"But—"

He slammed the door shut. "Lock it."

She watched until he turned the corner of the barn. She pulled up the leg of her pants. Blood flowed down from her knee. Looking for a first aid kit in the glove box, she opened it. And slammed it shut. A box of condoms right there in front only reinforced her opinion. Nicholas McFadden was nothing more than a womanizing playboy.

Pulling a napkin from the drink bag, she wiped the blood off her leg then glanced at her watch. Had it only been two minutes? It seemed like an eternity. *Please God, let him be safe. Put Your protecting arms around him.* Her heart froze as she saw him running toward her. She jumped out of the car and ran to him. Choking back tears she said, "I was so worried."

"Get back in the car. This is only round one."

Driving by the motel, Brittany asked, "Won't they see us?"

"They're taken care of."

"I didn't hear any gunshots."

"A gun isn't the only way to stop a man."

Brittany stared at him. He patted her leg. "They aren't dead, just unconscious long enough for us to get away."

She breathed a sigh of relief. Enough people had died already.

After a few miles, Nick winked at her. "So, you were worried about me?"

"Yes, but I don't know why. You're the best, aren't you?"

Nick laughed. "How's the knee?"

"It's fine."

"Humpf," he said, punching the phone button on his car, calling Carl.

Brittany kept looking over her shoulder at the road behind them.

"Sorry to wake you, but you need to know Vincent's goons found us."

Carl's voice came wide awake. "How?"

"I don't know how they found us. We weren't followed, and not even you knew where we were."

"You're wrong. James Hathaway informed me last night of your exact location."

"What?" Nick glared at Brittany. "You made a call while I was moving the car last night?"

"Yes, to my grandfather."

"I told you no phone calls!"

"Brittany," Carl said, "I know this is all new to you, but you have got to listen to Nick. He knows what he's doing." He paused. "Things could have ended a lot worse."

"I'm sorry." Brittany lowered her head.

"Find a place to lay low, until Miles and Frank can catch up to you." Before hanging up, Carl told Nick to put his earpiece back on. "I'll let you know where to meet them."

Nick ended the call, and immediately turned to Brittany. "Who else did you call?"

"What? You think I called Vincent?"

"He's your buddy."

"For the last time, I don't know him. And if I did, I wouldn't be calling him. Have you forgotten he wants me, not you?"

"Are you sure?"

"How do I know *you* didn't call him? You did do business with him."

"You know full well I was undercover."

"Do I?"

"You blew the bust. Remember?"

"If you worked for the D.E.A., then why didn't they question me?"

"They were sent to."

"Well, they never showed up."

"Guess your grandfather pulled some strings and cleared your name." Nick gave her a long stare. "Or maybe your pal Vincent did something to the officer."

Brittany glared at him. "I can't believe you think I'm capable of such—"

"Deceit?" he questioned.

"Don't you trust me?"

"No!"

"How can you say that?"

"Easy, I don't trust you, and that call you made last night when I told you *no calls*, makes it quite clear why."

"Let me get this straight, you think this cross-country chase is some elaborate scheme to get you killed?"

"It's possible."

"And I'm not an innocent victim, but one of the chief players in this game?"

"Could be."

Brittany placed her arms across her chest. "Other than the phone call, what have I done to make you think that?"

"Ten years ago you were pretty chummy with Vito Capri."

"So were you."

"How do I know you still aren't?"

"I'm not." She almost spit the words out.

Nick shook his head, "Vincent has been after me for years. What better way to get me off my guard than to send you."

"You're the biggest, most egotistical jerk I've ever known."

"And you are deceitful..." Nick stopped himself.

"What?"

"Forget it."

"No, I'm not going to forget it. Ten years ago, yes, I had a fake ID, but I never lied to you. And when you asked how old I was, I told the truth."

"In my book, deception is the same as a lie."

"And in my book, anyone who believed I was twenty-one without questioning it is a fool." She stared out the window. After that night, she had vowed never to deceive another soul again. If only she had kept that promise. Lies and acts of omission had a way of haunting you for the rest of your life. And if Nick ever found out about what happened in Cancun, she would never be able to convince him she wasn't the devious woman he believed her to be.

They rode in silence. Other than the occasional glance over her shoulder at the road behind them, Brittany just stared out the side window.

A few hours later, Nick pulled up to the gas pumps at a roadside diner. "Looks like we haven't been followed, so I think it's safe to stop and eat." She ignored him. Nick placed his finger under her chin, and turned her face to him. "Time to call a truce." Holding out his hand, he said, "Can we be friends again?"

"Were we ever friends?"

He grinned. "If I recall, we were more than friends." Opening the car door, he said, "Some things never change. You're still adorable when you blush." After he pumped the gas, he pulled in front of the diner between two other black sports cars.

"How strange," Brittany said.

"What?"

"We're in the middle of nowhere and the only other cars in the parking lot are black sports cars. You don't think that's strange?"

"No." Nick winked at her. Opening the door, he said, "I'm starving. How about you?"

Brittany could have sworn Nick knew at least one of the men in the diner. He hadn't looked at either of them, yet she sensed a silent signal. All through breakfast, she kept glancing at the two men. Trying to enjoy her pancakes, she attempted to convince herself she was the one being paranoid now. If Nick didn't care, why should she? Just because they drove a car similar to Nick's, and just because one of the men had a ponytail and scruffy look, didn't mean Nick knew them. The other man looked like he had stepped right out of a Columbo lookalike contest. Taking a deep breath, she tried to calm her nerves. She was in good hands—God's and Nick's.

Suddenly it dawned on her, "Is that the guy from the house?"

Nick nodded. "The cavalry has arrived." Before leaving, Nick ordered two large coffees and a bag of freshly baked donuts. "Might be a while before we stop again."

A few miles down the road, one of the cars from the diner passed them, followed by the other. Nick sped past the last car.

"What are you doing?" Brittany couldn't keep the panic out of her voice.

For the next twenty minutes, they played this cat and mouse game.

"I feel like I'm in a shell game."

"That's the idea. Don't want anyone knowing which car you're in." He gently squeezed her leg. "The last thing I want is for you to fall into the wrong hands."

A few miles later, they came to a crossroad, and all went their separate ways. "Aren't they supposed to be following us?"

"Don't worry they'll meet up with us on the other side of the mountain."

Brittany relaxed her grip on the door's armrest then released a deep breath. She stretched her fingers; she hadn't even realized she had been holding on so tightly. They drove quietly through the countryside, both wrapped in their own thoughts.

It was late in the afternoon when they stopped in Tennessee for lunch, and gas. Before leaving the restaurant, Brittany stopped at the adjoining general store. "Oh, this looks like you," she said, laughing as she picked up a porcelain figurine of a knight. "Did you pose for this?"

He took the item from her. "It does look like me, doesn't it?" He winked. "So is this what you think of me, the white knight riding in to save you?"

"More like the black knight." She giggled, then with a defiant air added, "But no, that isn't what I think of you."

Nick placed his hand over his heart. "I'm crushed you don't think I'm your savior."

"Definitely not."

"You need anything while we're here?" He looked around, "Doesn't look like they have any clothes other than t-shirts."

"Have you forgotten I don't have a purse, which means no money?"

"I have money." A few minutes later, Nick paid for their purchases. Brittany took the sketchpad and pencils from the bag, before Nick dropped the bag behind his seat. Closing his door he sang, "On the road again..."

Brittany started to draw Nick driving. She smiled softly. Could she capture his raw strength on paper?

Nick glanced at her sketch and laughed. "Is that me?"

She felt her face flush.

He pointed to her drawing, "I don't have a dimple."

"Oh yes, you do." She touched his cheek, "Right there."

He placed his hand over hers and winked, "Not as cute as yours are."

She felt his body go rigid. He reached behind his back pulling out his Glock.

"Why did you do that?"

"Getting prepared."

"For what?" Looking behind, she saw nothing but the curvy mountain road. The increased speed and the firm set of his jaw alarmed her even more. Panic rose in her voice as she repeated, "For what?"

"We're being followed."

Brittany glanced behind again, "I don't see anyone."

"Take my word for it."

"Maybe it's your friends."

"Wrong color car."

"How—"

"Put your seat back as far as it will go." He patted her leg. "Don't worry, you're in good hands."

Brittany hoped so. Within minutes, a green sedan sped past them. Brittany gave a sigh of relief. "False alarm?"

"No, that was one of Capri's goons."

"But he..."

"He passed us so he could block the road ahead to try and ambush us."

She grabbed his arm. "Shouldn't we turn around?"

"No, that's what they want us to do." He glanced in the rearview mirror. "There's another car a few minutes behind. Either way, they came looking for a fight."

"What are we going to do?" she asked.

"Fight."

Chapter 4

Brittany saw the instant change in Nick—the firm set of his jaw, the cold blackness of his eyes, the gun that seemed to belong in his hand. Gone was the relaxed man from a few moments ago, replaced by a tiger ready to devour its prey. How many men had felt that cold stare before death greeted them?

This dark part of Nick was a side she did not want to see. Brittany watched his finger wrap around the Glock's trigger. Her heart froze, and she placed her hands over her mouth to suppress the scream she felt rising.

"Hang on." Rounding the bend, Nick slammed on the brakes. The green car blocked the road ahead. The Porsche came to a screeching halt.

Brittany braced herself for an impact that never came. She sunk down as far as she could while bullets bounced off the windshield. The cold November wind swept over her as Nick opened the sunroof. "Stay down," he ordered. He undid his seatbelt, lifted himself though the sunroof, and fired. A deafening explosion was followed by pieces of green metal hitting the hood of his car.

Yea, though I walk through the valley of the shadow of death, I will fear no evil: for thou art with me; thy rod and thy staff they comfort me. She repeated the verse over and over again.

Slipping back into his seat, she felt him touch her arm. A sob escaped her lips.

"We aren't out of trouble yet."

Nick looked in the rearview mirror. He cautiously drove around the wreckage, before flooring it. Beyond the next curve, Nick spun the car around. With squealing brakes, they came to a halt. A few minutes later, the second car rounded the bend. A passenger leaned out the window, shooting.

Nick fired one shot, hitting the front tire. The car spun out of control, crashing into an embankment. Nick turned the Porsche, and they sped away.

Brittany jumped when he touched her hair. "It's over."

Looking out the back window she cried, "Stop, they could be hurt."

"They tried to kill us."

"But—"

"They have cell phones. They can call for help."

"What if they can't?" Brittany stared at the road behind them. No one could have survived that crash. How many more must die before they made it safely to Colorado? Hugging her arms around herself, she tried in vain to stop the shaking. Closing her eyes, she fought the tears.

Nick pushed the speak button, "Call Carl." The car dialed the number. Nick quickly brought him up to speed and hung up. "He's sending the police to check on them." He reached for her hand, giving it a soft squeeze.

Nick drove as fast as the road would allow. When the car slowed and turned, Brittany opened her eyes.

Tree branches blanketed the vehicle. The scream she had been holding in let loose. She threw her arms over her face. Had they survived a gunfight only to crash into the woods?

He patted her leg. "Guess it's a good thing I never got around to trimming these bushes. They make the perfect cover. If Capri has anyone else out there, they'll never know where we went."

After several miles, Nick pulled into a clearing, stopping in front of a stone cabin with a wraparound porch.

"Honey, we're home." He winked.

Brittany tried to stand, but her trembling legs refused to support her.

Nick ran around the car, grabbing her before she fell to the ground, and carried her into the cabin. When the door shut behind them, relief flooded through her. *We're safe.* Like a bursting dam, the tears came.

Nick sat on the sofa holding her, caressing her hair. "It's okay, angel. You're safe now."

Burying her face into his chest, she whispered, "I'm sorry," between sobs.

"I promise I won't let anyone hurt you." Laying his face into her hair, he whispered again, "I promise."

His emotions were swirling. Holding her next to his heart, his arms around her protectively, was exquisite torture. Tenderly, he stroked her hair. His heart was pounding. He had to get out of here, get away from her before he got lost in the raging storm.

Gently, he placed her on the sofa. "I have to put the car in the garage. Not that anyone knows how to find this place, but I don't want to take any chances." He all but ran out of the house.

Shutting the door behind him, he took a deep breath, hoping to calm his racing heart.

In the safety of the outdoors, he laughed at himself. The crying damsel in distress was nothing new to him. What was new was his walking away before the early morning sunrise. He shook his head. She wasn't the young college student anymore. She was a full-grown woman—a woman who still had the power to put him under her spell. He knew that one touch of her voluptuous lips and he'd be lost forever in paradise.

Before he could experience the ecstasy of her, he had to... He mentally gave himself a solid shaking. *The ecstasy of her?* Was he crazy? Never again would he accept an assignment while suffering from jet lag.

Nick jumped down from the porch and started running. He needed to clear his head. Moreover, he needed to double check the perimeter.

After a few laps around the edge of the woods, he pulled the car into the garage. Grabbing his duffel bag and rifle, he took a deep breath at the door and walked in.

Brittany was curled in the corner of the sofa, her face lying on her knees.

Nick walked over to the bar. "Would you like a drink? I know I could sure use one."

"Water would be fine."

"I was thinking about something stronger." He picked up a bottle of Jack Daniels. "Something to calm the nerves."

She shook her head. "I don't drink anymore."

"What? Why not?"

"I'm a Christian."

Nick laughed. "Little miss party girl, a Christian. How did that happen?"

"The path I was heading down ended up not being very fun. It almost got me killed." She rubbed her shoulder where Vincent had shot her. That wasn't the reason she had changed. It was Cancun, but he didn't need to know about that.

"Looks like the path you're on now is trying to do the same thing."

Brittany sighed. "Lucky I have God and you on my side."

Nick laughed. "Don't know about God, but you got me." He downed a shot of Jack. "Sure you don't want one?"

"A good prayer is better than alcohol any day."

"So, what," he said walking to the refrigerator, "are you one of those born-again Christians?"

"Isn't that what being a Christian is?"

"I guess." Nick shrugged. "There's Coke if you would rather have that."

"No, water is fine." He grabbed two bottles of water and returned to the sofa. When he handed her one, she looked into his eyes. "So, are *you* a Christian?"

"Me?" His hand slipped into his pocket, his fingers wrapping around his lucky rock. He chuckled, "Not hardly."

"Oh."

"Can you blame me? Every day I see the evil in the world."

"Yes, there's evil in the world, but there's also good."

"Maybe, but the evil's winning."

"It didn't today." She laid her hand on his knee. "God protected us. How else do you think we survived?"

"My skills."

She smiled. "Where do you think you got them from?"

"The Army." He glanced at the rifle lying on the coffee table in front of them.

Brittany shook her head. "When did you join the Army?"

"Left shortly after we parted ways."

"Oh." Picking up a picture from the end table she asked, "Are these your parents?"

"Yup."

"You look nothing like them."

"I look like my Dad." Seeing the puzzled look on her face, he added, "That's my step-father in the picture. My dad was killed a month before I was born." Nick took the picture from her hands and sighed. "And my step-father died about a year ago."

Brittany touched his arm. "I'm sorry."

"Me, too. If I'm half the man he was when I become a father, then my kids will be some kind of lucky." Nick returned the picture to the coffee table.

"I actually knew him."

"You did, how?

"He remodeled my house. If I had known you were the son he kept trying to pawn off on me, I might have said yes."

"You *might* have?" He grabbed her to him and started to tickle her. "Might have!" Laughing, they rolled off the sofa, and she begged him to stop. "Not till you say you *would* have."

"All right, I would have."

"That's more like it," he grinned. Their eyes locked in an embrace. As if in a trance, his lips moved toward hers. His pounding heart drowned out all reason. Her breath gently brushed his lips as she whispered his name.

A heartbeat away from ecstasy, the door flew open with a bang.

Nick jumped up to one knee, grabbed his rifle, and aimed at the door in one fluid motion. He watched as it swung back and forth in the wind.

Ordering Brittany to stay down, he crouched low and ran to the door. Had they been followed? Or was it the wind? He had to make sure. Slipping out the front, he made a thorough search of the area before returning to the house.

He glanced around the room, "Brittany, where are you?"

She stood up from behind the kitchen island.

He smiled. "Smart girl."

Brittany ran to him, throwing her arms around him. "I was so afraid someone had gotten you."

"No need to worry yourself, it was just the wind. By the looks of things, we're in for a big storm."

The look in her eyes was unmistakable; there was more than one storm brewing.

She softly traced the deep dimple in his cheek. He longed to kiss her, to feed the hunger in her eyes. With a sigh, he gently removed her arms from around him and stepped back. Whatever was going on within him must be stopped. She was distracting, clouding his judgment, and that could very well get them both killed.

If that hadn't been the wind... well, from here on out, she was off limits. "I need to get some wood before the storm hits."

Brittany watched the door close behind him. There was no denying he felt the same as she did. She groaned. *God, what's wrong with me?* Her desires and his were not the same. She wanted a life with him; he was looking for a one-night stand.

She sat down on the sofa, and bowed her head. *Why can't I control these feelings? Please help me. I am so weak. No man has ever made me feel this way, and I know his walking away was for my own good, but it still hurts. He doesn't even believe in You, so I know that means he's off limits, and yet I can't stop wanting him. I need extra help fighting this battle. Amen.*

She jumped up and ran to open the door when she heard Nick step up onto the porch.

"Thanks, this ought to keep us warm tonight." He dropped the wood by the fireplace before removing his coat. Stooping down, he started to stack the wood. "After I start the fire I'd like to jump in the shower."

What about the fire you already started! It should be a sin to fill out jeans the way you do. "I could go for one myself." *A long cold one.*

He nodded, "Then I'll fix us something to eat."

"You know how to cook?"

"Of course." He patted his stomach. "A man has to eat, doesn't he? Out here it's learn to cook or starve. I always keep a stocked pantry and freezer, so there's plenty of food. What would you like?" He nodded toward the kitchen. "That NuWave oven comes in handy. Can take the meat from freezer to table in no time."

"Never heard of that."

"Not much to do late at night, so sometimes when I can't sleep I watch infomercials." He chuckled. "And sometimes I buy the product."

She laughed. "Can't picture you as an infomercial guy."

In no time, he had a roaring fire going. "Time to get this road dust off."

"That would be nice but my overnight bag is back at the house. Is there anything I can change into?" She lowered her eyes from his. "Like maybe one of your shirts?"

He nodded to a door to the right of the kitchen. "Help yourself. The bathroom adjoins that room, and the towels are in the closet."

Brittany barely glanced at the king-sized oak bed. She didn't want to see where he slept. And she didn't want to imagine how many women he had shared it with. She grabbed the first shirt she could find and quickly left the room.

The shower calmed her jangled nerves. She picked up Nick's flannel shirt and put it on. All her senses came alive. She hugged the shirt to her face. His warm masculine scent wrapped around her, making her body tingle with the knowledge that this shirt had covered him as it would cover her. She groaned. *So much for the cold shower.* She looked up to the heavens. *Please Lord, help me.*

She rolled up the sleeves and bunched up the hem of the shirt tying it in a knot. She looked in the mirror, and laughed at the too large shirt. Way to make an impression. Brittany opened the bathroom door, but stopped when she heard Nick on the phone.

"I want to know what's going on." His voice was low and hard. "This was supposed to be an easy job? Just grab her and go? But around every corner, Capri's stooges are waiting for us." He paused. "Life was easier in Mexico. At least I knew who the enemy was."

Brittany gasped; did he still think she was the enemy? Tears stung her eyes. Stepping back into the bathroom, she slid down to the floor.

Nick thought he heard the bathroom door open, but when he looked up it was still shut. "Other than you, Miles, and Frank, who else knew where we were going?"

"No one," Carl said.

"Well, someone is tipping Capri off to our location."

"That has me worried, too. Is it safe to stay there tonight?"

"Yes, other than family there are only a few people who know about this cabin, and I trust each of them with my life." Nick rubbed the back of his neck. "Hopefully, that trust isn't misplaced."

"What's your plan? Will you fly the rest of the way?"

"Most likely, but honestly I'm not sure. And the way things are going, I think everyone needs to be on a need-to-know basis. I'll inform you tomorrow what the plan is. Just get Miles here by six. He knows the way."

"You don't trust me?"

"You're one of the only people I do trust, but someone's tipping Capri on my whereabouts. Don't know if the phone is bugged or what, but somehow he keeps finding us." For a moment, there was silence. Nick ran his fingers though his hair. "Other than you and Miles, does anyone else know about Heidi's place?"

"Not that I know of." Carl cleared his throat. "You could be to Heidi's place in fifteen minutes. Don't you think it would be wiser to leave now?"

"I've barely slept in three days. I'm in no condition to be flying tonight." He stirred the potatoes he had frying. "I'll call you in the morning with the plan." He looked toward the bathroom door.

Had Brittany used the phone while he was outside earlier? He shook his head. Even if Brittany was the informant, there was no way she could tell Vincent where they were.

He knocked on the bathroom door. "Hey, dinner's almost finished."

Brittany inhaled deeply and opened the door. The breath caught in her throat. Nick stood inches away, wearing just his jeans. Black hair graced his chest like a welcoming playground, his long wet hair hanging loose over his shoulders. She grabbed the door.

"Sorry, didn't mean to frighten you." Nick laughed. Following her eyes to his chest, he laughed again. "I showered in the other bathroom. Didn't want to risk going into my room for clothes in case you were dressing in there. Not that I would have minded." He winked. "By the look in your eyes, I don't think you would have minded either."

Brittany scooted past him. "I think you're mistaken."

"You're not a good liar." He touched her arm. "But you're adorable when you blush."

"What's for dinner?"

"Steak and fried potatoes." He filled her plate. "Hope you don't mind canned potatoes."

"At this point, I'd eat anything. I'm starving." After a few bites she said, "Who would have thought you could cook so well?"

He winked. "I do everything well."

She laughed. "I'm sure you do."

After the dishes were washed and put away, Nick pulled out a package of zip ties from the tool drawer. "Come here. I want you to put this around my hands."

"Why?"

"I want to show you something."

Nick held out his hands. "Pull it tight," he said. She did as he asked. Within moments, he broke free. "Now I want to teach you how to do what I just did."

"Do you honestly think someone's going to grab us here?"

"No." He took her hands. "But every woman should know how to protect herself. You never know when it might come in handy." While tying her hands together he added, "If you're going to spray mace at someone, you need to aim higher. Granted I'm 6'5", but you were aiming at my chest, not my face."

She shook her head. "A lot of good the mace was. You didn't even cough."

He laughed. "I've had worse things than mace thrown at me, I know not to breathe." He pulled the zip tie tight.

"Ouch."

"Sorry, sweetheart, but a criminal is not going to be gentle."

It took her a few tries before she was able to break free.

"Good, now turn around. You need to know how to do it from behind, too."

This took longer.

"Let's do it again." They spent the next hour practicing, until she was able to break free with ease.

"Is this how you normally spend your evenings? Breaking free of zip ties?"

Nick grinned. "I have a feeling you wouldn't be up to my normal activities."

Brittany felt her cheeks grow red. "No, I think not."

He handed her a glass of water before leading her into the living room and turning on the TV. Nick sat on the sofa, cleaning his rifle, while Brittany took the overstuffed chair closest to the fire—and farthest away from him. She tried not to watch his hands as he caressed the long barrel. If only she was that rifle. She closed her eyes. *Get a grip.*

She needed to get her mind off him. She glanced around and noticed her sketchpad and pencils on the table by the door. She smiled. "Wow, you thought to bring in my stuff."

"Of course I did." He winked, "You do have to finish your picture, don't you?"

She giggled, "Maybe." She sat back by the fire, pencil poised to draw, but it never moved.

When Nick finished cleaning his rifle and gun, he said teasingly, "Can I see your drawing?"

Embarrassed, Brittany looked down at the paper. She couldn't concentrate with him so near. Her face felt flushed. It was a good thing he couldn't read minds, or he would know she had been fantasizing being held in his strong arms, touching the tiger tattoo on his shoulder, and the pleasure of running her fingers though the hair on his chest.

She shook her head. What was wrong with her? His lips hadn't touched hers in ten years, and yet, he had control of her emotions like no one else.

Grinning, he stood and stretched his legs. Brittany gazed at the fire. She couldn't keep her thoughts from wandering to that night on the beach. Something ice-cold pressed against her right cheek, making her jump.

"Hey!" She pushed the soda can away.

"That should cool you off."

"I don't need to be cooled off," she said with as much dignity as she could muster.

"Really, well your eyes tell a different story."

"Oh! And what story is that?"

"Those icy blues melted like a spring thaw. Are you inviting me in, or are you like a siren, tempting me to drown?"

"What?"

"Your eyes are dangerous waters, Brittany. Waters where even a brave man is afraid to go."

"What's there to be afraid of?"

He knelt down in front of her, placed a finger under her chin, and gently lifted her face. "I'm not the man you're looking for. Part of me wishes I were but..."

She pulled back from his hand. She had heard this all before.

"Oh Brittany," he pulled her into his arms. Slowly, his hands traveled down her face to the opening of her shirt. *His shirt.* She pushed him away.

"Stop, you're right. This will never work." Brittany dashed to the front door. "I need some fresh air." She glanced at the rifle. "It's safe, right?"

Nick nodded and added more wood to the fire before following Brittany outside. She didn't even glance at him as he crossed the porch. Sitting on the railing, he said, "I'm sorry. I don't know what came over me. I promise I won't touch you again."

He saw tears glisten in her eyes. *There ought to be a law against eyes like that.* Eyes that could freeze a man's heart or make him desire things he had never wanted before. He lived his life with no regrets. No, that wasn't totally true. His one regret was not fighting for her after he found out she wasn't dead. And now she was an arm's length away, yet still worlds apart. What was wrong with him? Yes, she was beautiful, but beautiful women were a dime a dozen.

Just a few days ago, he held Rosita in his arms... and Heidi was only three miles away, where he came and went as he pleased, no strings. Moreover, if their paths never crossed again, there would be no tears, and no remorse.

He glanced at Brittany. With her, on the other hand, he knew there would be tons of regrets. Regrets he wasn't willing to encounter. He glanced across the yard at the setting sun. He had a feeling it was too late for that. His heart was already regretting chances not taken.

Two deer grazed near the edge of the woods. "Look over there," he whispered.

Brittany smiled and nodded. She had already seen the buck and doe, two beautiful animals from God's creation. Animals that had no problem with wanting different things in life. They were just happy to be together. *Why are you letting Nick affect you like this? He's playing a game you can't win. So, stop fantasizing about the wonderful moments you once had, and remember the heartache that followed.*

Brittany bowed her head and prayed, *Please, deliver me from temptation. I know I've been wrong to fantasize about Nick all these years, instead of taking heed of your words. Proverbs 23:7 says: "For as he thinketh in his heart, so is he..." and so I'm trapped to the desires of my heart. My heart already knows I can't trust him. Please take these desires away from me.* She shivered and sighed.

"It's getting a little chilly out here. Let's go back by the fire." Nick held the door open for her.

Brittany caught her breath as she brushed his arm on the way into the house. *Hurry, God!* She raced to the chair by the fire, once again trying to get as far from him as possible. Before Nick sat down she asked, "Do you have a Bible?"

He laughed. "The house is still standing, isn't it?" Nick went into the kitchen, "Want a snack or something?"

"No, thanks." She hugged her arms to herself. She didn't want anything from him. Maybe if she said it enough she would believe it.

Brittany glanced around the large cabin, trying to keep her mind off Nick. Everything from the oak bar in the corner, to the plush furniture and bearskin rug, had to cost a fortune. And his car... How could he afford such luxuries?

She cringed, remembering ten years ago when she had overheard Vito telling Nick how much money he could make working for his brother. *Is that how he can afford these things?* Was Nick taking her straight into Vincent's hands? *No!* "Maybe I will have a cup of tea."

"Sure." He opened the cabinet. "What kind would you like? My mother likes it all, so you can have your pick—black, white, green?"

"White, please." When the whistle blew on the kettle, she joined him in the kitchen. While the tea steeped she said, "You must really make good money working for PSA."

"I do." He gave her a puzzled look. "You're the last woman I would have thought would ask that question."

"Just this cabin, it has everything... and your car. How can you afford it?"

Nick chuckled. "Well, the car I bought at a government auction, for next to nothing. And this cabin was built by my dad and his construction company." He took a bite of a Hershey bar. "Trying to figure out if I really work for Vincent or not?"

She lowered her eyes.

"Don't worry, sweetheart, I don't." Holding up a second Hershey bar he asked, "Sure you don't want one?"

"No thanks, I try not to eat much candy."

"How about some TV?"

They watched for an hour before he clicked it off. "We're getting an early start tomorrow, so I think it's time to get to bed." He nodded toward his bedroom. "You can sleep in there." He laid one more log on the fire. "That ought to do it for the night." He stood, watching it burn for a few minutes, before checking the windows and doors.

Brittany brushed her teeth, before taking off her pants. She kept Nick's shirt on since it was long enough to serve as a nightgown. She was surprised to see Nick sitting on the edge of his bed, removing his jeans. "What do you think you're doing?"

"Getting ready for bed."

"In here?" She tried to keep her voice steady.

"This is my bedroom."

"Then where would you like me to sleep?"

Nick patted the sheets beside him.

"You're crazy. I'm not sleeping with you."

"How am I supposed to protect you if you're in another room?"

"Cut the crap. You said we're safe here." She glared at him. "You must have an awfully short memory. I told you last night I wasn't sleeping with you, and as far as I can see, nothing has changed that fact."

"It's late, I'm tired, and don't feel like arguing about it. Just get in the bed."

"No!" She started past him, but he grabbed her arm.

"Get in bed. I'm not going to touch you if that's worrying you." They both looked at his hand on her arm. He dropped it quickly to his side.

"Of course not, I'm just a *job*." She started out of the room. "But I'm still not sleeping with you."

"It's just sleeping." He smirked. "You can't tell me you've never shared a bed with a man before."

She quickly lowered her eyes.

"You've not still a virgin, are you?"

She could feel her cheeks redden.

He laughed. "How is that possible?"

"I made a promise to God to wait until marriage."

"That's taking religion a little too far, don't you think?"

"No, I don't."

He shook his head. Walking out of the room, he mumbled, "It's the twenty-first century, not the ice ages." Brittany breathed a sigh of relief as she heard him open another door. But her relief was short-lived as he returned a few minutes later, carrying a body pillow. He pulled back the covers and placed it in the middle of the bed.

"I don't think your God will object to this. Get in."

With a flounce, she got into bed, lying as close to the edge as possible. Whether she wanted to or not, her body trembled as he lay beside her and turned off the light. This wasn't the way it was supposed to be. The man of her dreams lay a few inches from her, but she was not his wife, not the love of his life. *Nothing but a job*. A sob caught in her throat.

She crawled from the bed, and knelt beside it.

Nick turned the light back on. "What are you doing?"

"Praying."

"Why?"

"I pray every night before I go to sleep."

"Hmm…"

She said a quick prayer before returning to the bed.

She was just about settled, when Nick spoke. "Let's say that today I didn't do my job, and you died, and you discovered that there was no God, no Heaven, no Hell. How would you feel knowing your life was lived believing in a hoax?"

"If there were no life after death I wouldn't be feeling anything. I would just cease to exist." She rolled over to face him. Even in the dark, she could tell he was looking at her over the pillow barrier. "Honestly, if the Bible isn't true, then what have I lost? I've had a happy life, have helped others when I could, loved with all my heart, and have done my best to live by the golden rule. There would be no regrets." She sat up, trying to see his face in the dark. "On the other hand, what if it is true? And I died not believing in Jesus only to discover it was all true. Would an eternity in Hell be worth the vices of this world? I don't think so. So, yes, I choose to believe that the Bible is true, that there is a Heaven, and one day I will be standing proudly before my Lord and Savior. Living eternally in glory. Believing makes me a winner no matter what."

"Well, I may not believe in God." He leaned across the pillow and kissed the top of her head. "But I do believe in angels."

Chapter 5

"You better have good news for me!" Vincent Capri shouted into the phone.

"The tracking device I planted on his car has them outside of Midland, Tennessee, about ten miles from where your men were found."

"Who has her?"

"McFadden."

Obscenities flew from his mouth. "I want him dead. Do you hear me? Dead!"

"That wasn't the deal."

"I pay you to do what I say, not what you want." Vincent laughed. "Of course you always have a choice. It's McFadden and the girl... or I send someone to your house, and we start with that pretty daughter of yours." Vincent didn't wait for a reply. He slammed down the phone. "Sonny, get in here."

The door slowly opened.

"We know where she is." Vincent's fist hit the desk like an erupting volcano. "McFadden's got her." Vincent grabbed a dart, throwing it at a photo of Nick's face hung on the wall. "He has messed with me for the last time." He picked up another dart. "I want the girl dead... She's useless to me."

"I thought the plan was to hook her on heroin and leave her strung out and naked in a crack house?"

Vincent shot a death glare at Sonny, "You question me?"

Sonny held both hands up, "No, never."

A slow sinister grin spread across Vincent's face. "I should have killed her ten years ago for choosing McFadden over me."

"If I remember correctly, she hadn't even met you yet. McFadden stole her away before you even got there." Sonny chuckled. "Funny how he has a habit of doing that."

"Shut up!" Vincent snatched the paperweight off the desk and threw it at Sonny's head.

Sonny ducked. "You know, you need to watch that temper of yours. It's not good for your blood pressure."

Vincent threw his hands in the air. "I'm surrounded by morons." He took a deep breath. "McFadden has messed with me for the last time." He pointed a finger at Sonny. "I want him brought to me alive."

"I thought you wanted him dead?" Sonny shook his head.

"I don't pay you to think, I pay you to do what I say."

"Actually, you don't pay me at all." Sonny stood tall, "My father, your uncle, the same man who pays you, pays me."

Vincent pointed the gun at Sonny. "You are lucky we aren't in the West Virginia kill house, cause cousin or not, I'll put a bullet through your head if you don't deliver him. I'll be the one to kill McFadden!" He smiled and caressed the gun. "He'll die looking into my eyes, knowing I defeated him. If I'm denied that pleasure, mark my words, you'll take his place."

Sonny backed out of the room. "Don't worry, we'll take him alive."

Vincent poured himself a glass of Bourbon. Propping his feet on the desk, he leaned back in his chair. For years, he had tried to wipe McFadden from the face of this pathetic world. He would have succeeded ten years ago, if Brittany had not interfered.

He had known McFadden was an undercover D.E.A. agent, the fool. The plan had been perfect: lure him to an abandoned dock, get the money, and then shoot him before anyone could come to his rescue. He just hadn't counted on lover girl showing up.

Vincent cradled his head between his hands. It had happened so fast. One moment she was waving at them from the water, the next she was slamming her boat into the pier. She'd been like a cat, jumping from the boat and diving between them, knocking them both over. The bullet meant for McFadden had hit her instead. The force had sent her flying off the pier and Nick dove after her.

Vincent shook his head. *What had gone wrong?* They both should have been dead. He'd emptied his semi-automatic into the water. The water ran red with their blood. And yet, somehow, they both had survived. McFadden obviously had a lucky horseshoe around his neck.

He laughed; the perfect plan did have a happy ending. Thanks to Brittany, he'd been able to escape in her motor boat with the money. Which was the only reason he'd let her live once he found out she wasn't dead. No one in the family knew he'd gotten away with the money.

Snatching a Cuban cigar from the box on his desk, Vincent took a long puff. If he was honest with himself, he'd let her live because he was sure the day would come for a second chance with her—and this time she wouldn't run off with someone else.

Vincent swung his chair around and admired himself in the mirror. He was handsome and he knew it. His father was Italian, but his mother was Russian. The combination of black hair and blue eyes drove women crazy. One look and they were falling all over themselves to be with him. Brittany Fitzpatrick would have been his if he hadn't been late for their blind date. Anger raged through him. It might have been the first time, but not the last, that McFadden subjected him to the family's ridicule.

McFadden had a history of messing up the best-laid plans. The memory of the most recent offense hung around Vincent's neck like a noose. McFadden had set a bonfire with an entire shipment of cocaine. The cost to the family, though astronomical, was nothing compared to the embarrassment it caused him. After the incident, McFadden had disappeared, leaving Vincent to face six long months of family scorn. There had been talk behind his back that he wasn't capable of running the business with his uncle. And now McFadden reappeared... foiling an easy kidnapping. He would definitely enjoy killing the man.

Vincent banged his fist on the desk. *It's Vito's fault this is all happening.* For a hundred years, the family had run the east coast, having someone in their pockets in every state law enforcement agency from Maine to Florida. No one in the family had ever gone to jail. Some of their men, maybe, but never a family member. Until Vito and Dmitry. *All because of a skirt.*

Vito, the charmer, could sell sand in the desert. He had persuaded the family to expand to Colorado, convincing them that many of their customers vacationed in Aspen and it would be easy to set up shop there. Vincent knew the real reason Vito wanted to be in Colorado—Carissa Hathaway. Their on-again off-again relationship was driving Vito insane. The stupid sap had really thought once he was in Colorado, she would be his forever. Little did he know she would be his downfall, sending him and Dmitry to jail. She'd been caught with cocaine, and quickly rolled over on Vito.

Carissa was the one who was supposed to be sent back to the honorable judge—dead. How dare she think just because she was the granddaughter of a judge that she was safe from the wrath of the Capris? But Vito had refused. Said he would not allow her to be harmed in any way. Apparently, he didn't hold it against her for turning State's evidence. Swearing any of them would have done the same thing to her. He even went so far as to warn that if anyone touched Carissa, they would be answering to him.

Stupid boy. Lust was a dangerous enemy. Since he couldn't touch Carissa, now he would be forced to kill the feisty one.

Vincent laughed one last time. They had come full circle. Brittany Fitzpatrick and Nicholas McFadden... finally, he would get his revenge. He raised his glass in a mock toast. "To what could have been, and to the death of a formidable adversary."

Chapter 6

Nick woke with a start. He lay motionless, trying to hear the sound that had stolen his dream. There it was again. *Was that a car door shutting?* He looked at the alarm clock—five A.M. Would Miles be here yet? He lay there listening. Nick slid a hand under the pillow for his Glock.

"Brittany?" He reached over to shake her gently, but she wasn't there. Was that what had woken him, Brittany in the other room? No, he could still hear her soft breathing. He glanced over the side of the bed. Brittany was asleep on the floor.

He slowed his breathing, and listening, he picked out three sets of footsteps. With his left hand, Nick reached for the rifle beside the bed, rolled out the other side, and dropped to his knees beside her. He laid the rifle on the floor, before softly touching her shoulder. "Wake up, sweetheart, we gotta go."

The words were barely out of his mouth when the bedroom door flew open. Brittany jumped.

"Stay down." Nick aimed his Glock at the gunman and fired with deadly accuracy. The man grabbed his chest and fell backwards.

A second gunman appeared and opened fire into the room. The glow from the fireplace allowed Nick to see the man clearly. He aimed and fired dead center. The gunman fell to the floor alongside the other intruder. Where was the third man?

He could hear muffled voices coming from near the front door. "Crawl to the bathroom," he ordered, putting the rifle in Brittany's hand. "If anyone but me tries to get in, shoot them."

She timidly closed her hand around the weapon. He wanted to reassure her, but what could he say? He waited for the sound of the bathroom lock before belly crawling across the floor. A third person was right inside the front door of the cabin, talking to someone outside.

Nick sprinted out of the bedroom firing his Glock, his aim again perfect. The fourth man peeked around the open doorway, and peppered the room with semi-automatic fire. Nick rolled behind the sofa, barely avoiding being hit. Heart pounding, he waited for the shooting to stop. He lay quietly until the man entered the house. When he did, Nick jumped up firing. Crimson exploded on the man's leather jacket and he fell to the pinewood flooring with a heavy thud.

Cautiously, Nick approached the front door. He squatted to check the pulse of the fallen gunman. Nothing. He listened for the slightest sound in the house. It was too quiet. He looked outside and spotted two cars. Vincent always sent teams of two. That would account for the four men.

Slowly, he stood. A bullet sped by, inches to the right of his head. Nick dropped to the deck for a moment to regroup. How many more were there? He crept around to the side of the porch. Using the night as cover, he slipped into the dark.

The shot had come from the woods. His bare feet and body barely registered the cold. He circled around through the woods, until he was certain he was behind where the unknown gunman had fired. He listened for any movement, but heard nothing. He glanced at the house. Had this gunman circled around? Car lights were coming up the driveway. Nick started running toward the house, a bullet whizzing past his shoulder. He hit the ground and crawled back to the cover of the woods. He made a silent plea that the car was Miles and not more of Capri's men.

"What a mess," Miles said as he stepped over the body on the porch. At the sound of footsteps on crunching gravel, he spun around, gun drawn.

"Hey man, take it easy," Frank said. "It's just me."

"I saw your car parked back there near the woods. Thought you were already in the house."

"Nope, when I got here I saw Nick running into the trees, so I followed, but lost him."

Miles put his back to the wall, quickly looked into the house, and drew back. He motioned for Frank that it was clear, and both men slowly entered with guns drawn.

In the bedroom, Frank kicked the body of a dead man, rolling him over. "Nick's alone in the woods, and the girl's not among the dead, so she has to be around here someplace." Frank flipped on a light, and opened the closet door. Brittany wasn't hiding in there. He turned to Miles. "You find McFadden. I'll find the girl." As Miles started out the door, Frank called over his shoulder. "And don't let him shoot you."

"Don't plan on it. You'd better worry about the girl. If Nick left her alone, you know he gave her a gun."

"I can handle the girl." Frank watched as Miles left the house then glared at one of the dead men on the bedroom floor. "It was a simple job, you idiot." He kicked the body and looked around. *Where is she?* He turned the knob to the bathroom.

"I know you're in there. Open up."

The turning of the doorknob startled Brittany. She jumped from her knees where she had been praying. The door jingled again.

"Open the door!" a male voice called.

"Nick said not..."

"Nick's dead, I'm here to help you."

"Nick's dead?"

"Good thing, too. He led the Capris right to you."

The man must be lying; Nick would never have done that. She sank to the floor as the words pierced her heart. Laying the rifle down beside her, she cradled her face in her hands. *No, God! No!* Her body racked with sobs. *It can't be true. Please, God. Please, let it be a mistake.*

She jumped as the man violently body slammed the door.

"We need to get out of this house now." He yelled.

Taking a deep breath, she wiped the tears from her eyes, and aimed the rifle at the door. Nick had died protecting her. She pushed herself up, not wanting to let his death be in vain. Somehow, she would make it out of here alive. "I have a gun, and I will use it."

She clutched the rifle in her hand. Did she have the nerve to kill another human being?

"Just open the door and no one gets hurt."

"No."

"Fine, stay in there until Capri's men storm the house." He waited a minute before body slamming the door again. "I'm tired of playing games," he warned, abandoning all pretense of being there to help her. "Open the door. If I have to knock it down, I'm going to be angry and you don't want to see me angry. I promise you that."

Unless she was willing to use the gun, she was a sitting duck in this bathroom. Her stomach churned at the thought of firing at a human being, much less killing someone. She couldn't do it. Glancing out the window, she noticed the woods were only a short run away. She was fast enough to outrun most people... *but a bullet?* She prayed, *God, please guide my way.* A peace came upon her, and she knew she would survive.

"Who are you?" she asked, diverting his attention and, hopefully, buying a precious minute to flee.

"I'm Frank Talonge. I'm with PSA."

Brittany stopped with her hands on the window. "Why didn't you say that from the start instead of beating on the door?"

"Capri could have more men on the way. It's my job to get you out of here as quickly as possible. If you don't open it, I have no choice but to knock it down."

Brittany hesitated. Was he really there to help her? No. Her gut told her she would not be safe opening the door. "How did you know we were here? Nick said no one knew about this place." She slowly opened the window, praying it wouldn't squeak.

"I was at the diner yesterday morning. He told us to meet him here."

"Who's your boss?"

"This is ridiculous." The man crashed against the door. "Open the door; we don't have time for this silly game."

"If you want me to open the door, tell me who your boss is."

"Carl Miller."

"What does he look like?" Brittany lifted herself onto the windowsill.

There was another hit to the door. "Open the door! Now!"

"Not until I'm satisfied you are who you say you are. Now tell me everything you know about Carl Miller. I know him personally so don't think you can make something up."

The man swore, then started talking.

From the woods, Nick watched Brittany open the window. She pulled herself up, straddling the windowsill, then reached back into the room, her hand emerging with the rifle. She leaned out laying the rifle against the house, before jumping. For a moment, she hung in midair. His shirt billowed above her hips, revealing her pale skin and white underwear before she yanked the shirt down. He groaned.

Brittany landed on the ground, grabbed the rifle and ran toward the woods, heading straight to where he'd last heard Capri's man. He couldn't call out a warning. If by some stroke of luck the thug hadn't seen her escape, he didn't want to alert him.

Nick ran toward Brittany. He dove, knocking her to the ground just as his shoulder was ripped by searing hot pain. "Stay down," he ordered, rolling off her body.

She stared at him with wide eyes. "You're not dead."

From the corner of the house, another shot rang out in the night. A scream followed by the sound of a body hitting the ground came from the woods. Nick threw his body back over Brittany. Turning, he aimed his gun at this newest threat that had sneaked up behind them.

"Having trouble with the lady?"

"Miles," Nick said with relief.

"At your service. I believe that was the last one." Miles reached out his hand to Brittany. "Once this oaf gets off of you, I'll take you inside before you freeze to death."

Nick slapped Miles' hand away and helped Brittany up himself.

She threw her arms around him. "You're alive."

"Of course, I am." He unwrapped her arms. "Miles, give her your coat."

Miles draped his jacket across Brittany's shoulders. Glancing at the shirt she wore, then at Nick in his underwear, he winked. "I see why Capri's men made it inside. You were a little distracted." He left his arm around her as he guided a dazed Brittany toward the house.

"It's not what it looks like."

At the corner of the house, Brittany pulled back. "There's someone in there."

"That would be Frank. He's with us." Miles grinned. "Is he the reason you climbed out the window?"

Knocking Miles' arm off Brittany's shoulders, Nick scowled at him. "You saw that, too?"

Brittany pulled the jacket tightly around her. "You know this man?" She touched Nick's arm. "But he told me you were dead."

"Why would he tell you that?"

She shrugged her shoulders. "I-I thought he was going to kill me." Brittany's voice broke.

Miles snickered, "That's Frank for you, he's too gruff for his own good."

"Not a good reason to frighten her." Nick swallowed the anger he was feeling toward Frank.

Brittany gasped as they neared the porch. A body lay on the ground. Nick scooped her up and carried her past it. "Don't look." She buried her face into his shoulder, but tensed as he said, "Put the gun away, Frank. Everything is fine." Nick deposited her on the sofa. "I'll get your clothes out of the dryer." Over his shoulder, he glared at Frank. "I said to put that away before I make you eat it. She's rattled enough without you pointing a gun at our backs."

"Looks like you're the one who's rattled."

"What's that supposed to mean?"

"You let them get all the way in here." Frank glanced at the body by the bedroom door. "I've never known you to be so sloppy."

Nick advanced on Frank, his fists clenched. "And what exactly are you insinuating?"

Brittany's gasp stopped Nick in his tracks. He spun back toward her.

"You've been shot," she cried.

"It's a scratch." He barely glanced at his shoulder. "The bullet just winged me."

Brittany reached out to him. "Let me look."

Nick jerked his arm away. "I said it was nothing."

"It's bleeding."

Nick went to the oak bar in the living room, opened a bottle of whiskey, and poured it over the wound. He grimaced in pain. Gritting his teeth, he slammed the bottle down. "Now it's taken care of. Satisfied?" He stormed into the laundry room, grabbed her clothes, and tossed them at Brittany. He pulled on his jeans, grabbed a shirt, and slipped into his loafers. "Move it, sweetheart, unless you want to wait around for the next round." He glanced at the bodies blocking the bedroom door. He grabbed her by the hand and walked her into one of the other bedrooms.

"Get dressed or go as you are," he said without turning. "You have two minutes." Then he slammed the door shut.

He stormed out of the cabin. Trained to hear any unusual sound, Nick never should have let those men make it to the front porch, much less into the house. Frank was right. He was lucky he hadn't gotten her killed. He had allowed his dreams to pull him away from the job at hand. From here on out, he had to get control of his emotions. No more dreams of yesteryears. No more thoughts of picking up where they had left off. Nothing. She was a job, and the only way he would keep her alive was to remember that.

A sob caught in her throat. Why was he being so mean? Why had he jerked away from her twice? She quickly dressed. When she came out, Frank was standing there, gun in hand.

"You could have opened the door when I told you to."

She eyed the gun. "Nick," Brittany called out. PSA agent or not she didn't trust him.

"He's outside and can't hear you."

Brittany tried to sidestep around him, but he grabbed her arm. "Nick won't be around forever."

She jerked her arm from his. "What's that supposed to mean?"

The front door opened. "Brittany, let's go," Nick said.

Frank quickly holstered his gun. Brittany dashed by him, wondering what he would have done if Nick hadn't arrived.

At the front door, she stopped midstride. A dead man laid there with his eyes staring up at her. She started to sway.

Nick picked her up again and carried her to the sofa.

"I'm sorry." Her voice broke. "There are bodies everywhere."

"I'm the one who's sorry. I should have covered them up." He ran his fingers through her hair.

Another wave of nausea swept over Brittany. She would never make it to the bathroom. Instead, she ran into the kitchen and used the trashcan. Nick followed and knelt beside her as she slumped to the floor. "You're safe now," he murmured, handing her a wet paper towel. "You have three of the best guarding you. I promise on my life no one is going to get to you."

Brittany managed a slight smile. "I'm sorry for being such a baby."

"Things never should have gotten this far." Nick's voice was full of anguish. "I almost got you killed."

She placed a hand on his leg, "But you didn't. God protected us."

Frank laughed. "God, ha! It was us who saved you."

Nick glared at him. "Where is Miles?"

"Outside."

"I have to make a phone call." To Brittany he said, "Are you okay here?"

She nodded.

"I'll be right out on the porch."

Brittany watched Frank inching his way toward the door, straining to eavesdrop on Nick's call. Back within moments, Nick said to Frank, "I don't see your car out there?"

"I'm parked near the woods."

Nick scowled.

"I thought I heard someone so I stopped to see."

Nick nodded. "Well you better go get it, we're leaving now."

Brittany waited until Frank left the house. "You sure you can trust him?"

"Carl does, that's good enough for me."

Brittany shook her head, "He threatened me again."

"What?"

"He said you won't always be around."

Nick stared at the door, "I'm sure he didn't mean it like it sounded." Nick scooped her up and headed toward the garage door.

"I can walk," Brittany insisted.

"And I can carry you," Nick retorted. "Just lay your head on my shoulder and don't look around."

"But your shoulder's hurt."

Nick lay his face into her hair. For a moment, he said nothing, then whispered, "Let me be your hero, if only for this moment."

Brittany ran the back of her fingers down his cheek. "My valiant knight, you already are." She buried her head into his shoulder, his strength wrapped around her like a protective cover. She felt safe in his arms. Nothing else mattered.

Opening the door to the garage, he glanced over his shoulder at the bodies littered between the front door and the bedroom. Putting her down he said, "I think you need to go in the other car with Miles. He'll keep you safe."

"I'm going with you."

"Look around." Nick waved his hands. "You aren't safe with me."

Brittany pushed away from him, and hurried to the passenger door. "I started this nightmare with you, I'll end it with you."

"Brittany, you're safer with Miles."

She looked from Nick to Miles, who stood by his car. Whatever was down the road didn't much matter at this point. For all she knew it could be Capri waiting around the bend. The one thing she did know was that God was on her side. And if she was meant to make it, she would. If not, then she would die by Nick's side.

Brittany entered the vehicle and locked her door. Nick hesitated, and then climbed in as well. "If I'm going to die today it will be with you," she said.

"I don't plan on dying."

"Good, neither do I." She bowed her head, said a quick prayer, then breathed a sigh of relief as Nick backed away from the cabin of death.

She covered her face, not wanting to see anymore. With a deep sigh, she reviewed the last few days. Colorado was still a long way off. Would they make it? Or would their bodies be counted along with the others? *No!* That was a thought not worth thinking. God was her protector; He had not gotten them this far for them to die now.

She wasn't sure where they were, or how far from her grandparents' compound, but she did know that when they arrived, Nick would once again walk out of her life, taking her heart with him. She glanced at him, swallowing the lump in her throat. *Why can't you be my hero for all times?*

The car stopped at a small airport. "Let's go."

Brittany gave him a questioning look.

"It will be safer for us to fly from here."

"Do you trust the pilot?"

"I hope so, it's me." Nick laughed. "Don't look so surprised."

The sound of car doors slamming reminded Brittany of the others. "Why did you lie to your friends and tell them we were driving?"

"Who said I lied? Maybe I changed my mind."

"Don't you trust them?"

"In this business, too much trust will get you killed."

"What's going on?" Frank demanded as he got out of his car.

"Just a pit stop. I need to get this shoulder looked at before we go any farther."

"Here?" Brittany and Frank said together.

"My friend Heidi was a medic in Iraq. She was in med school before her father died and left her this place." The words were barely out of his mouth, when a beautiful blonde came running from the hanger. "Nick!" She leapt into his arms, wrapping her arms and long legs around him.

"Hello, sweetheart."

"I've missed you so much."

Their kiss told Brittany more than she cared to know. So, this bimbo was his type. *No, Brittany. All women are his type. Don't you know that?* She barely managed a smile as Nick introduced them.

Heidi turned her back to Brittany, linking her arm with his. Suddenly, she stopped short. "You're bleeding."

Brittany felt nauseous watching Heidi fall all over Nick. "It's only a little scratch," Brittany said.

Heidi turned on her, fire flashing in her green eyes. "A scratch! A scratch wouldn't bleed like that. You insensitive little..."

"Heidi!" Nick grabbed her by the elbow. "It's nothing."

The flash of anger on Heidi's face froze at Brittany's cold stare. Without batting an eye, Heidi turned back to Nick. "Come inside, I'll fix you right up." She kissed his shoulder. "There, does that make it all better?"

Nick chuckled. "Sure."

"Nice girl." Heidi spoke loud enough for Brittany to hear. "You should let me shoot her in the shoulder and see how she likes the little scratch."

Nick looked back at Brittany. "Miles, take care of Brittany."

Miles jumped off the hood of his car. "Thought you'd never ask." He laughed as he picked Brittany up and sat her on the hood of Nick's car. "She'll be fine with me." Miles leaned in as if to kiss her. Brittany placed her hands on his chest to stop him. He winked and whispered, "Don't worry, darling. I'm just playing with Nick."

"Miles!"

Miles gave Nick a big grin. "Go get fixed up. Everything's under control here."

Miles let out a loud whistle. "I've never seen Nick fall for anyone." He gave Brittany a long lingering look. "And two days after meeting you, no less. How did you do it?"

"One... he hasn't fallen anywhere," Brittany huffed. "And two, we met ten years ago."

Miles let out a long whistle then gave her a big hug. "No wonder I recognized your name. You're the one that got away, the one that broke his heart." He pulled back, "What? I thought you were dead."

"Not yet."

Frank kicked a stone across the driveway. He was pacing like a wild man.

"What's got you all riled up?" Miles asked Frank.

"What are we doing here?" Frank glanced at his watch. "We're supposed to be on the road."

"Nick said we would be flying from here," Brittany said.

"What?" Frank slapped his hand on the car. "This was supposed to be easy."

From the corner of her eye, it looked like Frank was pulling his gun, but he quickly moved his hand back into his pocket when the door to Heidi's house opened.

Nick and Heidi walked out. His arm was around Heidi's waist.

A sob caught in Brittany's throat.

Miles patted her leg, "Don't worry, darling, I'm sure the best girl's going to win."

Chapter 7

Brittany watched Heidi run her hand down Nick's shirt. It was a different one from what he'd been wearing when they arrived. "Humpf," she said angrily, tossing her hair over her shoulders. She jumped down from the car's hood and turned her back on them.

So, he keeps clothes at her place. Well, Brittany certainly didn't care. No more than she cared he'd allowed that bimbo to doctor his shoulder when he wouldn't even let her look at it. He could bleed to death before she'd ever offer to help him again.

Miles put an arm across her shoulder. He leaned down and whispered in her ear, "She doesn't own an inch of his heart."

Brittany looked back at Nick and Heidi in disbelief.

Nick hurried over and knocked Miles' arm away from around Brittany. Miles laughed and winked at her. "Trust me."

Frank pointed at Brittany. "She is under the impression that you're flying from here."

"We are," Nick answered.

The vein in Frank's temple bulged. "Why the secrecy?"

"You know the drill, strictly need to know."

Frank kicked a rock toward Nick. "So, you dragged us out here just to play nursemaid while you could go off playing doctor?" He stormed back to his car, slamming the door. Nick and Miles stared at him.

"What's eating Frank?" Nick asked.

Miles shrugged his shoulders.

Nick placed his hand on Brittany's arm. She yanked it away, glaring at him. He raised an eyebrow and grinned. "Let's go."

Taking Brittany firmly by the arm, he headed behind the barn where a blue helicopter waited. Heidi moved in close to Nick. Shrugging loose, Brittany walked away from them. She would not be part of this threesome.

Nick opened the door to the passenger side and lifted her in. Before he closed the chopper door, she heard Heidi say, "I'll see you tomorrow night."

"Maybe," he responded.

"No maybes," Heidi pouted. "You promised to dump your baggage and come back to me. I'll have your two favorite things, me and Jack Daniels, waiting for you." She reached up and kissed him.

Brittany hugged her arms to herself. How much more of this could her heart take? Nick shut the door and walked around the helicopter, inspecting it. When he finally climbed into the pilot's seat, she let out the breath she hadn't realized she'd been holding.

Nick handed her a headset. "Put these on."

Brittany gripped the edge of her seat as the helicopter lifted off. Nick patted her leg. "Don't look so nervous. I'm an excellent pilot."

"Of course, you are," Brittany snapped.

He smirked.

"I'm not worried about your flying ability; I'm just relieved you left your *friends* on the ground."

"Green is not your best color."

She crossed her arms. "What's that supposed to mean?"

He nodded toward the ground. "Obviously, you're talking about Heidi."

She lifted her nose and sharply turned to look out the window. "I was referring to your *other* friends."

Nick clenched his jaw. "Did Miles make a pass at you?"

"Not Miles, Frank."

"Frank made a pass at you?"

Brittany rolled her eyes. "No one made a pass at me. I told you I didn't trust Frank."

"In this world, you're lucky if you can trust yourself."

"Do you have a problem with trusting yourself?"

Nick was quiet for a few minutes. "Life is strange. You go along content with the way things are, knowing what and who you are. Then suddenly you run into something—or someone—that sends your life into a whirlwind, changing everything." He fiddled with the instrument panel. "Everything you thought you believed in is swept into turmoil and you end up doubting it all."

"Does this happen often?"

Nick laughed. "Fortunately, no."

Brittany gazed at the clouds. She knew exactly what he was talking about. Life had been going along just fine until Nick and Capri showed up, sending her emotions on a roller coaster ride. Her safe little world had become anything but safe. "How did Vincent find us?"

"Obviously someone told him where we were."

Her voice rose. "You don't think it was me?"

He brushed her cheek. "No."

She breathed a sigh of relief. "Good. But what changed your mind? At the hotel, you certainly thought it was me."

"Because those men back there were after you, not me."

"Weren't they shooting at you?"

"Capri's men are better shots than that. If they wanted me dead I would be."

"But they did shoot *you.*"

"Only because my shoulder happened to be where your head was a moment before."

The realization of what he said hit her. Brittany wrapped her arms around herself hoping to stop the shaking.

Nick gently squeezed her leg again. "We'll be at the compound soon and this ordeal behind us."

She touched his shoulder. "Funny how every time we're together, one of us gets shot."

"Or both of us." Nick reached over and pulled her gently toward him, in a side hug. "I never thanked you for saving my life ten years ago."

Brittany's heart skipped a beat. Those were the words she had longed to hear so long ago. "I was surprised you never came to see me in the hospital."

"I couldn't."

"Why not?" She couldn't keep the resentment out of her voice.

"I was in a medically-induced coma for weeks."

"But..." Brittany paused, shocked at the revelation. "I was the one who got shot."

Nick clenched his fist. "After you nose-dived into the water, I dove in after you." He took a deep breath. "Vincent emptied his gun into the water after us. I was shot multiple times before I was able to get us under cover of the pier."

Brittany glanced toward his back, remembering the bullet scars, and gasped. He nodded. She grabbed her chest. "I didn't know." A soft sob escaped her lips. "I didn't know." She hid her face with her hands. "They told me you pulled me under the pier until help got there, and they had to pry your arms from around me." Her voice quivered. "But they never told me you got shot."

Nick hit his fist on the steering column. "All this time, I thought you didn't care."

She took a deep breath. "Is that why you didn't look me up after you came home?"

He shook his head. "I thought you were..." His voice broke. "...dead."

"What?"

"When I came out of the coma, the first thing I did was ask about you." He ran a finger under his sunglasses. "They said you were gone. I took that to mean you were dead."

"That's crazy. How did you find out I wasn't?"

"Three years ago I saw your picture in the paper when you opened the arts center. Thought I was seeing a ghost."

"Why didn't you look me up then?"

"I went to the opening." Nick fiddled with the instruments on the dash, avoiding her eyes. "You were with some Ken lookalike. So, I left."

"I was with a guy?" Brittany asked puzzled. She giggled, "Oh, that must have been Mike. I wasn't with him. At the time he was an employee." She shook her head. "So many misconceptions." She leaned against the cool window pane and sighed. "Would things be different between us if we'd known the truth?"

He reached across the cockpit and lifted her face, turning it gently toward him. "I believe so."

Her lips quivered. Ten years of heartache washed over her.

"So, is there a guy in the picture now?"

"No."

"What about this Mike?"

"He is my best friend."

He raised an eyebrow. "Just a friend."

Brittany smiled, "Yes, just a friend."

"Maybe after all the smoke clears we can finish what we started ten years ago?"

If things had been different, would they be married with kids? Or would something else—most likely *someone* else—have broken them up? Brittany shook her head. "I don't think that's a good idea." Love hadn't been enough to keep them together, and now life had put them on two different paths.

"Sweetheart..."

"I'm not Heidi."

He chuckled. "Is that shades of emerald I see in those eyes of yours again?"

"Of course not." Brittany stared out the window.

"When you get back to Maryland, we could do dinner and a movie or something."

It was the *something* she couldn't deal with. The something he found with Heidi. No, this would not work. "If you think we can pick up where we left off, you are sadly mistaken." She was being irrational and she knew it. Nick wanted to see her. Isn't that what she had always wanted? She hung her head.

"Why not? You can't deny there is still something going on with us."

"No, I can't." She stared at the clouds, "The problem is you don't believe in God." She wrung her hands together. "And that is a deal breaker for me."

"Are you serious?"

"Yes."

Nick stared at her in disbelief. "Whatever you say, *sweetheart.*"

For the rest of the flight neither talked, which was just as well. In a few hours, she would once again say goodbye to him. Only this time it would have to be forever. *Forever* ripped through her heart like a jagged knife.

She leaned her head on the back of the seat, looking at him from the corner of her eye. It was just as well. He could never be true to one woman. Here he talked about starting a relationship with her, after he had already made plans with Heidi. No, she didn't feel bad about ending this before it started. Better end it for God than over Heidi or someone else. *Someone like her cousin Carissa.*

The family beauty with her long blonde hair and emerald eyes would capture Nick in seconds. It happened over and over again. Why would this time be any different? Brittany groaned inwardly. It already was different. This time she cared. And Carissa would know it.

Her heart ached. She closed her eyes and prayed. *Dear Heavenly Father, he doesn't love You, so I can't love him. But it hurts so bad. Help me get over him.*

"Are you okay?" Nick said.

"Yes," she mumbled through her hands.

"Need an air bag?"

She attempted a smile. "Now that I'm almost home, I guess the tension of the last few days just hit me." Brittany wished that were true, but the stress of her trip was nothing compared to the emotional roller coaster of her heart.

"It has been a rough few days." Nick laid his hand on hers. Part of her wanted to pull away, to save herself from more pain. The other part wanted to throw both arms around him and never let go. What kind of fool had she become?

"I have a thought. One I'm sure your God won't object to. We can be friends." That thought hung between them as they flew over a mountain and the compound came into sight.

He whistled. "No wonder they had me bring you here. This place is a fortress." An endless stone wall weaved around the mountain. A driveway curved its way up the mountain to the front of a massive stone mansion. No one could get in without going through the front gate, or flying in. "You definitely won't be needing me anymore."

I do need you! she wanted to scream. Instead, she said, "It's more like a resort." She pointed. "There's a swimming pool, tennis courts, a track for running, horses, snowmobiles, and whatever your heart desires. Even our own private mountain for skiing."

"Didn't realize a judge made that kind of money."

She laughed. "My grandmother's from old money. Her great-grandfather struck it rich in the gold rush. With all the shady characters back then, he was afraid for the safety of his family, so he built a wall around his mountain. Over the years it's been added onto, but it still keeps out shady characters."

Nick nearly had the helicopter down on the front lawn when a team of men surrounded the chopper with guns aimed.

"They're going to shoot us!" Brittany screamed.

"Just precautions. They know it's us."

Brittany closed her eyes and held her breath, praying until Nick finished landing.

"You can open your eyes, angel. You're safe."

Before Nick turned off the propellers, Carl had Brittany out of the chopper. Ducking down, he guided her away from the helicopter. Once out of the propeller's range, he hugged her. "So glad you're safe."

Brittany glanced over her shoulder. "Thanks to Nick, I am."

Carl took her by the arm and started walking toward the house. "Your grandparents are anxious to see you."

"I'm sure they've been worried sick." Brittany paused, patting Carl's arm. "I'll be right back." She hurried back to Nick who was exiting the chopper.

"Thank you." She hugged him. Laying her head on his chest, she enjoyed the feel of his arms around her for just a minute. Pulling away, she whispered, "I really wish it would work, but it won't. We're as different as champagne and beer." She kissed him softly on the lips before running toward the house. She had to get away before the tears started.

Nick was taken by surprise. The soft brush of her lips had ignited a flame. "Brittany," he called, starting to follow her, but a firm hand on his arm stopped him. Turning, he saw his boss, Carl.

"I have a crew heading to clean up the mess at the cabin. They will also fix the dent in your car, and will return it back to Heidi's for you to pick up."

Nick nodded.

"The pictures arrived moments ago. Looks like you had trouble everywhere you turned."

"Yeah, and I want to know why." Nick glanced at Brittany's retreating back. If she disappeared into that mansion, he would never see her again. He brushed Carl off. "We'll talk about it later." He ran and caught up to her as she entered the house. Brittany barely acknowledged him.

"Brittany!" A young blonde rushed down the steps and threw her arms around Brittany. "I thought those nasty Capris had gotten you."

Nick looked from one to the other. They looked almost identical.

Brittany hugged her cousin in return. "Lucky for me, PSA sent the best. Nick, this is my cousin Veronica, Carissa's sister. This is Nicholas McFadden."

"Nice." Veronica started to giggle uncontrollably.

"What's so funny?" Brittany asked.

"Carissa's going to be furious. They sent an old man for her."

Brittany didn't want to think about what Carissa would do when she saw Nick. "Where is everyone?"

"Not totally sure, but I think Grandfather is in his study. I was up in my room when I heard the helicopter." She snickered. "Sort of avoiding a certain someone." She looked over her shoulder. "I'm surprised they all didn't come running."

No sooner were the words spoken than Brittany's grandmother came hurrying down the stairs. She hugged Brittany in a tight embrace. "Thank the good Lord you are safe." She looked at Nick. "And thank you for bringing my little girl home."

"My pleasure, ma'am."

"Call me Lillian."

"Yes, ma'am, um Lillian," Nick stammered.

"Your grandfather is anxious to see you both." Lillian kissed Brittany on the cheek, "Come to my sitting room when you're finished." She patted Nick on the arm, "We can never thank you enough."

Brittany guided them down a long marble hallway, stopping in front of the third oak door.

"Grandfather!" Brittany hurried across the room.

James Hathaway rose to greet them. He came around the desk with outstretched arms. "We've been so worried." He hugged her tightly then looked at Nick. "So, this is the young man responsible for getting you here safely."

"Grandfather, this is Nicholas McFadden, my valiant knight."

"Glad to meet you, Nicholas." They locked eyes during a firm handshake. Looking down at Brittany, James asked, "I'm sure your grandmother will want to count all your fingers and toes. Try to avoid Carissa and your Aunt Constance. They're both in foul moods." Kissing Brittany's cheek, he added, "Your being here has made a tired old man happy. Now, run along to your grandmother. I need to talk to your young man."

Nick watched her go, wondering if this would be the last time he saw her. She paused and turned at the door. Their eyes locked and his heart swelled. He took a step toward her, but she bolted out of the room. His heart felt as if the closing door had ripped his soul from his body. He stood frozen, staring at the door.

Okay you sap, emotions are for fools. You've been trained to ignore everything but the job at hand. And unless Carl walks in and fires me, I'm still on the job. Get your act together. He closed his eyes, inhaled, and felt the calm return. He heard James. "Marcy, bring Mr. Miller to my study, please." He turned and faced her grandfather. Time to face the music.

James put an arm across Nick's shoulder. "Nick, may I call you Nick?" Nick nodded. "How about joining me in celebrating the safe return of my favorite granddaughter?" The judge led Nick over to the bar in the corner. "What would you like?"

"I'm not sure if I'm still on duty. Water would be fine."

He watched as the judge set three glasses out on the bar. Though his hair was white, the face and body were untouched by signs of age. He wasn't exactly a "tired old man." Tall and lean, the laugh lines around his blue eyes were his only wrinkles. Nick guessed him to be about seventy, and 6'2". But this warm and loving grandfather had a reputation for turning into a raging bull.

The judge handed Nick a glass of bourbon. "I'd wager you are off the job. Have a seat and tell me what happened."

"Okay..."

The study door opened again and his boss, Carl, entered. James handed him a drink as well, and they all took seats on leather chairs around the coffee table. Nick went into detail about their trip. What had Brittany called him? *Her valiant knight?* He certainly didn't feel valiant now as he confessed the details of multiple attacks on Brittany's life. He downed his drink. He had gotten sloppy, let his emotions cloud his judgment, and for that he deserved whatever punishment he was about to be dealt.

James poured each of them another drink. "The Capris are a bad lot, and Vincent is the worst of them. I am forever indebted to you for saving Brittany." James raised his glass in a toast. "Carl tells me that you're going to leave right away. Can I talk you into staying on to protect Brittany until this is over?"

Nick glanced from James to Carl. Had he heard right? They wanted him to continue to protect Brittany. Isn't that what he wanted? He shook his head. "For her safety, you'd be better off assigning someone else."

"Looks to me like you saved her life more than once on this trip."

"The Capris never would have gotten as close if I hadn't been distracted. In this work, the slightest loss of focus can get you killed."

"And what was the distraction?"

Nick sipped his drink. How do you tell a man his granddaughter is so desirable that your job was the farthest thing from your mind?

James chuckled. "And does she find you to be a distraction, too?"

Nick ran his finger around his collar, "You'll have to ask her that yourself."

James pulled a cell phone from his shirt pocket. For a moment, Nick wondered if he would call Brittany. "Set another plate for dinner," the judge said and hung up. A mixture of relief and disappointment washed over Nick. "I see no reason why you can't stay the night. The least I can do is offer a good meal and a warm bed to the man who saved my granddaughter's life."

Carissa was furious. How did the Ice Maiden get assigned a gorgeous body guard? Someone would be hearing about this. How dare they send an old weasel for her and give Brittany a drop dead gorgeous hunk? *Veronica had better be lying or heads will roll.*

Carissa placed an ear to the thick study door, straining to hear what was being said. Disappointed, she hurried next door to the library and out through French doors to the patio. By squeezing behind the bushes and squatting down below the window, she could hear some of the conversation.

The deep sexy tone of the stranger thrilled her. With a voice like that, he had to be gorgeous. She listened for a few more minutes. Hearing enough, Carissa hurried back inside, threw open the study door, and breezed in.

One look at Nick and she practically purred. "Grandfather, you are being simply awful. How could you be so selfish, keeping this gorgeous creature to yourself all afternoon?" She brazenly waltzed over to Nick.

"Carissa." Her grandfather gave her a look of displeasure.

With a toss of her long blonde hair, she joined the stranger on the leather sofa. Breathlessly she introduced herself. "Hello, I'm Carissa." Her eyes ran seductively over him. *Veronica wasn't lying.* If anything, she had understated his magnificence.

"Yes, I know. We've met before."

"I don't think so. I would have remembered someone as gorgeous as you," she said before examining his face for familiar signs. "What did you say your name was?"

"Nick McFadden."

Carissa's hands flew over her mouth. "*No!*" Then she softly giggled. "You've aged well." A gleam of pure delight shone in her eyes.

The love of Brittany's life had just been tossed at her feet. She noticed her grandfather's gaze on Nick. With satisfaction, she saw a look of displeasure cross it. "I didn't realize you two had met before?" he said.

"Grandfather, this is the guy who broke poor Brittany's heart."

James looked from Nick to Carissa. "The D.E.A. agent?"

Nick held his breath.

"Yes, Grandfather," Carissa said impatiently.

He turned to Carl. "Did you know this?"

"I'm just as surprised as you are."

James reached over and took Nick's hand. "Twice you have saved my granddaughter from the Capris. How can I ever repay you?"

Carissa reached out for Nick's hand and tried to pull him up from the sofa. "Be a dear and give Nicky to me. That old man guarding me would be much better for the Ice Maiden."

"That will be enough, Carissa. Run along. We have things to discuss."

"What else could you possibly have to talk about?" Pouting, Carissa sat back down beside Nick. "It's time Nicky had some fun."

Nick shifted away. Her emerald eyes sparkled as she reached across the couch and fingered the buttons of his shirt.

In a voice that boomed with authority, James said, "Enough."

Carissa jumped up and hurried to the door, giving Nick a last smile before flouncing out of the room. Before the night was over, Brittany would know how it felt to have the man of her dreams in the arms of another. Revenge was about to be served.

Chapter 8

Brittany hurried to her grandmother's sitting room. When she didn't answer the knock, Brittany opened the door and peeked in.

"Grandmother?" She wasn't there. Brittany gave a heavy sigh. She had hoped to avoid Aunt Constance, but without a doubt, that's where Grandmother would be.

The sun danced across the flowered wallpaper as if mocking her. The warmth of this room is what she needed, not the cold dark of Aunt Constance's room. She glanced across the hall at her own bedroom. If she curled up there she would sleep for a year. Unfortunately, sleep would have to wait.

Wearily, she turned and headed toward the east wing. Though her aunt and uncle didn't live here, even when they weren't present, that wing was off limits to anyone but them. Reluctantly, she knocked on her aunt's door. A feeble voice said, "Come in."

Please protect me from all evil before entering this dreaded room, Brittany prayed. She entered. Her eyes were involuntarily drawn to the hideous bedside lamp fashioned like a black cat with glowing green eyes. The eyes seemed to stare at her, and she shivered. As a child, Aunt Constance told her that they'd had another daughter before Carissa. That child had been so naughty she'd been turned into a lamp. The threat was obvious—if she and Carissa didn't behave, the same would happen to them. Brittany tried to laugh away the childish fear.

She hated this room with its dark green drapes pulled tight, a pale green rug, and ivy wallpaper. Even the wingback chair her grandmother sat in while visiting her daughter-in-law was green. The four-poster had a sheer green canopy and curtains that draped down the sides, only the white bedspread broke the monotony. The only light shone from the cat lamp.

In the bed, among a dozen pillows of various shades of green, lay Aunt Constance. Lillian rose to greet her. Hugging her close, she whispered, "We will talk later." Louder she said, "We were so worried about you."

"There was no need to worry. I was in good hands."

"That's not what we were told," Constance snapped. "From the reports, we thought surely they would have to send the National Guard."

Brittany smiled at her aunt. "It wasn't that bad. Nick had everything under control."

"Well, you're here now." Lillian stroked her hair. "You're safe and that is all that matters."

"I knew those reports were being exaggerated." Constance laid the back of one hand to her own forehead. "Since you're here, you might as well massage my temples."

With her other hand, Constance patted the bed, her red nails vivid against the white sheets. "It's the least you can do after this needless worrying. It caused me a tremendous headache." She made a big production of rearranging the pillows so Brittany could sit behind her.

Brittany glanced at the door then sent a pleading glance toward her grandmother. Lillian smiled. "You do give such wonderful massages."

"What are you waiting for, child?" Constance patted the bed again.

Walking slowly, Brittany took a deep breath then gently sat down.

"Brittany, please," Constance whined, "don't bounce."

Lillian returned to her chair and picked up her notebook. "Since you are safe, now we can plan Thanksgiving dinner. Anything special you want?"

"The usual."

"That's what's wrong with you," Constance scolded. "You're so conventional and boring. If you would just..."

Brittany tuned out the prattling. Constance could go on and on, never expecting or accepting any comments.

"Maybe it's fashionable to fly around in a noisy helicopter on the east coast, but not here. Why didn't you just fly in your own private jet? I really don't know what's come over you. What will the neighbors think? I doubt if my headache will go away for days after all that racket."

Brittany tried not to laugh. They were near the top of the mountain; their nearest neighbor was her great uncle on the other side of the mountain. As for the racket, here in the back of the house the only noise would have been a dim roar.

"Why don't you go and rest before dinner?" her grandmother suggested, "I know you've had a stressful few days."

Brittany gave her grandmother a look of gratitude. "I really could use a nap. I haven't slept much lately."

She kissed the top of Aunt Constance's head before leaning over to kiss her grandmother's cheek. "I'll see you at dinner."

Closing the door behind her, Brittany gave a sigh of relief. If she were lucky, she could make it to her room without running into Carissa. Opening the door to her bedroom, she grinned at the familiar woman inside.

"Nannie." Brittany rushed across the room, and Nannie turned with outstretched arms.

"They said my wee lassie had come home, but—" She sniffed back her tears. "I just couldn't bring myself to believe it 'til I saw it with my own eyes." Hugging Brittany, she laughed. "Look at me, crying like a wee babe." She wiped the tears from her face with the corner of her apron. "Ah, we were so worried about you."

"It seems everyone was..." Brittany giggled. "Including Aunt Constance."

"*Humph*, I'll bet. It just gave her a good excuse to stay in bed. Have you been to see your *Maimeó?*"

"For a few minutes. Unfortunately, she's in Aunt Constance's room." Brittany opened the French doors and walked out onto the balcony. She breathed in the fresh mountain air, glad to be alive. *Thank you, God. If not for Nick...* She shivered.

"Dear child, come in before you catch your death of a cold."

"I'm fine."

"Well, put this on," Nannie said, draping a jacket across Brittany's shoulders.

She turned and hugged the older woman. "You're always looking out for me."

"As if you were my own." She rubbed Brittany's hair. "Just like I did your mother. I got down on my hands and knees and prayed to the good Lord that He wouldn't see fit to take you like He did your mother."

Brittany smiled, "And here I am, the answer to your prayers. Thank you." She looked out over the estate. In the spring, the gardens would be alive with color, but today it was dead. Her heart fluttered as she thought of the men Nick had to kill to protect her. The tennis courts were empty, horses grazed in the fields, not a soul in sight. She glanced at the track where they trained the horses. "I was going to take a nap, but honestly with all that has happened I don't think I could." She walked to her dresser, taking out a pair of yoga pants and sweat shirt. "I think I'll go for a run. Care to join me?"

Nannie patted her round hips. "Me and these hips have a date with a piece of Abby's chocolate cake."

Brittany pointed her finger at Nannie. "Not before dinner."

Quickly, she donned running shoes and hurried outside, eager to exercise and relieve the tension of the past couple days. The familiar rhythm of her pace relieved a bit of the stress. As she rounded the bend of the track, her eyes drifted toward her bedroom window. She stumbled, almost losing her balance at the sight of him on the balcony next door to her room. He was so striking. The setting sun glistened in his long black hair like specks of gold. The rays caressed his flesh, making him look more like a god than a man. For a moment, their eyes met and held. Brittany smiled and waved.

Like lightning, Nick disappeared. The slamming door filled her heart with anguish. She stared at the closed door and knew it only reinforced the words her heart knew to be true. Without God in Nick's life, that door must remain closed. She slowed her steps. The joy of running had sunk along with the setting sun.

Nick stepped out of the shower and dried off. Pulling on a clean pair of jeans, he walked over to the balcony. Spellbound, he watched Brittany run around the track, her grace and beauty flowing. Forgotten were his wet hair, bare chest, and feet. He stepped outside. The desire to be near her filled his heart. Time stood still. He knew he wanted her as much today as that first moment he saw her.

Out of the corner of his eye, he caught a movement in the garden below him. *Carissa.* He groaned, dashing back inside and slamming the door behind him. Nick stood against the closed door hoping he had ducked in before Carissa had seen him. The sugary sound of his name shattered that hope.

"Nicky darling, come out."

Nicky? Did she actually expect him to answer to that childish name? Well, she would be waiting a long time. He lay on the bed and closed his eyes, drifting off to sleep, dreaming of Brittany.

He woke with a start and watched the bedroom door slowly open. He reached under the pillow for his gun. Nick was relieved to see a stout elderly gentleman rather than a thug. *Or Carissa.*

"Pardon me, sir. I knocked, but no one answered."

Nick sat up and put his feet on the floor.

"It's almost time for dinner." The butler laid a jacket on the end of Nick's bed, then went to the closet and chose a shirt to match the tie he'd brought with him.

Nick looked at the clothing.

"Compliments of the judge. He didn't think you would have a suit with you."

Nick laughed. "No, I don't."

"I'm Douglas. If I can be of any assistance, just ring." He pointed to a button on the wall beside the bed.

"Thanks," Nick said as Douglas left the room. He quickly dressed, but stared at the tie. He hadn't worn one in years and doubted he remembered how to tie one. Standing in front of the mirror, he got the knot lopsided then tried again. The next time it looked even worse. He glanced at the button for Douglas, but decided he wasn't going to be that guy. He smiled. *I bet Brittany knows a thing or two about ties.*

Nick pulled his hair back into a ponytail and left the room. He looked up and down the hallway, wondering how he would ever find Brittany in this palace. There were ten doors in this wing alone, five on each side of the hallway. Starting to turn back, he saw Veronica swing around the corner.

"Wow." She smiled. "You dress up nice."

"Thanks, so do you." He winked. "Other than the hair color, you could pass for Brittany at seventeen."

"Everyone says that. We both look like our grandmother."

"Do you happen to know where your cousin is?"

"Probably hiding out in her room." Veronica knocked then opened the door adjacent to Nick's. "There's a hunky guy looking for you."

"Let him look." Brittany's icy tone sent a chill through him.

"Is she decent?" he asked. Veronica nodded. Nick pushed the door open wide and entered. "My search is over."

Brittany was seated at her vanity. She refused to look at him in the mirror, reaching instead for a tube of lipstick.

"You don't need that. Your lips are perfect the way they are." Her eyes drifted up to his. Icy blue and cold. He pulled at the collar of his shirt. "I was wondering if you knew how to tie this confounded thing."

"Of course, she does. We all learned on grandfather," Veronica chimed in. "And since three's a crowd, I'm out of here."

"It's been a long time since I have had to wear a tie." Nick laughed, trying to warm her mood.

"Not surprising." Brittany's hands were shaking. "You seemed to have made quite an impression on Grandfather."

Nick took her hands in his, drawing Brittany to her feet. "He isn't the person I care about impressing." He placed a finger under her chin and gently raised her face. Her eyes told him there was still hope for them. His arms tightened around her as he hungrily captured her lips.

Brittany's hands went inside his jacket, around his waist, as her body melted into his.

The door flew open. Nick spun, reaching for his gun, but it wasn't there. He pushed Brittany behind him.

"Nicky, darling," Carissa purred. "Veronica says you need help with your tie." She glided across the room. "Oh, you're already done." She stroked the crisp Windsor knot. "Next time come find me. I'm much better than her."

She eyed Brittany suspiciously. Nick wondered if she noticed her cousin's flushed cheeks. With a smug look, Carissa linked her arm with his. "You will escort me to dinner, won't you?"

"I'm sorry. I've already promised Brittany."

"Oh!" Carissa's eyes threw daggers at her cousin. "Well, duty goes only so far. After dinner, we'll go for dessert." Playing seductively with his tie again, she pressed her body against his. "You were naughty this afternoon, ducking in from the balcony like that. Didn't you hear me calling you?"

Nick stepped away from her. Holding his arm out for Brittany, he asked, "Are you ready?"

Carissa glared as they left her standing in the room alone. She followed them out, slamming the door as she went. Nick hurried them down the stairs then let out a breath when they reached the bottom and Carissa passed them. Instinct told him she was someone to never turn your back on.

In the sitting room, Brittany introduced Nick to her uncle Jim Jr. and his sons, JB and Frederick, before pointing to the corner bar. "Would you like a drink before dinner? Carlos will make you anything you want."

Nick shook his head. "Nothing for me, thanks."

"Don't tell me you are a teetotaler too," Carissa said with a sneer.

"No, I'm not." He turned his back. He didn't have to explain his actions to her.

Jim Jr. asked Nick a question about their trip. Before he could answer, James and Carl entered the room. Brittany rushed to give her grandfather a big hug.

Carissa smiled smugly at Brittany and waltzed over to Nick. She ran her long nails down Nick's arm. "Nicky dear, did the Ice Maiden treat you nicely or—"

"Who's the Ice Maiden?"

"Brittany, silly." Carissa smiled slyly. "But I'm sure you're just being polite."

James kissed his wife's cheek when she entered the room. Taking her arm, he led her to Nick. "Lillian, have you had the chance to meet Nick, Brittany's valiant knight?"

Brittany blushed.

"Yes, for a few moments in the hallway." She hugged Nick. "I will forever be grateful to you for saving my granddaughter."

"Mother Hathaway," Constance said coming into the room, "the poor boy doesn't want you hanging on him."

"You can hug me anytime." Nick winked at Lillian. "My arms are always open to beautiful women."

Lillian laughed. "Why doesn't that surprise me?"

Carissa slipped under Nick's arm once more and cuddled in close. "No need to hug anyone else when you have me." Glancing up through mascara-covered lashes, Carissa added, "I assure you, if we were together, you never would have asked to be reassigned."

"Who asked to be reassigned?" Constance asked.

"Nicky did. It seems he was unhappy with the Ice Maiden." Carissa's eyes sparkled with joy.

"That's not true," Nick said quickly.

"Nick had just stepped off a plane from six months undercover in Mexico when I got the call about Brittany. As his boss, I've ordered him to return home for some much-needed rest."

"Grandfather did ask him to stay on and he refused. Didn't he?"

Brittany sank down onto the sofa. Her pale face said it all. Once again, he had hurt her. If Carissa had been a man, he would have belted her.

Taking a step toward Brittany, Nick stopped when Carissa's long nails planted on his arm. "Since Brittany has failed to impress you, maybe I can change your mind about staying."

"If I were staying, it would be for Brittany." He stepped back from Carissa. "Brittany..."

"Dinner is served," Douglas announced.

Brittany whispered something to Douglas as they entered the dining room.

"Master Nick, you may sit here." Douglas pointed to the chair beside Carissa.

Nick glanced across the table to where Brittany sat, but she refused to glance his way. With dread, he took a seat.

Nick was getting a headache listening to the senseless babble of Carissa and her mother. Not once had Brittany glanced his way. He knew because he watched her intently.

Finally, the ordeal of dinner was over and they adjourned to the sitting room for after-dinner drinks. Now was his chance to talk with Brittany, but by the time he escaped Carissa's clutches, Brittany had already seated herself between Veronica and her grandmother.

Constance spoke. "Instead of the normal holiday parties, I was thinking it would be nice for everyone to fly down to Cancun for New Year's."

Carissa choked on her drink. Brittany's hands clutched the edge of the sofa. They both screamed, "No!" at the same time. All eyes turned to them in surprise.

Nick glanced from Brittany to Carissa. Why were they overreacting?

"Of all times for the two of you to agree on something, it has to be now," Constance said in a huff. "Are we to be banned from the island just because some boy you once dated died there?"

"He wasn't some boy." Carissa's face had paled and her knuckles were white around her glass. "He was the love of my life." She glared at Brittany. "He didn't die, Mother." Pure hatred filled her eyes as she leaned toward Brittany. "He was murdered."

Nick was taken aback by the animosity Carissa aimed toward Brittany. What was going on with these two? Ten years ago, they were best friends. Now they were enemies.

Constance waved her hand in the air as if to dismiss Carissa's outburst. "Well, I, for one, am tired of being exiled from such a wonderful place just because the two of you have bad memories." She smiled at Lillian. "Don't you remember how grand that boy's family resort was?"

"That boy had a name!" Carissa was near to hysterics. "Alexander Rolands."

Constance kept talking as if she hadn't heard her daughter. "Wouldn't it be wonderful to have New Year's there and put all this drama behind us?"

Lillian put her arm around Carissa. Carissa shrugged it off. "Constance, I really don't think that is a good idea."

"Why not?"

"At this late notice, I'm sure they are booked up."

"Of course they are, but I'm sure for Carissa's family they would find accommodations for us."

"How do you think your friends would feel being treated like an afterthought?" Lillian smiled sweetly. "You know that is what they will think. A party like this would have been planned months ago and the invites already sent out." Lillian paused to let her words register. "You know full well anyone receiving an invitation at this late date will automatically assume you forgot to invite them and they are just filling a vacant spot. They would never believe you waited this late to plan a party in Cancun."

"Oh my." Constance apparently hadn't thought of that. She sighed. "So, what shall we do? I'm simply bored with the usual events. This year I wanted something grand, something everyone will be talking about for years to come."

While the women discussed the upcoming holiday, the men—eager to hear more about the events of the last few days—drifted toward the bar. Carissa's younger brothers crowded around Nick. "Geez," JB said looking at Brittany. "You're lucky. Nothing exciting ever happens here." His eyes grew wide as he asked Nick, "Did you really shoot a man right between the eyes?"

"Gross," said nine-year-old Frederick, as he moved closer to hear Nick's reply.

"Where did you hear that?" Jim Jr. asked. JB shrugged his shoulders.

"He was hiding behind the sofa in the study listening to Uncle Carl's phone conversation," Frederick said. JB jabbed him with an elbow. "Ouch!"

"JB, for the life of me, I don't know where you learned such behavior," Constance said indignantly.

"You and Carissa do it all the time."

"JB!" She grabbed her throat. "I have never hidden behind a sofa in my life."

"No, but you stand outside the door all the time."

"Go to your room, young man."

Before leaving, he said to Frederick, "Ask him to show you the pictures of the one he shot in the head."

Brittany visibly paled and apologetically said, "I'm sorry. I can't handle this conversation. If you will excuse me, I think I will go to my room." She kissed her grandparents on the cheek and practically ran from the room.

Nick started after her, but Constance's hateful laugh stopped him. "No wonder you asked to be reassigned. The baby probably cried the whole way here."

Carissa snickered.

Nick spun on his heels, contempt for mother and daughter burning in his eyes. "Let's get this straight. I did not ask to be reassigned!" He glared at Constance. "Brittany is a very brave and remarkable woman. I wonder how you would have reacted to being shot at again and again, not to mention being dragged through the woods, chased out a bathroom window, and having to step over dead bodies."

"Young man, there's no need to exaggerate. Brittany already told us it was nothing."

"I assure you, I do not exaggerate."

"I'm growing weary of this whole conversation," Constance said with a wave of her hand. "Why everyone wants to make more of this than what it really was is beyond me."

"Uncle Carl has pictures that show what happened," JB said, jumping up from behind the sofa. Nick wondered how he had slipped back into the room.

Carl shook his head. "They're nothing you would want to see."

Carissa jumped up. "I want to see the pictures."

"No one is seeing those pictures," James said.

"Oh, come on, Grandfather. I'm not a child."

"If there are pictures of Brittany's so-called ordeal, I would most definitely like to see them," Constance said.

"Suit yourself. Either way, we end this topic once and for all." James motioned to Carl.

Pulling the photos up on his phone, Carl passed it to James saying, "You sure you want them to see these?"

James scrolled through the photos. "No, but I'm tired of this bickering."

Constance grabbed the device from James' hand and Carissa looked over her mother's shoulder. They smiled smugly at the picture of the bullet-ridden bed.

"No one was in the bed, I see," Carissa purred.

"We were, just a second before."

Carissa's head jerked up. "You slept with the Ice Maiden?"

"No." Nick straightened his tie. "One of us slept on the floor."

Carissa scoffed, "Why am I not surprised?"

Constance flipped forward to other photos. "These don't look—" She gasped at the photograph of the first dead man. With a scream, she tossed the phone and started to swoon. Her husband Jim Jr. caught her before she fainted. Carissa adeptly caught the cell before it hit the floor. One look at the graphic image and she fled the room.

Nick excused himself. He took the stairs two at a time and made a beeline to Brittany's room. Lifting his hand to knock, he wondered what he would say to her.

Could he tell her he couldn't stay on because she was too much of a distraction?

He stood with knuckles paused a few inches from her door. How could he tell her he didn't mean to hurt her, but there was no way he could stay on? Would she understand? His courage failed him. He turned away, stopping at his own door, but briefly glancing back. What was wrong with him? He faced bad guys every day and never felt as afraid as he did right now. No, it wasn't the idea of facing her that frightened him. It was the thought of never again seeing the ice melt from her eyes when she looked at him.

Nick tossed his jacket and tie on a chair, unbuttoned his shirt, and walked to the balcony door. His heart stopped beating. Brittany hadn't gone to her room after all. He could see her racing around the track in the moonlight, running much faster than she had earlier. Why did the sight of her always make his heart do that?

There was a knock on his door and he went to answer it.

"Mr. Nick." Frederick lowered his eyes to the floor, "My cousin sent me to see if you would meet her in the garden behind the house in five minutes." His eyes darted around the hall. The second he said yes, Frederick pointed to the back hallway. "She said to take the back stairs. It will be easier to find her." Then he ran down the hall and out of sight.

Nick grabbed his jacket off the back of the chair, glancing out the balcony door to see that Brittany had just finished her run. Hurrying down the back stairs, he rushed to meet her.

He arrived in the garden. The cobblestone path leading toward the track was dimly lit with solar lights. He was startled when Carissa came up behind him.

"So, you got my message." She walked up to him, running her long nails down the front of his jacket. "I wasn't sure if you would come."

Nick grabbed hold of her hands. "I misunderstood. I thought Brittany was the one who wanted to meet."

Carissa threw back her head and laughed. "The Ice Maiden? What a silly thought." She smiled smugly, threw her arms around his neck, and kissed him just as Brittany rounded the curve of the garden.

Gasping, Brittany's hands flew to her throat. She stood frozen, staring at them.

Nick awkwardly pushed Carissa away. "Brittany," he said, taking a step toward her.

Carissa wrapped her arm around Nick's, holding him back. "We weren't expecting to see you." She ran a hand down the front of his shirt.

Nick grabbed her hand by the wrist and wrenched it away, glaring at Carissa. "Stay away from me." He turned to move toward Brittany, but she was already running, tears glistening in her eyes.

Chapter 9

Nick hurried after Brittany. "Wait," he called. The sound of Carissa's sinister laugh sent a chill through him. Brittany was just a few paces ahead, but somehow, she had disappeared.

"You won't find her."

Furious, he spun back to Carissa. Her smug face was his undoing. He leaned down staring her in the eyes. "I don't know what your game is, but I'm not playing."

Fear flooded her eyes momentarily, then the smugness returned. "Too late."

"Stay away from me," he warned.

"Or what?"

"You think you're hiding your drug habit—"

"I don't have—"

"Don't even try to lie. Why your family doesn't see it, I don't know, but I promise if you mess with me again I'll make sure you're arrested. And this time, you won't be making any deals with the D.A."

Carissa backed away from him with fear returning to her features.

Nick took a step toward her and grabbed her arm. "You will tell Brittany that nothing was going on between us." Tightening his grip, he finished. "Is that understood?"

Carissa tried to pull away. "You're hurting me."

He loosened his grip and she pulled free and ran.

Nick felt hopeless. Why should he care? There were plenty of other women. All he had to do was pick up the phone. So why did his heart ache so badly? He had to make this right with Brittany.

Once again, the back stairs were empty. Each step toward Brittany's room felt like a thousand. Would she ever talk to him again? He had lost her once. Could he stand to lose her again? His heart screamed, *No!*

Lightly, he knocked on her door. No answer.

"How could you?" Nick turned to see Veronica, storming down the hallway. "I thought you were different." She bit her lip, as though trying to hold back tears.

"It wasn't what it looked like."

She stood with her hands on her hips. "Brittany saw you kissing Carissa."

"I wasn't kissing Carissa." Nick swiped the back of his hand across his mouth. "She was trying to kiss me."

"That's what they all say." Veronica stomped her foot.

"We weren't kissing." Nick leaned his head against Brittany's door. "She set me up." He glanced down, then back up at Veronica. "I don't get it. Why would she do that? They used to be best friends."

"Ever since Cancun, they've been mortal enemies."

He rubbed the back of his neck. "Somehow, I have to convince Brittany I wasn't kissing Carissa."

"Good luck with that." Veronica smirked. "She isn't in there."

"Where is she?"

"You'd be the last person I'd tell." She started toward the east wing and mumbled under her breath. "Men. You're all alike."

Nick leaned against the door frame. He would just have to wait for Brittany to come back.

A few minutes later, Frederick came up the stairs. Seeing Nick, he turned to hurry back down.

"Come here," Nick said firmly.

Frederick skirted along the wall, staying out of Nick's reach.

"Why did you tell me your cousin wanted to meet, when it was really your sister?"

Frederick stuttered. "*Ummm, ummm*, she made me."

"You do know it's wrong to do something when you know it's meant to hurt other people, don't you?"

"I didn't want to hurt Brittany." The boy looked up and down the hallway. "But I don't want to be turned into a cat."

"What?"

Frederick whispered, "Carissa said if I didn't tell you that my cousin wanted to see you, then she would turn me into a matching cat lamp for my mother's room."

Nick touched Frederick gently on the shoulder and knelt in front of him. "You do know she can't really do that..."

"Oh no, she can. My mother told her how." Frederick started to cry. "I don't want to be a lamp."

Nick wiped the tears away. "I'll make you a promise, but you have to make me a promise, too."

"What's that?"

Nick reached into his pocket, pulled out a stone, and handed it to Frederick. "I've been carrying this around since I was a little boy. My grandfather gave it to me.

When I was afraid, he told me a story about how God made rocks to help people. There are many different kinds. He said some rocks are for climbing, so we can move up higher, some are for shelter, and some like the rock that David used, are to save us. David's little rock defeated Goliath. He was just a boy, maybe not even as old as you, but he was brave because he had a rock, and since God created the rock, David knew he would be safe. Whenever you're afraid, just touch the stone and the strength from it will help you be brave. Because you see, nothing can hurt stone. It's too strong." Nick took the rock from Frederick.

"Not even Carissa?"

Nick ruffled Frederick's hair. "Watch this." He put the stone in his fist and tried to smash it with both hands, then placed it on the ground and stomped on it. "I can't break it. What is for God's use cannot be broken. And I know you can be strong like this rock." He placed it back into Frederick's hand and closed the boy's fingers around it. "It's like carrying a piece of God's love with you always."

Fredrick looked at the stone in awe. "Brittany says God loves me, but Carissa says He isn't real. Do you think He is real?"

Nick's heart contracted. He rubbed the back of his neck. How could he crush this child's hope? He took a deep breath. "Yes." He felt a burning in his chest. He shook his head. *Heartburn.* "Now to the promise. If Carissa, or anyone else, ever threatens to hurt you again, I want you to call me." Nick pulled out his business card and wrote his home number on it. "And I will take care of it. I won't allow Carissa to turn you into a cat..." He bit the inside of his jaw, trying not to smile. "...or anything else for that matter."

Frederick wiped the back of his hand across his watery eyes. "Promise?"

"Promise." Nick laid his hand on Frederick's shoulder. "Now it's your turn."

"Okay."

"You need to tell Brittany why I went to the garden."

Frederick looked at the stone in his hand. Holding it tight he said, "I'll be brave and tell her. I promise." Frederick threw his arms around Nick's neck. "I'm sorry."

"You're forgiven." He patted the boy's back. "Now run along. It's getting late."

"Brittany's not in there, you know."

"I know, but she has to come back sometime."

"She won't come in this way."

Nick raised an eyebrow. "What other way is there?"

"She'll use the secret hallway."

"Where is that?"

"No one will tell me, but I know there's one. Sometimes Brittany and Carissa will be in the garden and they just disappear. Other times, I'll see them upstairs and then they're downstairs without coming down the steps."

"Hmm, well I'll wait here anyway."

"Night, Mr. Nick." Frederick ran down the hall, but before rounding the corner, he held up the rock. "Thanks."

Nick leaned back against the wall, smiling. It had been a long time since he'd thought of that story. His pocket felt empty without his grandfather's rock. *Someone needed it more than me.* Then Nick's smile turned to a frown. He didn't know what Carissa's problem was, but he was going to see she never hurt Brittany again.

Chapter 10

The helicopter lifted from the ground. Nick couldn't stop himself from glancing back at her window. His heart skipped a beat. Was the moonlight playing tricks on him? Was she there on the balcony? He squinted into the darkness. Would this be the last time he lay eyes on her? The thought choked him. It was ten years ago all over again. The love of his life was taken from him. He hovered inches off the ground. Did he dare go to her? He swallowed hard. The swirl of the blades seemed to say 'love' was a word for fools... Well, this fool had survived before, he would survive again. He turned his helicopter south, refusing a final look back. He had done nothing wrong. He adjusted the collective lever and the copter rose quickly. He took a deep breath as he flew over the mountain. Soon he would be at his cabin. Alone—just the way he liked it.

Yet he was still disheartened when he landed at Heidi's airstrip. No sooner had he gotten his bag and started toward his car when Heidi came running. "Nick!" She tried to jump into his arms, but he sidestepped her. "You aren't coming in?"

He shook his head. Ignoring him, she linked her arm through his and pulled toward her house. He withdrew.

"What's wrong?"

"Nothing." He tossed his duffel bag into the trunk of the Porsche.

As he started toward the driver's side, Heidi grabbed his arm. "What you need is a drink."

Like a lost puppy, Nick let her lead him.

"Make yourself comfortable, I'll be back in a flash." She leaned against the doorframe. "I know exactly what will make you feel better."

As if on autopilot, he sat on the sofa and propped his feet on the coffee table. His mind swirled with unanswered questions. What was Brittany doing? Was she thinking about him? Had Frederick told her the truth? *Would it matter?* He kicked himself for dwelling on her when he had Heidi to make him happy.

Heidi welcomed him with open arms, never asking or caring about the other women in his life. He came and went as he pleased. No strings, no questions, just his freedom. Where Brittany on the other hand... *Brittany.* His heart skipped a beat. *Get out of my head!*

He leaned his head back on the sofa. A headache was coming on.

Heidi returned wearing only one of his shirts, carrying a bottle of Jack Daniels and two glasses. Nick took the whiskey and glasses from her. Filling them, he handed one to Heidi and downed the other. The liquid warmed its way through his body. *What do you know? I can feel something besides misery.*

He poured another glass and started to down it, when Heidi placed her hand over his. "Talk to me."

He polished off the second drink and then leaned his head back on the sofa.

"Did something terrible happen after you left here?"

Yeah, I fell in love. His mind started spinning. "No!" he snapped and reached for the bottle. Heidi grabbed his hand.

"I've never seen you like this. Talk to me." She rubbed his arm. "What happened that's so terrible you need to get drunk in order to face?"

Nick laughed. "I'm not trying to get drunk." He moved his hand from the bottle. He was acting like a sap and he knew it. What difference did it make whether Brittany hated him or not? Right in front of him was a beautiful woman anxious to please. "You did invite me in for a drink, didn't you?" He pulled Heidi into his arms. "The whiskey's warm. Are you?"

His kiss searched her as never before... searching for the ecstasy he had tasted in Brittany's lips. Thirsting for fulfillment, he almost called out her name. Disappointment washed over him and he opened his eyes. For the first time in his life, the sweetness of a woman's lips left him cold.

"Sorry, sweetheart." The words escaped him as if from another man. Brittany was right. He did use that endearment too freely. "I have to go."

"Why?" Heidi ran her nails down his chest. "We were just getting started." She grabbed his hand before he could get up to leave. "Stay. I can make whatever is bothering you go away. You know I can."

"I can't." He strode to the door. "Good-bye, Heidi."

"You mean, see you later, right?" she cried in dismay. Heidi rose from the sofa and reached for him, but he kept walking. "You're serious, aren't you? This is really goodbye?"

Nick shrugged. He wasn't sure what he was doing. He did know that it wasn't Heidi's arms he longed to be in. Maybe he was going crazy. He rubbed the back of his neck. He had only felt like this once before—confused, out of control, sick to his stomach —and both times the reason was Brittany.

Heidi ran to keep up with him as he left the house and walked to his vehicle. As he opened the car door, she pleaded, "Please don't go." A sob caught in her throat.

Nick barely glanced at her. "I need to go." He felt relieved as he backed the Porsche around and started down the driveway. With each turn of the wheel closer to his house, a calmness came upon him. At the front of the cabin, he finally took a deep breath. *Home*. That's what his weary soul needed. Some much-needed rest.

Grabbing his bag, he started up the porch stairs. Carl's crew had done their job. Not a trace of yesterday's battle remained. Had it only been yesterday? It seemed like weeks ago. Nick walked into the cabin. Not a speck of blood, or even a remaining bullet hole was left.

Brittany would be pleased. He mentally kicked himself. Why must he keep thinking of her? Would his life ever be the same? He grabbed a soda from the fridge and drank it straight down, then burped. He grinned. At least now he had a good reason for his stomach to feel like revolting.

Brittany, Brittany, Brittany, what have you done to me?

Nothing. Absolutely nothing. That is what she'd done. Other than being the most exasperating woman he had ever met. Nothing. It was jet lag, pure and simple. He'd been foolish to take this job right after landing from Mexico. But the moment he'd heard her name, he knew he had no choice. He had to see her one last time, see the woman she had become. See if that spark was still there.

Nick groaned. Boy, was it ever.

Stop being a sap. There is no spark, no anything. *You're just tired.*

Every muscle in his body ached. His brain was on overload. He grabbed the duffel bag and headed for the bedroom. But first he needed to brush his teeth, get that taste of Jack Daniels out of his mouth. Or was it the taste of Heidi?

Unzipping his bag, he was surprised to find a Bible sitting on top of his things. He pulled it out and opened the cover. Inside was a note.

What if it is true?

He dropped down on the bed, staring at the piece of paper. A Bible was supposed to bring comfort to old people and children, not sensible adults. But Brittany was sensible. What made her believe in God?

He glanced again at the note. *What if it is true?* Lying back on the bed, he sighed. *If it's true, then I'm in big trouble.*

"It's not too late." Where had that thought come from? Was he hearing voices in his head now? Nick rolled over, hugging the Bible to his chest. Somehow, it made her feel closer. Her lingering scent drifted over him. That was impossible—the mattress and bedding weren't even the same as yesterday. Carl's crew had changed it all. And even if they hadn't, she'd never slept in this bed. Virtuous Brittany had slept on the floor.

He rolled over into the oversized pillow and smiled, pulling Brittany's barrier toward him. He wrapped his arms around it and drifted to sleep.

Nick's dreams carried him to a star-filled night on the beach. Brittany was in his arms, their lips joined in a heated embrace. His heart felt the swell of the gentle ocean waves, until suddenly the waves knocked him to the ground. When he reached out for Brittany, it was Carissa in his arms. "*No!*" he screamed, scrambling to his feet to save Brittany.

The waves carried Brittany away from him. He tried to run toward the water, but sand gripped his feet, holding him in place. He called out her name. Suddenly, he could no longer see her. He dropped to the ground.

He felt a gentle touch on his shoulder and hope filled his heart. *Brittany!* He looked up, only to see Carissa, Heidi, Rosita, Maria, Angie, Michele... all the women in his past. Then Brittany was there, standing in the middle, accusing him, *"You love them all?"*

He laughed. "Love is a word for fools."

Brittany backed away. "*Is that what you believe?*"

He reached for her, but couldn't touch her. *You're different*, he wanted to say, but the words wouldn't come. She was slipping away like the sand on the beach, being carried farther and farther away.

Brittany, he lashed out at the waves separating them. The harder he fought, the stronger the waves became. He watched in horror as she was swept out to sea. Carissa's evil laugh drowned out his cry.

He woke in a sweat, heart pounding. Nick swung his feet onto the floor and put his head in his hands. Every inch of his body ached with the loss of her.

Rising, he staggered to the bathroom. He splashed cold water on his face before downing some aspirin. His reflection stared back. It wasn't pretty. His eyes were bloodshot and he was in dire need of a shave. He ran his hand though his shaggy beard. What a mess. He looked like a pathetic dog with his tail between his legs. He cursed. *Are you man enough to fight for what you want, or are you going to allow evil to destroy any chance you have with Brittany?*

The only way to defeat your enemy was to know your enemy. Nick grabbed his cell phone from the nightstand and dialed PSA. "Lisa, I need your expertise."

"Hello to you, too," she replied coolly.

"Sorry. How are you, sweetheart?" *There's that term again.*

She giggled. "You sure know how to make a lady feel special."

"You are special, darling. Hey, I need some information."

"You and everyone else."

"I'll be away a few days, so take your time. Just not too much time. I want every crumb you can find on Carissa Hathaway. You're probably going to have to dig for it because her grandfather is Judge Hathaway and her father is a D.A. They might have covered things up. I know for a fact that Judge Hathaway covered up at least one granddaughter's misdeeds."

"If you're talking about Brittany Fitzpatrick and how she saved your life ten years ago, I don't think that was a cover up."

"How the heck do you... Miles. Boy, does he have a big mouth."

"You should have known better than to tell him anything about your past."

"Well, we were in Iraq fighting. Who would have thought he'd remember all these years later?"

"You are talking about Miles, you know." She chuckled. "He forgets nothing. So do you want me to run a check on Ms. Fitzpatrick, too?"

Nick paused. She had deceived him once. "No, she's clean." He started to hang up, then reconsidered. "Lisa, wait. Check Cancun—I have a feeling something happened there. Thanks."

He hung up, grabbed a water, and headed to the front porch. Ten years ago, Brittany had come into his life like a breath of fresh air. Air that quickly turned him inside out. For two weeks, she'd lied to him until the truth exploded in his face. Then she'd foiled his drug bust by saving his life, but ultimately, in his attempt to save her, he almost lost it anyway. The only difference in this windmill battle was this time his heart was in jeopardy.

Nick needed a run. He hadn't exercised in days. A jog around the property always cleared his head. Setting off toward the woods, his foot kicked a small stone. A rock with yellow and red markings flew out in front of him. His heart skipped a beat. *It looks just like my grandfather's rock.* Nick picked it up and rubbed the yellow line. His grandfather's voice echoed in his memory. *"You know what that yellow line is?"*

"Gold?"

"No," laughed Grandpa. *"It's your life. See how the line is straight for a little bit, then it's broken and goes off into another direction?"*

Young Nick nodded.

"And you see how the red runs alongside and through the yellow? That's the blood of Jesus. There will be times in your life when you won't be sure if He is real or you just don't care. Because it's easier to walk the

path of the world than to walk with Him. During those times, the blood of Jesus covers you. No matter what, He will be with you. Carry this rock with you and remember He is always there waiting to guide you home."

Nick stared at the stone in his hand. He had totally forgotten that part of the story. He flipped it in the air and looked skyward. "Thanks, Grandpa. I remember now."

He flashed back to sitting in church beside his grandfather, suddenly not able to sit still. A warmth filled his heart and body. He remembered walking the aisle and giving his heart to Jesus. *Was it real? Was Jesus real?* A large buck sauntered out of a copse of pines. For a moment, it stared at Nick, then nodded its head before turning back into the woods.

For the first time in years, Nick sank to the ground and prayed.

Brittany lay in bed, curled up in a ball, but sleep refused to come. She wanted to storm into Carissa's room and confront her once and for all. Make her listen to the truth. Brittany punched the pillow. Carissa knew the truth. She just refused to let the animosity go. Revenge was all she thirsted for. Brittany rolled over and stared at the ceiling. She whispered into the darkness. "Was the kiss worth it?" A sob caught in her throat. "I never touched Alex." She groaned. "Your payback was for nothing." The sun's rays mocked her as they danced along the ceiling. She could hear her grandmother's warning it was okay to sleep in, but she was expected at breakfast. Forcing herself to get up, she vowed not to let Carissa know the agony she had caused.

On her knees, she prayed. "Please, bless this day and give me the strength to face what lies ahead. Amen."

Brittany dragged herself to the closet for a jogging suit. No point in messing up her morning routine. Once at the track, barely managing a jog, she noticed the curtain to Carissa's room move slightly. With a burst of unexpected energy, Brittany sped up. *You can't beat me*, her mind screamed.

After the sixteenth lap, she slowed to a cool-down pace. She would have just enough time to shower and get ready for breakfast. Carissa would be there, even though normally her cousin never made it out of bed before noon. Today, Carissa would be there to gloat over Brittany's heartache.

"Good morning, everyone." Brittany breezed into the dining room with a smile. The look of surprise on Carissa's face was worth the charade. She kissed her grandparents before heading to the buffet. "Boy, am I hungry," she said, filling her plate. Sitting across from Carissa, she smiled broader. "What a pleasant surprise to see you this morning." Carissa only glared. "Would you please pass the salt and pepper?"

Carissa slammed the shakers down in front of Brittany.

She forced herself to eat every bite. No way she'd allow Carissa to know that the food tasted like sawdust to her today. "Isn't this breakfast wonderful?" she asked, though the food hit her stomach like rocks. Within ten minutes, Carissa stormed out of the room, the thrill of victory no longer shining in her eyes.

Later that day, Brittany's grandfather came looking for her. "I'd like to talk with you, if you have a minute."

"Sure."

"Let's go to my study."

They walked in silence. When the door was shut and they were seated on the sofa, he spoke. "I was proud of you this morning at breakfast." He took her hand in his. "I wish I knew how to heal this rift between the two of you, but without knowing what caused it—"

"It's not my story to tell," she interrupted.

"I assume it has something to do with the murder of her boyfriend."

Brittany lowered her head. How could she ever confess that she was the reason Carissa was a heroin addict? That Alex was in a wheelchair because of her? She couldn't lie to her grandfather and so she said nothing.

"You know sometimes the telling of the story helps to heal the wounds."

Brittany pulled her hand back. "Like I said, it's not my story to tell."

He put an arm around her shoulder. "Someday the truth will come out. But I see that won't be today." He sighed. "The reason I called you in here is to talk about Nick. I think you owe it to him and yourself to talk about what happened."

"No!" She jumped up.

James patted the sofa. "Brittany, sit back down." She did as she was told. "You had the courage to face Carissa. Why don't you have to courage to face Nick?"

"There is nothing to talk about," she sniffed. "I saw him kissing Carissa."

"Maybe it wasn't what it looked like."

Brittany stared at her grandfather in disbelief, "I saw them."

"Did you?" He squeezed her hand. "I think if you were to search your heart, you will find the truth. You know Carissa's game and you know Nick. Which one is more likely to be telling the truth?"

"Nick's a playboy. There's no reason for him not to be attracted to Carissa. She's beautiful."

"And so are you." He smiled, "It doesn't matter how beautiful someone else is, when a man falls in love there is only one beautiful woman."

"Love, ha," Brittany scorned. "Nick doesn't know the meaning of the word." She wrung her hands together. "I'm sure once he landed at Heidi's, the playboy didn't miss a beat. Nothing will change his nature."

"Men can change. Ask your grandmother."

Chapter 11

Vincent was about to make a birdie on the ninth hole when Sonny sped up alongside him on a golf cart. Vincent patted his gun and said to the others in his foursome, "If he wasn't my cousin, I'd be tempted to shoot him."

They all laughed. Vincent took one look at Sonny's pale face and grinned. *So they found her already.*

He held up a hand. "Whatever it is can wait until I make my shot." Vincent lined up his putt and watched as the ball rolled into the hole. "Now that's how it's done, boys." Turning to Sonny, he growled, "This better be good for you to disturb our game."

"It's bad, real bad." Sonny was shaking as he got out of the cart. "You need to come now."

"What's so bad that it can't wait until I'm finished?" Vincent watched Sonny tremble. "Spit it out, man. I don't have all day."

Sonny kicked at a blade of grass. "It's your sister." Without looking up, he took a step backward and mumbled, "She's dead."

"What did you say?" Vincent advanced toward his cousin.

"Maria..." Sonny choked back a sob. "...was brutally murdered."

"You're lying."

"I'm sorry," Sonny touched his arm. "Your mother..." He gulped. "...found her."

"Mama found her?" Vincent threw his club, barely missing Sonny, and then grabbed him by the shirt. "What do you know?" He pulled Sonny so close he smelled cigarettes on his breath.

Sonny tried to twist out of his grasp. Vincent shook him. "Tell me!"

"She was..." Sonny whispered, "...raped."

"What did you say?" Vincent's hands shifted from Sonny's shirt to his throat now. "I want him found." He started to shake Sonny. He clawed at Vincent's hands. "I want him dead. Do you hear me? Dead!" Vincent squeezed hard. Sonny's face started to turn blue.

One of the golf partners stepped up, "Don't kill the messenger." Vincent glared at him, but released his hold. Sonny dropped to his knees, coughing.

Vincent kicked Sonny, "I want every man looking for whoever did this to my sister!" He climbed into Sonny's golf cart and took off toward the clubhouse. *Sonny can find his own way back.*

Out of sight, Vincent laughed. No one would ever find out who killed Maria. He spit on the ground as her name entered his mind. The lying traitor deserved what she got. And that fool, The Butcher, was shark bait. After all, no one did that to Maria and lived to see another day. Didn't matter that Vincent had paid the man to do it. The Butcher knew the rules. No one touched the Capris and lived to see another day. Stupid sap. He sighed. *It's a shame, really.* He had loved his sister, until he discovered she was sleeping with the enemy. He shook his fist at the sky. Treason had a quick and harsh punishment.

He hit the steering wheel. As if he needed another reason to hate McFadden. He thought back to last night. The family had gathered for Maria's birthday dinner. They were all having a good time, until Vito mentioned Nicholas McFadden. Vincent had been sitting right across from Maria when she said. *"Oh, is he back?"* The second the words left her mouth she must have realized her mistake, because she swiftly added, *"I didn't know Rick Macover was back from Italy."*

Vito laughed. *"Not Rick, sweetheart. Nick. You don't know this guy."*

But he saw the look in her eyes. She did know McFadden. And he was going to find out just how well.

After the party, he followed her home. She had made it easy for him, by taking a shower the minute she returned home. He sneaked up behind her and thumped her head against the wall, knocking her out. By the time she came to, he had her tied to the bed.

First things first, he turned on the video camera before putting a glass of wine to her lips. "Drink up, little sis."

When she refused, he forced her mouth open and poured it down her throat. She spit most of it in his face.

Vincent laughed. "Good girl. Now you'll know exactly what I do to traitors. If you swallowed it all you'd have passed out and missed the best part." He patted her leg. "Don't worry, you only need a little bit in your system to make you too weak to fight him."

Vincent opened the door to her bedroom and motioned for The Butcher to come in. "Do what you want with her."

The Butcher entered the room grinning. "You sure you're okay with this?"

Vincent's laugh filled the room as he noted the look of horror cross Maria's face.

Maria screamed, "I'm your sister!"

"You stopped being my sister the minute you took Nicholas McFadden into your bed." Vincent shook his fist at the sky. "You made me do it." He smiled to himself. He could use this to his advantage. He would pull everyone in to look for Maria's murderer. That would make PSA think Judge Hathaway's family was safe.

Vincent chuckled. He would allow them to enjoy Thanksgiving dinner, maybe even Christmas... after all, this was the season to be merry. Then when their guard was completely down, he would make his move. What The Butcher did to his sister was nothing compared to what Vincent would do to Brittany Fitzpatrick.

Brittany twisted her hands together. She was glad to be home, and yet dreaded what waited inside. When Carl pulled into the driveway, she groaned. "My keys are inside with my purse."

Carl patted her shoulder. "No problem. We re-keyed the locks when we installed the alarm system."

"What?"

"Nick insisted." He winked. "He wasn't happy with your current lack of security."

Brittany gasped when a car pulled in beside them.

Carl opened his car door. "That's Annabelle. She's here to give you your new keys." A tall woman got out of her car and opened Brittany's door. Brittany paused before following Carl up the walkway with Annabelle behind her. Was she still in danger?

Annabelle unlocked the front door and quickly explained the alarm system before handing Brittany the keys. A cold wind blew hair across Brittany's face. Carl took her by the arm. "Let's get in where it's warm."

Brittany hesitated.

Carl patted her arm. "Sweetheart, it's safe."

She closed her eyes and took a deep breath before crossing the threshold. Carl put his arms around her. "You know I would never have brought you home if I didn't believe you would be safe. Don't you?"

Brittany nodded warily and looked around. She ran her hands across the wall. "I thought for sure at least one bullet hit this wall."

"My clean-up crew fixed it," he said. "I assure you the house is just the way it was before Capri's men showed up." He walked through the rooms with her. Back at the front door, he hugged her goodbye. "If you need me, I'm just a call away."

Brittany locked the door behind them. She stood watching them pull out of the driveway and away from the house. She was alone. The silence echoed in her mind. She had always felt safe here, but now—she squeezed her eyes shut. "The Lord is my Shephard..." she prayed as she headed to the kitchen. A good cup of hot tea would calm her nerves.

Next morning, Brittany pulled herself out of bed too late for her run. Thank heavens for automatic coffee makers. She poured herself a cup and raced out the door to school.

Though they had three days left, her students had already mentally gone home for the holiday. After a long day, she looked forward to an afternoon run and then heading to the Arts Center to deliver Thanksgiving food baskets to the students' families.

As she crossed the parking lot, she pulled out her cell phone and texted Mike: Did the turkeys arrive?

"So you do have a cell phone?"

Brittany's heart skipped a beat. There was no mistaking his voice. She tried to keep the smile from her face as her eyes traveled past his arms folded against a lean muscular chest, past the hair peeping from under the top button of his shirt, and past the long dark hair gracing his shoulders. Her gaze continued upward, past his five o'clock stubble and on up to his rich brown eyes. "Nick." Even in a whisper, her delight must be evident. She stopped short, looking around the parking lot. "Are you here to kidnap me again?"

He laughed. "No," he said, holding out an apple. "Brought something for the teacher."

She reached for the apple, fingers brushing his. Her heart pounded wildly. Nick's fingers wrapped around hers and gently pulled her to him. "Did Frederick talk to you?"

"Yes." Brittany pushed away. "But does that really change anything?"

"Why wouldn't it? You know I'm not interested in Carissa."

"Maybe not Carissa," she said scornfully, "but what about Heidi..."

"What does Heidi have to do with anything?"

"You couldn't wait to rush back into her arms, could you?"

"I told you before that green is not your color."

Brittany glanced at her watch. "I really need to go. Thanks for the apple." She tried to reach around him to open her door. He didn't move.

"We need to talk," Nick said.

"There's nothing to say."

"We both know that whatever we had ten years ago is still alive and well. Don't you want to explore this thing between us?"

"Why? We're too different. You're the all-American playboy and..."

Nick threw his head back and laughed. "Is that how you see me, as a playboy?"

Brittany nodded.

"Want to be my bunny?"

"No." She pressed the unlock button on her key fob. "I can't be just a number for you."

Nick stepped away from the car door as she opened it. "Brittany, I'm not walking away from this. I lost you once. I don't want to lose you again." He ran his fingers through her hair. "We could go to dinner as friends, no strings, no expectations." He chuckled. "If it would make you feel better you can even pay."

She glanced up at him. Was his arrival an answer to her prayers? She couldn't keep a giggle from escaping. *Those turkeys are heavy.* She touched his bicep. "I do have dinner plans tonight. You are welcome to join us." She smiled softly.

"Us?"

"Just a few friends and myself." She winked. "And believe me, I'm paying."

At five-thirty on the dot, Nick rang Brittany's doorbell. She opened the door immediately.

"Brittany," he scolded, "never open until you know who's there."

She started to slam the door, but he stuck his foot in the opening and pushed through. "See how easy that was? Less than a week ago you were almost kidnapped..."

"Almost?" Brittany interrupted. "Seems to me I was kidnapped... By you."

"Well, it could have been someone less appealing." Nick grinned.

"Who said you were appealing?"

"Your eyes."

Nick pulled her into his chest, holding her as if he were afraid she would disappear. "And the feeling's mutual." He lowered his lips to hers. He could feel the pounding of her heart, or was it his? For a moment, he felt her surrender, before the wall came crashing down between them once again.

"I'm sorry. I can't do this." She pushed away, then picked up her purse and coat. "I understand if you don't want to come with me tonight. I'm sure you can find something better to do." She hurried toward her car.

Nick set the alarm, shut the door, and rushed to reach her side.

Taking her by the arm, he said, "I'm driving," as he led her to his car. Other than directions, neither said a word. As they pulled into the alley, Nick looked at her in surprise. "We're having dinner here?"

She grinned. "Yes." She pointed to three vans being loaded with food. "First we deliver food to the neighborhood, and then we eat."

Nick opened his car door. "I'm game." He walked around to her door, helped her out, and whispered in her ear, "I still would have said yes, if you had told me, you know."

She quickly introduced him to her staff. Nick glanced into the vans.

"Who pays for all of this?" he asked.

Dan, one of the young men, pointed at Brittany. "She does."

Nick shook his head. "Why not just have a big community dinner like other places do?"

"I believe every family deserves to sit down to a nice Thanksgiving dinner," Brittany added, "at their *own* table."

"But..."

"If you're her friend, then you know nothing you say will change her mind."

Nick turned toward the voice and his heart sunk. Walking toward them was the all-American quarterback kind of guy, with sandy blond hair, blue eyes, and perfectly white teeth that almost sparkled when he smiled. The newcomer held his hand out to Nick. "Hi, I'm Mike."

Nick's heart sunk. So this was Mike.

They firmly shook, neither willing to be the first to let go, as they sized each other up.

Brittany coughed. Mike smiled and let go of Nick's hand. Mike gave Brittany a big bear hug, lifting her from the ground. "So, glad to have our angel of hope back safe and sound."

The second Mike put Brittany down, Nick quickly pulled her to his side, "Angel of hope?"

Mike nodded, "A few years ago, she picked me up off the street and gave me a job and a place to live. She opened this art center, not just to give these kids a chance to find a talent, but to help the neighborhood at the same time." He touched her face. "We're all grateful that God brought Brittany to this community." He took her by the hand and started walking toward one of the vans. "This little lady is one amazing woman."

Nick took her other hand. "More than I knew."

Brittany pulled both hands free. "Enough chatting, let's get moving," Brittany said, climbing into the driver's seat of the nearest van. They left in teams of two. As Brittany backed their van out, Nick nodded toward Mike still standing at the back door of the center. "What's his story?"

"It's not my story to tell."

"He said you picked him up off the street."

"I did."

"Come on. A nice-looking guy like that living on the street?"

"He didn't look so good when I found him." Brittany pulled up in front of a row house and climbed out.

Nick followed.

"This is the easy street," Brittany said. "Three of our families live next door to each other."

He grabbed a box from the back while Brittany carried the pies. Before she could knock, the first door opened.

"Mom, Ms. Brittany's here," a boy of about six yelled to the back of the house.

His mother yelled in reply, "Well, let her in."

The child led them down a dark hallway into the kitchen. Nick set the box on their table. "I'll be back with the turkey." Nick headed down the hallway and returned in time to see the boy tug at Brittany's arm. "You said to tell you if we knew someone that needed help, right?"

"Yes, Tyrone. Do you know someone who needs us?"

"Tyrone," said the boy's mother. "Ms. Brittany has helped enough people."

Brittany knelt down in front of the boy. "When someone's in need, and you can't help them yourself, you can tell someone who *can* help. That's the same as if you were helping that person. Do you want to help someone?"

Tyrone jumped up and down with excitement. "I want to help Mrs. Polyakov. She lives next door and she doesn't have no electricity. Somedays I give her my sandwich so she has something to eat."

"That's very nice of you. I'm so proud of you for helping her." Brittany stood up, "Why don't you take me next door to meet Mrs. Polyakov?"

"She only speaks a little English," the boy's mother said. "I don't think she understands why her electricity was turned off."

A few minutes later, Brittany tried to explain to Mrs. Polyakov that she wanted to help, but she wasn't having any success.

"Here, let me talk to her," Nick said.

Brittany's mouth gaped as he started to speak Russian. After a few minutes, the lady walked into the house, leaving the door open.

"You speak Russian?" Brittany whispered.

"See how handy I am to have around?" He winked. Mrs. Polyakov returned and handed Nick her electric bill.

Brittany reached for the paper. "Tell her tomorrow her electricity will be turned back on. In the meantime, ask her to pack a bag and I'll have Mike come take her back to the center. There's a nice bedroom where she can be warm tonight."

Nick translated Brittany's message. The Russian woman threw her arms around Brittany and squeezed.

Their next few deliveries went quickly. Then they pulled up to a dark house. "Guess no one's home," Nick said.

Before Brittany could answer, the door opened. "And this is why we deliver at night. The first year we delivered right after school, while it was still light. I was unable to see who was without electricity. So now if there are no lights on, I have a couple of days before Thanksgiving to get the power turned back on for them."

"You pay their electric bills, too?" Nick let out a loud whistle. "I knew you had money, but not so much that you can support half of Baltimore."

"I don't support half of Baltimore," she scoffed.

"Okay, a quarter."

"What good is money if you can't help people with it?"

Nick smiled. "The moment I laid eyes on you, I knew you were an angel."

It was late by the time they had delivered all the boxes and returned to the Arts Center. The smell of chili filled the air. "Man, that smells good," Dan said. "I don't know about anyone else, but I'm starving."

Everyone else chimed in, "Me too."

Mrs. Polyakov was dishing out bowls of soup. Mike held up two hands when Brittany flashed him a puzzled look. "She insisted on helping."

In broken English, Mrs. Polyakov spoke. "I'm no lazy free loader. I work for my keep."

"You are a guest here." Brittany put an arm around the old woman's shoulder and led her to the table. "Sit down and enjoy the meal with us."

Once everyone was seated, they bowed their heads in prayer before hungrily devouring chili, corn bread, and hot apple cider.

"Man, this is the best chili I have ever eaten," Nick said.

Brittany smiled. "Mike used to be a chef at the fire hall."

Nick looked up in surprise.

"Yeah," Mike said with a shrug. "I used to be a fireman. The short story is that there was a chemical fire and it messed up my lungs. I got addicted to pain pills and alcohol, but once the doctor stopped giving me pills, I found heroin. My wife forced me into rehab, but I walked out and found myself homeless. Until one day, this lovely lady picked me up off the street and took me home with her."

Nick's expression morphed from awe to anger. He spun in his chair to face Brittany. "You brought a drug addict home with you? Are you crazy?" He saw Brittany send an apologetic look across the table to Mike. Nick looked at Mike and said, "Sorry, man."

Mike replied, "I said the same thing. When we pulled up to her nice house in that rich neighborhood I asked her, *'Are you stupid or something?'*" He started laughing. "And you know what? She looked me right in the eyes and said, *'No, I'm really quite brilliant'.*"

Brittany giggled. "And under his breath Mike said, *'Doesn't look like it to me'.*"

Mike's face broke out in a big grin. "Then she said, *'I trust God and he told me to help you, so that is that'.*"

Brittany reached across the table and patted Mike's hand. "And what a brilliant move that was." After they finished eating, Brittany collected the electric bills from each team. In all, her staff had found six families without electricity. "Thanks for all your help tonight." She handed each of them a stack of pies. "Tomorrow night's dinner is on me."

It was late when Nick drove Brittany home. At her door, he said, "Tonight was amazing. I never knew how good it felt to be helping people… and all I did was carry food." He pulled Brittany to him, lowering his lips to hers, and whispered, "Thank you for being such an amazing woman."

Brittany welcomed his lips and her body melted into his. Within the swirl of passion, a tiny voice broke through. *Not now.* She pushed him away. "I can't do this. It's not right."

"What isn't right about it?"

"We can be friends, but we can't do this." She turned to unlock the door.

"What's so wrong about this?"

"I can't be with a man who doesn't believe in God."

He grinned. "I *do* believe in God."

"Really?" She raised an eyebrow. "A few days ago, you didn't."

Nick took the stone from his pocket.

Brittany stared at it, recognition dawning in her eyes. "Isn't that the stone you gave to Frederick?"

"Funny thing, I went for a run at my cabin and found another one just like it." He told her the story, twirling the rock between his fingers. "It was as if God was telling me he was real."

Brittany threw her arms around him. "I'm so glad you found God." On tiptoes, she smacked a quick kiss on his lips, then pulled away to look into his eyes. "What about Jesus?"

Nick stared back, his hesitation speaking volumes.

Brittany shook her head, opened the door, and walked in alone. "Goodnight, Nick." Closing the door before she had a chance to change her mind, she slid the deadbolt into place and dropped to the floor. On hands and knees, she prayed, *God, you know that I love him. I have from the day we met. Please bring him to know your son, Jesus. Not for me, but for him. Please, God.*

She sat there for a long time, waiting for that sweet peace she usually received when she knew God had heard her. But tonight, there was no peace, only silence.

Chapter 12

Brittany smacked the snooze button and sank back under the covers. She wasn't willing to give up her dream just yet. Soon enough the clock screamed out again, doing its best to keep her out of Nick's arms.

Dressed in her jogging suit, and after doing some stretches, she put her cell phone in her pocket, grabbed her water bottle, gloves and earmuffs, and headed out the door. The sun just barely peeked over the horizon. She stood on the porch waiting for her vision to adjust to the darkness. From the corner of her eye, she caught movement. A man stood in the shadows. In an instant, her heart recognized Nick.

"What are you doing here?" Her voice could not hide her delight.

He met her halfway across the yard. "Thought I would run with you this morning."

"How did you know I would be running?"

"Miss predictable, remember?" Nick took her in his arms and started to lower his face to hers, then stopped. "Sorry, forgot myself. No kissing." He pulled her body tightly into his. "But you didn't say no hugging."

What a perfect way to greet the day. She felt his fingers caress her cheek.

Looking serious he asked, "Do you ever listen to anyone?"

"About what?"

"I told you it's dangerous to run so early. You never know who could be lurking about."

"You're right." She smiled sweetly. "Look who I found this morning." Laughing, she asked, "Can you handle six miles or should I cut it to three?"

"Sweetheart, I can handle anything you give me." He picked her up. "Want me to carry you the whole way?"

Brittany giggled. "Put me down, you big goof."

"Goof, huh?" The second her feet touched the ground she took off. "See if you can keep up. I don't wait for stragglers."

Nick easily caught up to her and passed her. As he rounded the corner he slowed and let Brittany pass him.

The last half mile Brittany said, "Last one to the house has to cook breakfast." She took off as fast as she could, but she was no match for Nick's long legs. He passed her with ease and stopped in the driveway.

"What's for breakfast?" he joked. "I'm starved."

"Me too," she smiled as she passed him and opened the door. "The deal was to the house, not your car. Looks like you're cooking."

Laughing, Nick grabbed her by the waist and pulled her close once more. Every inch of her screamed for him to feel his lips on hers, to feel the beat of his heart next to hers. It took every ounce of strength to pull away. With pounding heart, she pointed to the kitchen. "You know your way. Fix whatever you like. I'm taking a shower."

Alone in her room, Brittany dreamily leaned against the door, hugging her arms to herself. Nick's earlier hug had left a trail of fire. There was no denying her lips hungered for him. Her eyes drifted to the bed and she suddenly longed to rekindle that night from the beach.

The Bible on her nightstand came into focus. *Yes, I know. Be strong. But that doesn't mean I have to like it.* Brittany's eyes looked up to the heavens. *I need you now more than ever.*

The smell of pancakes and bacon greeted her when she stepped out of the shower. Walking into the kitchen, she said, "I could get used to having you around," as she combed her fingers though her wet hair.

They laughed through breakfast and after loading the dishwasher Brittany said, "The paper should be on the front porch by now if you want to catch up on the news." She made a beeline for her bedroom, then returned and sat in the breakfast nook. "I always read a little before I start my day. You're welcome to read along."

Nick glanced at the Bible in her hands. "I'll get the paper." He returned a few minutes later and pulled out the sports section. "What turned you from the party girl I knew to this Jesus person?"

Brittany half smiled. "Long story. Someday when we have time I'll tell it to you."

"What about the short version?" he teased.

"My college roommate was tired of hearing me cry myself to sleep, so one day when I came back from class there was a bible on my bed, with a note that read, *'This will help.'* And it did."

"Is that why you hid a bible in my duffel bag? You think it will change me?"

"God can only change you if you are willing." She closed the book and met his gaze. "Have you read any of it?"

"Haven't had much time, but I'll check it out."

She laid her hand over his. "I hope you do." She opened her bible, closed her eyes, and silently prayed, *Please open his heart to You and mine to Your word.* She read a few chapters, glanced up at the kitchen clock, and sighed. "As enjoyable as this is, I need to get going." She slipped on her heels. "One more day of classes before Thanksgiving break." At the door she hugged him a little too tightly. She really didn't want this morning to end.

Nick waited until Brittany backed out of her driveway, before pulling out behind her. He followed her to the corner. She turned right and he turned left, but at the next block, he made a U-turn and waited. It had been too dark during their run to tell for sure, but he could have sworn he saw Vincent Capri parked near her house. His heart dropped when a car stopped at the stop sign. That was Vincent's car all right. He tailed Vincent a few blocks before he was sure he wasn't following Brittany to school. Nick drove to MICA checking to make sure Brittany had gotten there safely.

Brittany was about to leave the classroom for lunch, when Nick walked in. "Ready for a picnic?"

"Are you crazy, it's freezing out," Brittany answered.

"Don't worry." He slipped his arm around her. "I'll keep you warm."

Of that, she had no doubt. Outside, the cold air took her breath away. "We're going to freeze."

"I have plenty of hot chocolate and then, of course, you have me." He kissed the tip of her nose, but she pushed him away. He winked, "That doesn't count as a kiss. It was just your nose."

In the park, it was easy to find a secluded spot. Nick spread out a blanket, then took another out and wrapped it around her. "So this is how you plan on keeping me warm?" she teased.

He pulled her toward him. "Do you have another idea?"

She laughed. "The blanket is perfect." She scooted out of his grasp.

He touched the tip of her nose. "You are no fun."

"So I've been told." She grinned. "So what's for lunch?"

Nick opened the basket and pulled out fried chicken, salad, rolls, and two thermoses—one of soup and another of hot chocolate. She looked around. "Are you expecting an army?"

"I don't want you to go back to school hungry."

"If we eat all this, I won't be going anywhere because I won't be able to get up. Did you cook this yourself?"

"No, my mother. She's a food pusher."

Brittany's head jerked up in surprise. "You live with your mother?"

"After my stepfather died, I asked her to come stay with me."

Brittany touched his hand. "That's so sweet of you."

He shrugged. "It makes her happy." After they ate, Nick reached into the picnic basket and pulled out a blue rose. "Blue, because that's how I feel when I'm not with you."

"Oh, Nick." She leaned into him. Her embrace took him by surprise and they toppled to the ground.

Her breath caught as Nick rolled her over, his weight supported above her by his arms. "I gather you like the rose." His finger traced the outline of her lips before he lowered his face to hers. Hungrily, she drank the passion of his lips. Her heart was on fire and she was spinning out of control. She gasped for air, pulling herself from the intoxicating kiss. She barely managed a whisper. "I love you, Nick." She lay her head on his chest. "But I can't do this."

I love you, three little meaningless words. Nick held her tight. Meaningless? Were they? Something had changed. His heart had never felt so alive. Slowly, he stood up, pulling her up with him. "I know, baby." Kissing the top of her head, he stepped back and reached into the inside pocket of his bomber jacket. He pulled out the strip of pictures he'd taken from her book. "Is that why you kept these all these years?"

"I..." Brittany stammered.

Nick kissed the tip of her nose once more. "You are so cute when you blush." He smiled, looking at the pictures. "If I remember correctly, I paid for these, didn't I?"

He tore the strip in half and Brittany gasped, "Nick!"

He handed her half and put the remaining half back in his pocket. "Now we both have something to remind us of the best weeks of my life. Of course mine was followed by the worst weeks ever."

"The best..." Brittany mumbled incoherently.

He nodded, "If I hadn't thought you were dead, we would be married with a dozen kids by now."

The smile on her face warmed his whole being. "Really?"

"Why do you look so surprised," he said flippantly, "weren't we young and in love?"

"You never said..."

"Didn't know it until I thought you were dead." He knelt down and started packing things up.

She helped him. "And now?"

He shrugged his shoulders. "Little hard to tell with this Jesus fellow standing between us." He grabbed her by the hand and pulled her to her feet with him. "So, how about dinner tonight?"

"I'm taking my staff out. You're welcome to join us. Be at the center by 6:30 if you want to come."

Nick waved as she walked into the school. "I'll be there." Even in her heavy coat, he could see the soft sway of her hips. Never had he wanted anyone more than he wanted Brittany. Was this just leftover regret for what could have been? For years, he had asked himself if it had been lust or had he really loved her. He still didn't know the answer to that question. He watched the door to the school close behind her.

Vincent sat in his car, laughing to himself. He watched as Nick whistled and drove off. This was too easy. Twice today, he could have easily taken them both, but what fun would that be? No, he had plans for the two of them. For now, he would sit back and enjoy the show.

He threw back his head and laughed again. *McFadden, I have finally found your Achilles heel.* Oh yes, this was going to be fun. He pulled out of the parking lot. No need to hang around here. The bug he'd planted on her car would pinpoint her location when he was ready to grab her. Meanwhile, he would return home and pretend to be in mourning for his sister.

The last class at the arts center ended at 6:00 p.m. Locking the front door behind the final student, Brittany glanced at her watch. She couldn't keep the smile from her face. Nick would be here soon. In the restroom, she brushed her hair and applied lipstick, then shook her head at her reflection. *You're awfully excited to see someone you only want as a friend.* Who was she kidding? She wanted more. Brittany closed her eyes. *I know, God. Only friends.*

She joined the others in the kitchen and opened the back door to look out at the parking lot. Disappointment filled her. No Nick. She went in search of Mike and found him in his office off the kitchen.

"Hey, pretty lady." He waved her in. "What's got you looking so blue?"

"I'm not blue."

"Hmm, from where I'm sitting it looks like something, or someone, has taken the sparkle right out of those gorgeous eyes of yours." He leaned back in his chair. "My guess is lover boy." Mike firmly put his feet on the floor and stood. Walking around the desk he said, "If he's hurt you, I'll take care of him." He punched his fist into his hand.

"Don't be silly."

"You know I haven't given him my seal of approval yet." This made Brittany laugh. Mike hugged her and kissed the top of her head. "And you know I love you."

"Love you, too."

Nick's stomach hit the floor. Did Brittany tell everyone she loved them? Had she really meant it that afternoon? *Or was it just words?* He cleared his throat. Brittany looked up.

Pulling away from Mike, she rushed to Nick and she touched his arm. "You did come."

"Sorry, I'm a little late." He shifted his feet. "Traffic." He couldn't tell her the truth. At least not yet. Twice today, he had seen Vincent watching her, once at her house and again at the college. He was late because he'd been coordinating her protection detail. Mostly it would be him.

Mike slapped Nick's back in a false gesture of welcome. "Glad you could make it." He walked into the kitchen and did a head count. "We're missing two."

"Janet and Dan just pulled up," Amy said.

"That makes twelve." Brittany grabbed her coat from the back of the chair. "So let's get this party started."

At the restaurant, Mike pulled out the chair at the head of the table for Brittany and helped her shrug out of her coat. He glared at a scowling Nick before each took a seat on either side of Brittany.

After the waitress took their order, Dan cleared his throat. "Hey Mike, was that story true you told last night? Did Brittany really get you off the street?"

Mike frowned. "Unfortunately, yes."

"Brittany, weren't you afraid to do that?" Amy asked.

"Honestly, no."

"I would have been terrified," Janet said.

"I prayed about it," Brittany answered. "And had total peace. So there was no need to be afraid. God was with me."

"You really put a lot of faith in God, don't you?" Nick said.

"Hey, what about me? Don't you think I was afraid?" Mike chimed in.

"Afraid of Brittany?" Amy laughed.

"I watched Criminal Minds before I went on the streets," Mike said. "Do you know what they do to homeless people in that show?" Laughter broke out.

"So what's your story, Nick?" Amy asked.

Nick paused, his fork halfway to his mouth. "Mine?"

"Yeah, let's hear your story." Mike leaned his elbows on the table.

Nick put his fork down. "Short version? College, Army, and now I work for PSA."

"Were you in Iraq?" Mike asked. Nick nodded and they talked about the war for a few minutes, discovering they had both been there at the same time. "You can thank us Marines for paving the way for you Army guys."

"And you can thank me for flying in to rescue you when your sorry butts got into trouble."

Mike tilted his head and raised his eyebrows. "You were a pilot? So, what was the name of your plane?"

Nick smiled at Brittany. "Angel," he answered.

Mike threw his head back and laughed. "Oh man, you really did fly me out of there. I remember seeing angel wings on the plane by the door. And the crazy pilot said..." he made quotation marks with his fingers and narrowed his eyes at Nick, "...'Don't worry, boys, I have a—'"

Nick chimed in, "...Beautiful angel looking over me. We'll be out of here and back at base in no time."

They both laughed and Nick let go of his suspicion of the guy. Brittany stared wide-eyed at Nick.

He high-fived Mike. "See, I did save your butt." They shook hands, suddenly finding a bond that could never be broken.

Brittany couldn't keep the grin off her face, "You named your plane *Angel*?"

Nick lowered his eyes and sighed deeply. "I thought you were dead."

Mike frowned. "Glad we didn't know your guardian angel wasn't even an angel yet." He patted Brittany's hand. "But mighty glad she isn't."

The evening ended all too soon. Before Nick knew it, he was following Brittany back to her house. At the door, he hugged her good night. "How about a dinner with just the two of us tomorrow night?"

"Sorry." Slowly, she shook her head. "I'm flying to Colorado tomorrow."

Nick's shoulders sagged. He smiled halfheartedly. "Can I drive you to the airport?"

"Mike's taking me."

Nick mumbled, "Of course he is."

"Green is not *your* color." Brittany grinned.

He gently lifted her face, looking into her eyes. "Should I be green?"

She giggled. "Of course not. He's like a brother to me."

"Hmm..."

She placed her hand on the doorknob. "It's late and I have an early morning." She opened the door then turned back. "I'm glad you came tonight."

"Are you running in the morning?" Nick asked.

"No. I'll run once I get to the compound."

"Good, I don't want you to run alone."

"You worry too much."

"And you don't worry enough."

After a quick kiss, she shut the door and left him alone. He drove around the block to where Miles was waiting to exchange cars. Then he drove back and parked in a neighbor's driveway. Brittany had mentioned they were away. Nick had noticed them earlier putting their suitcases in a green Lexus. He hoped no one would think twice about an identical Lexus sitting in their driveway.

Nick staked out her house all night. He alternated between sitting in the car and running around her block. Fortunately, it was an uneventful night. He was in the neighbor's backyard when Mike pulled up to take Brittany to Baltimore Washington International Airport. A few minutes after Brittany and Mike left, Nick drove home and collapsed in bed. He woke around noon and listened to his voicemail—two from Carl and one from

Mike. *"Hey man, I don't know what your game is, but if you're stalking Brittany, you better think again."*

Nick shook his head. No way could Mike have seen him. He'd been in the neighbor's backyard when Mike had arrived. Nick showered and headed to the Arts Center where he rang the kitchen bell and waited.

Mike opened the door. Without wasting a second, he pointed his finger at Nick. "You have some explaining to do, buddy."

Nick rubbed the back of his neck. "How did you even see me?"

"I didn't see you per se. But between the Marines and the fire department, I have been trained to take note of my surroundings." Mike made a fist. "If you hurt her in any way, you'll be answering to me."

"Relax, bud." Nick threw his hands up. "It's my job to protect her. Mind if I come in? It's cold out here."

Mike hesitated before stepping back and letting Nick in.

He glanced longingly at the coffeepot. "Mind if I have a cup? I had a long night."

"Sure." Mike begrudgingly pointed to a bar stool, "Have a seat."

"So what triggered your suspicion that I was there?" Nick asked.

"The Lexus in the neighbor's driveway... it was the same year and model, but theirs has a dent in the driver's fender. So after we left, I pretended to have forgotten to set the Center's alarm. I pulled over and faked setting it with the app on my phone. Really, I was watching to see if anybody followed us. When the Lexus turned in the opposite direction, I saw another car pull from the curb. That car followed us to the airport. So, I put two and two together." Mike poured them both a cup of coffee. He slid the cup across the island to Nick. "So what's the deal?"

Nick took a long drink of coffee. "Yesterday, I caught Vincent Capri watching her."

Mike jumped up, "The guy that tried to kidnap her?"

"Yes. So I set up a twenty-four/seven watch on her."

Mike started to pace. "But she's traveling." He glared at Nick. "And you're here."

"I assure you I wanted to be on that plane with her this morning, but my boss thought otherwise." Mike's cold stare might have made most people squirm, but Nick had faced worse. So much for the bond of friendship they had last night. He shook his head. "The other car you noticed following you to BWI was a PSA agent. There was another inside the airport making sure she safely got on her plane. Once in Denver, she'll be followed to her grandparents' house."

"You thought of everything, didn't you?"

"It's my job."

"Is that why you're hanging around?" Mike scowled. "Because it's your job?"

Nick sipped his coffee, buying time. "Not completely."

"I hope not." Mike's jaw tightened.

Nick gave Mike a death stare. "Not that it's any of your business, but I really like her."

"Listen, you come waltzing in after ten years and think you can pick up where you left off." He leaned toward Nick. "Who do you think will be here when you waltz back out again?"

"I'm not..."

Mike held up his hand. "Don't make promises you can't keep."

Nick downed his coffee in one last gulp and thumped the cup on the counter. "Well, I better get going. Don't want to keep you from your Thanksgiving plans."

"No plans."

Nick headed out and then paused with his hand on the door. He turned, giving Mike a long hard look. What was his deal? Was there something between him and Brittany? He had to know. He withdrew a pen and notebook from his pocket and scribbled his address. Ripping out the page, he handed it to Mike. "You're welcome to have dinner with my family."

Mike stared at the paper. "Why would I want to spend my Thanksgiving with you?"

"You know the old saying, "Keep your friends close..."

Mike finished the sentence for him, "but your enemies closer."

Chapter 13

Brittany was surprised to find both Nick and Mike waiting for her at the airport when she returned home from the Thanksgiving weekend. Mike pushed Nick out of the way. "Hey man, if I let you hug her first, I'll never get a turn."

"Sure," Nick said, throwing his arms around them both.

"Okay guys, can I breathe?" Brittany gasped.

They both stepped back, but Nick kept one arm around her shoulders. "I missed you." He kissed the top of her head.

"Missed you, too."

"What about me?" Mike pouted.

"I missed you both," she said, eyeing them suspiciously. "You two BFFs now?"

"Seems we have a lot in common," Nick answered.

Mike smacked him on the back and bragged. "I even got Nick to go to church with me this morning."

Brittany's surprise slowly erupted into joy.

"Not really sure about this Jesus guy," Nick hedged, "but I'm willing to figure out what the two of you see in Him."

Brittany threw her arms around Nick. She had never felt this happy.

The next week passed like a whirlwind. Nick was with her every spare moment. When he wasn't at her house, he was at the arts center. He and Mike had their heads together often. They were up to something. She just didn't know what.

After their Saturday morning run, Nick and Brittany headed to the center for breakfast. Mike cooked from nine to eleven every Saturday and anyone in the neighborhood was welcome. It was a lot of work, but also fun. Mike kept the pancakes and eggs coming while Nick cooked the bacon and sausage. Brittany, Amy, and Janet took turns serving and clearing tables. Brittany was exhausted two hours later when Nick whisked her away.

"Aww," Brittany said, relaxing on the soft seat in Nick's car. "Feels good to sit."

Nick nodded in agreement. "I know one thing. I need a shower."

"You smell delicious." Brittany grinned.

He leaned over and kissed her cheek. "Maybe I ought to start wearing *eau de sausage and bacon*."

Brittany glanced down at her clothes spattered with food. "Who knew waiting tables was so messy?"

At her house, Nick walked Brittany to the door and gave her a hug. "I'll see you tonight about six."

Before heading home, Nick drove around the block a few times—just like every other day, there was no sign of Vincent. *I'm probably just being paranoid.* He shook his head. Carl might think the threat was over, but he felt in his bones that it wasn't. He parked at the end of her block and waited for Brittany to head back to the arts center. He followed her there, watching her enter through the back door. She was in Mike's hands now.

When he finally made it back to the house, Carl's car was parked out front. *This is it. Vincent must be back!* In the kitchen, he found Carl having a cup of coffee with his mother. "Hey, what's up, boss?"

"Grab your duffel bag. You're needed in Mexico."

"Now?" Nick could feel the air leaving his lungs.

"Max's cover's been blown. Juan Mendez's men dragged him off. Witnesses couldn't tell if he was still alive or not."

Nick frowned. "Give me a minute. I have to make a call." He pulled his phone from his pocket.

"Your plane leaves in an hour. You can call from the road."

Unperturbed, Nick dialed Brittany's number, but she didn't pick up. Then he remembered she always locked her purse and cell phone in the desk at the center. Mike never carried his while there, so Nick started to look up the center's number.

"We don't have time to waste," Carl huffed. "Get your stuff and let's go."

Nick left the kitchen and returned with his duffel in one hand. He always had it packed and ready to go at a moment's notice. In his other hand, he still punched numbers on the cell.

Amy answered his call at the arts center. "Brittany's teaching a class and Mike's outside shoveling snow." Nick hung up in frustration.

Carl pointed to the door. "Let's go."

Lucy hurried to her son's side. She reached up and cupped Nick's face between her hands. "You be careful."

He kissed the top of her head. "Always." Within the hour, he was in the air. Carl never had his agents fly the most direct route, so he would have a quick layover in Denver, before heading to Texas. Once there, he would pick up a jeep, his cowboy hat, and drive across the border.

He tried calling Brittany a few more times, but no answer. Finally, he settled on a text message: Sorry, have to cancel tonight. Job in Mexico. Then he left a voicemail for Mike. "Going to Mexico. Keep her safe."

At the Texas office, he tried Brittany's phone once more. He couldn't bring himself to leave another message. He wanted to talk to *her*. He wanted to hear her voice. Instead, he turned off the phone and put it with his ID in the lock box. From here on out, Nicholas McFadden didn't exist. He was now Nick Farley.

Once in Mexico, he checked into a motel. It wasn't much, but it was the best this old town had to offer. He threw his bag in the corner, then headed for the local saloon where he was no stranger. The bartender poured his whiskey before he'd even reached the bar.

"*Buenas noches,* **amigo**. What brings you back so soon?" The man beside him smacked Nick on the back. "Your boss afraid the American *policia* pointed a finger at him?"

Laughter filled the bar. At least his cover was still intact. One worry down.

"Yea, something like that." Nick drank his whiskey and ordered another. "Tell me what happened."

Two hours later, he had learned all he needed to know. He went back to his room to plan his next move.

Exotic perfume greeted him before he even opened the door. Lying on his bed was Rosita. A few weeks ago, he had considered her to be the most desirable woman in the world. *But now?*

"*Hola*, Nick." She spoke his name as if she were melting with desire. Rosita patted the bed and held her arms out. "I've been waiting for you."

Instead of moving toward her as normal, Nick crossed to the window and looked out. Feeling hot and trapped, he opened it for fresh air. His eyes drifted to the stars. He surprised himself with a prayer: *God, you know I'm not used to this, but please keep Brittany safe.*

The bedspring squeaked when Rosita rose from the mattress. He lay his forehead on the window frame, inwardly cringing as her arms wrapped around his chest. She lay her head against his shoulder blade. "You knew I would come as soon as I heard you were back. Why didn't you send for me?"

"I had things to do," he answered as gently as possible.

With practiced hands, Rosita turned him around and unbuttoned his shirt. She ran her hands through the hair on his chest.

"Rosita." Nick grabbed her hands. "I want you to go."

"Go?" she said in shock. "Go where?"

"Home," he commanded. "I can't do this anymore."

Rosita ran her long red fingernails down his arm. "You no longer find me desirable?" She looked into his eyes. Slowly, she moved her hips against his.

Nick backed away, falling into a chair while Rosita danced seductively before him. Her hands caressed her body, before letting her dress fall around her bare feet.

Her alluring eyes caressed his body. Brown eyes, not blue. Her skin was golden, not creamy. Her lips, though red, were not like strawberries, and her voice... What was he doing? There was no comparison. He closed his eyes and smiled as he thought about the way Brittany laughed, the gentle sway of her hips, the touch of her lips. Opening his eyes, he knew what his heart had known ten years ago. There was only one woman for him. He picked up the dress from the floor. "Get dressed, Rosita. This isn't happening."

"Is there someone else?" She reached for his hands and placed them upon her breast.

Nick pulled back and walked away.

"How is it possible that your heart has been stolen so quickly?"

"You need to go." He stared out the window and didn't look back until he heard the door open. "Goodbye, Rosita."

She ran to him, throwing herself at his feet. "But I love you."

Nick reached down and picked her up, wiping the tears from his former lover's face. "We both knew that one day this relationship would end. It just happened sooner than we thought."

"Do you love her?" Rosita pleaded.

One simple word sprang to mind. His heart burst into a thousand pieces and he knew without a doubt. "Yes."

Nick took the weapons from his duffel bag. He checked to make sure the pistol was fully loaded before strapping it to his ankle. Attaching the knife to his belt, he patted the Glock at his back, checked to make sure he had extra ammo, and slung the bag over his shoulder. He flipped off the light and snuck down the back stairwell.

He drove his jeep without lights down the dark alley. Once out of town, he parked a few miles from the Mendez estate, then hiked through the woods to the barn where Max was being held. Luck was with him. The barn door was unlocked. He crept in and stood still, listening for the sound of breathing. He zeroed in on Max. "Hey buddy," Nick whispered, "time to go home."

Max groaned.

"Can you walk?"

"Not sure."

Nick helped him to his feet and Max stumbled. "I got you." He lifted Max onto his back. "Hang on, buddy."

They were almost home free when Juan Mendez stepped from the woods. "Nice to see you back, my *amigo*." He snapped his fingers and two soldiers dragged Rosita from the bushes. Juan pulled her to him. "You have this beautiful *senorita* to thank for giving you away." Juan pushed Rosita to the ground and spit on her. "Get her out of my sight. Never trust a woman who out of one side of her mouth says I love you and the other she is handing you over to the devil." Juan laughed as they dragged her kicking and screaming to the woodshed. "I will have fun with her first, of course. Now to you, my *amigo*."

Nick didn't move. If he played this right, they just might get out of this alive. Mendez obviously thought he would be an easy kill. He had sent his two soldiers away, leaving just the three of them. Max would be of no help. He could barely move.

Mendez pointed at Max. "Put your friend on the ground." He kept his gun aimed at Nick. "Keep your hands where I can see them. I know you have a gun behind your back."

Nick put Max on the ground and slowly stood with his hands raised.

Mendez touched his chest. "It grieves me deeply that you are a *Federales*. It will hurt me to have to kill you, but kill you I will." He holstered his gun. "We shall play our little game, just you and me. On the count of three, we will both draw. Only this time we fire. Let no man say I killed you in cold blood."

Nick silently thanked God for all the times he had allowed Mendez to win at fast draw.

"*Uno, dos, tr–*" before Mendez had the word out of his mouth, the man started to draw.

Nick was faster and shot him through the heart. Mendez's eyes widened in surprise. He grabbed his chest, looking at the blood oozing though his fingers before he dropped dead to the ground. Grabbing Mendez's gun, Nick threw Max over his shoulder and ran for the woods. Good thing he'd staked out the woods beforehand. Quickly, he located his stashed backpack. He rolled Max into the thick bush before crawling in beside him.

Reaching into the backpack, he pulled out a canteen of water and handed it to Max. "Drink a little of this. Not too much, you don't want to get sick." He handed Max Mendez's gun. "Will you be able to use this?"

Max nodded.

"Okay, once it's clear, I'm going for Rosita." Nick patted his friend on the back. "We're getting out of here alive. I promise."

They held their breath as soldiers walked by their hiding spot. When he heard the order for them to search farther into the woods, Nick went back for Rosita. With his cover blown, the surrounding villages would be unsafe. Max needed medical attention immediately. And now that he had Rosita in tow, he had to figure out what to do and do it quickly. It wasn't safe here and there was no way the three of them were hiking out of Mexico.

Nick pulled his night vision goggles from his bag and put them on. When he was sure that they were safe to move, Nick put Max on his back and signaled for Rosita to follow. They had to stop often. The jarring of the rough ground was not helping Max's injuries. Nick found a small stream and they stopped to rest there. Rosita started to speak, but Nick put a hand over her mouth to signal silence. She shook her head no. She whispered, "My *familia*, we can make it there."

Nick shook his head *no*.

"They have no love for Mendez and there is *el doctor* there."

Nick thought for a few minutes. Could he trust her? *"Yes."* He nodded his head. Where had that assurance come from? His gut instinct had always seen him through. That must be what guided him now. He looked around, noting that sunlight was starting to peek through the trees. "Can we make it there before sunrise?"

"*Sí.*"

"Lead the way."

They made it safely to town and Rosita's family hid them.

"How did you know I was a cop?" he finally asked her on the second day with her family.

She shrugged and pointed to her heart. "I knew in here that you could not be a bad man like Mendez. I just guessed." She fell at his feet. "Please forgive me."

He lifted her up. "I do."

She started to cry.

Nick gently sent her away from him and paced the room. He felt like a caged animal. The doctor was doing his best, but Max needed to be in a hospital. There was no way they could drive out of Mexico without being caught by one of Mendez's brothers. It was only a matter of time before they avenged his death.

Chapter 14

The day Nick left, Mike decided to paint his apartment at the Center and stayed in Brittany's guest room while it was being done. She had a feeling it was more than that, she just didn't know what *it* was. Whatever the reason, she was glad he was there.

Decorating the Christmas tree had been so much fun with his help. Brittany stepped back to admire the seven-foot tree. Twinkling lights reflected off the Christmas balls. She smiled. It was almost perfect. Mike wouldn't let her put the tinsel on until he added candy canes and he'd gone to the store to purchase some. Brittany glanced at the angel on top. *Thank you, God, for sending me such a good friend.*

The lights on the angel shifted to blue, as if on cue. She curled up on the sofa, picked up her cup of hot chocolate, and took a sip. The fire glowed in the fireplace. On the coffee table, the dozen roses from Nick were wilting, but still beautiful. The smell of pine, along with the fire, made the room warm and cozy. The only thing missing was Nick.

Staring into the flames, she prayed he was alright. Other than his text, there had been no word. He'd warned her that he was often called away on a moment's notice and when he was undercover there would be no contact with anyone—not even Carl—until he was back in the States. He'd only been gone a week, and yet it felt like an eternity.

The doorbell chimed. Brittany's heart skipped a beat. *Could it be?* She hurried to the door, hoping, but instantly her heart dropped. It was her childhood friend, Chadwick Sinclair.

"Hello, darling." His thin lips barely moved when he smiled. Without waiting for an invitation, he waltzed inside. Tossing his coat on the back of a chair, he glanced around. "Nice tree. Needs some garland though."

Brittany followed him into the living room. "What are you doing here?" She narrowed her eyes. "Shouldn't you be in Colorado getting ready for your party?"

"I had some business here in Baltimore, so I thought I would stop in and see why you refused my invitation." He pulled a rose from the vase and flopped down on the sofa. Twirling the flower in his hand, he asked, "Is this new admirer the reason you aren't coming this weekend?"

Brittany sat down on the edge of the sofa. "I'm taking the dancers from the arts center to see the Rockettes on Saturday."

"How could you be so insensitive?" He smacked the rose against the coffee table. "And make plans on the weekend of my party?" he whined.

Brittany reached for her rose. "It's not like I was going to go to your party."

He held it out of her reach. "What's that supposed to mean?"

"Chadwick, you know full well what that means. I have no interest in being at a party where there are drugs."

"Who said there'll be drugs?" He laughed. "Oh, you mean the *marijuana*. That isn't a drug."

"It most certainly is." Brittany fumed.

"Well, it's legal in Colorado."

"Doesn't matter."

"Ever since you found God, you've become such a prima donna." He tossed the flower on the table. "It's the first party of the season and it's always a grand time. I can't believe you'd rather spend even an hour with those alley rats instead of your own kind."

"My own kind!" Brittany jumped to her feet. "I would rather spend a lifetime with them than another minute with you. How dare you call my kids names? They are beautiful human beings who deserve your respect, not your condemnation."

"Don't go getting all huffy about it. Sit back down." He patted the cushion beside him. "I apologize. I'm sure they are all fine, upstanding citizens." Chadwick pulled a cigarette from his pocket. "You know Mother expects you to be there. So you must come."

Brittany glared at the cigarette. "I hope you don't plan on lighting that in here." As if he didn't hear her, he lit the cigarette. Brittany reached over and yanked it from his mouth, sprinted to the fireplace, and tossed it in. "Not in my house, you don't."

"Guess your new beau doesn't smoke." Chadwick glared. "Does he have a name?"

"Nick."

"Wow, how strange is that?" He smirked. "Carissa's new beau's name is Nicky, too."

All the air left Brittany's lungs. She barely managed to say, "Really?"

"Yes." He toyed with his pack of cigarettes and looked down at the floor. "I was in Aspen over the weekend and Carissa was there with her new boyfriend."

"He was there?" Brittany folded her arms across her stomach.

"I didn't meet him, mind you." Chadwick ran a hand down his pants leg. "He'd just left." He cleared his throat. "But let me tell you that was all Carissa could talk about... how tall and handsome her new man was." Then he patted his stomach. "And boy did she go on about his six-pack abs."

Brittany gripped the edge of the mantle. Chadwick's voice had become an indistinct rumble swirling around her head. It couldn't be true.

"So are you?" Chadwick prompted.

"Am I what?"

"I asked you if you're coming to my party."

Brittany shook her head. "I already told you, *no.*"

"Don't you want to meet Carissa's new man?"

Brittany jerked her head around. "Nick's going to your party?"

"I would think so." He stood up to leave. "So, I can count on you being at my party this weekend?"

Brittany glared at him. For the life of her, she couldn't remember why she had ever been friends with him. She shook her head no. More like tolerated him, for Carissa's sake. She felt like her blood was about to boil over. The nerve of him coming here. Telling her lies. There was no Carissa and Nick. Was there? She swallowed hard. Brittany lifted her chin. "Chadwick, I have not been to your party in years. This year will be no different."

He rose to leave. He waved his hand around, "Why you choose to shun society and live like this is beyond me."

"I happen to like my life."

"Humph." He walked over to the Christmas tree. Eying the box of tinsel laying on top of a box of ornaments, he opened it and started throwing it.

Brittany gasped. She grabbed the tinsel from him. "What are you doing?"

"Decorating your tree."

"That is not how you do it." She started to remove the tinsel from the tree.

He laughed, "Oh yea, I forgot you like it one strand at a time." He shook his head, "I have no time for that nonsense." He grabbed his coat. Brittany followed him to the door. "You sure you won't change your mind?"

"No, Chadwick. I will not."

"Your loss." He leaned down and kissed her check, then planted a kiss right on her lips.

Brittany pushed him away. "What is wrong with you?" She wiped her mouth with the back of her hand.

He took a step closer and she put her arm out, stopping him. "You know I love you."

"Are you drunk?"

He winked, "Only with your presence."

She pointed at the door. "Get out."

As the door shut behind Chadwick, anger filled her. She stormed over to the tree and started yanking the tinsel off. The nerve of him, coming here, telling lies about Nick. Her heart flipped. *Was it a lie?*

Her mind drifted back to ten years ago, when Nick had left her crying at the beach party and walked away with someone else. Her heart said it wasn't true, but her mind couldn't forget how quickly he had left her for another. Hadn't he proven he was nothing but a womanizing playboy? She felt her heart break. *Nick is with Carissa, not in Mexico.* She spun from the tree, rushed to the coffee table, and with an angry sweep of her hand, she tossed all the roses into the fire. Tears streamed down her face while flames danced on the burning roses, mocking her. *You knew he was a womanizer.*

"Hey, what's wrong?"

Brittany jumped at the sound of Mike's voice. She wiped the tears from her face.

Mike quickly crossed the living room, pulling her to him. "What's the matter?"

She took a deep breath and told him what Chadwick had said.

Mike rubbed her back. "And you believed him?"

"Why would he lie?"

"Hmm... let's see. Maybe Carissa put him up to it." Mike put his hands on her shoulders and stepped back. Looking her in the eyes, he said, "Don't you think it's strange, him showing up here?" He handed her a tissue. "Wipe your tears. I'm going to make you a fresh cup of hot chocolate." He picked up her cup and headed to the kitchen. "Think about it, Brittany. Who do you believe—Nick, who says he's in Mexico, or Chadwick, Carissa's little pawn?" Mike put an extra spoon of whipped cream on top and handed her the mug.

"But..."

"No buts. I don't believe it and neither should you. Why would God bring him back into your life for him to end up with Carissa?" He took a sip from his own mug. "I bet if you prayed about it, you'd know the truth."

"You're right." She touched her heart. "I know it here." Then, she pointed to her head, "But up here, I just keep remembering that night on the beach."

Mike dismissed that with a wave of his hand. "I'm sure he just grabbed the first girl he saw to make you jealous. After all, your boyfriend had just shown up."

"*Ex*-boyfriend." Brittany emphasized the first syllable. She glanced at the fireplace. "I burned my roses."

"Well, they were almost dead anyway. But there's still one on the floor by the sofa."

Brittany bent to pick it up. As she stood, the angel lights once again changed to blue. "You're right. I don't know why he would lie."

"Carissa is up to something, mark my words."

Brittany nodded, then bowed her head and said a silent prayer. *Please give me the strength to deal with whatever lies ahead.* Taking a deep breath, she smiled. "Did you get the candy canes?"

Together they finished decorating the tree, after which they prayed and sang a few carols. Mike locked the house up for the night while Brittany washed the hot chocolate mugs.

The next few days were busy ones. Besides decorating the center for Christmas, the students took turns making cookies, each taking a dozen of each kind home. Food for the Christmas baskets had arrived and the staff was busy putting them together. Brittany had been almost too busy to think of Nick. *Almost.* Who was she kidding? Every moment, thoughts of him hovered near her heart.

Wednesday was turning out to be another whirlwind day. After her classes at MICA, she returned home for a quick run before heading to the Arts Center. She was looking forward to finishing up the art project the kids had started for Christmas. She was almost to her house, when she noticed a strange car in her driveway. Her thoughts quickly flashed back to a month ago. She slowed her steps.

Carl had assured her the threat on her life was over, but she wasn't totally convinced. Why else was Mike still here? And she had noticed strange cars following her. She started to pivot to run back the way she had come, when the driver opened the door and stepped out. Brittany almost fell when she tripped over her feet. *Carissa, what in the world are you doing here?*

Carissa called to her. "Hurry up. It's cold out here."

Brittany ran up to the front door. Her mind raced with a thousand questions. Carissa breezed in after her and tossed her fur coat across the loveseat. Pulling off gloves, Carissa asked, "Aren't you going to close the door? I have been sitting there waiting for you in the freezing cold. I really would like to warm up."

Flabbergasted, Brittany shut the door and stared at her cousin. "Carissa, what are you doing here?"

"Chadwick and I had some business in Baltimore. So I thought I would come see your house." She looked around and stuck her nose in the air. "You need a better designer."

Brittany folded her arms across her chest. "I don't think you came all this way to criticize my house."

Carissa rubbed her arm. "I think it's simply awful of you to refuse Chadwick's invitation. Everyone who is anyone will be there."

Brittany threw her hands up. "What's the big deal about me and this party? I haven't been to it in years." She eyed Carissa with suspicion. "And I'm supposed to believe you want me to go?"

Carissa waved her gloves in the air. After a feeble attempt at laughing, she said, "It suits me just fine not to have you there."

"So why are you here?"

"It's Chadwick. You know how sulky he is when he doesn't get his way." She flashed a fake smile. "And his mother. If you don't come, they'll both be in a mood. And if that happens, my whole weekend will be spoiled."

"I'm still not going."

"It's not like you to have anything better to do."

Brittany lifted her chin. "You have no idea what plans I might have."

Carissa eyed her suspiciously. "It's a shame Nicky's out of the country. Otherwise, I wouldn't care if you came to the party or not."

"Nicky?" Brittany closed her eyes. She knew the slightly higher pitch of her voice wasn't lost on Carissa. *Lord, give me strength.*

"You know, Nicky McFadden." Carissa flipped her hair over her shoulder. "Seems he discovered he doesn't really like the sweet, innocent choir girl type."

Brittany forced a laugh. "Is that so?"

"Your loss is my gain." She glanced at her watch. "Please do reconsider the party." Then she pulled her fur around her and waltzed out of the house.

Brittany gaped at the door. What was Carissa up to? She rubbed her head. It had to be big for her to make the trip from Colorado to Baltimore. Brittany looked up toward heaven. *I know Carissa is up to something. I have a feeling it's going to be earth shattering if she has her way. Please help me not to fall into her trap.*

A verse popped into her head—Romans 8:28. *"And we know that for those who love God all things work together for good, for those who are called according to his purpose."* With shaking hands, she sat down and opened her bible.

The month seemed to fly by. The Wednesday before Christmas, Brittany washed the breakfast dishes before getting ready to leave for Colorado. "You sure you won't come with me?" she asked Mike. "I hate the thought of you being alone for Christmas."

"Thanks, but I prefer to stay here."

"Are you going to make me face Carissa alone?"

"You won't be alone. Your whole family will be there." He winked. "And if it comes to a fight, you know they'll all be on your side."

She laughed. "There won't be a fight."

"You never know. I think the two of you are due for a real cat fight." He curled up his hands and swatted at her. "Meow."

Grinning, Brittany slapped his hands away. "And let Aunt Constance turn me into a ceramic cat?"

"Then Nick and I would come to your rescue."

"My heroes—the fireman and the cop. What more could a girl ask for?"

"I'm no hero," Mike scoffed.

"You've been clean for three years, you live in a neighborhood where the temptation is there daily, and yet you stay strong. I see you out on the street feeding the homeless and handing out Bibles. Yes, Mike, you're a hero to many people. I just wish your family could see you."

"They don't want to see me."

"How do you know? Why don't you visit your parents for Christmas? I'm sure they'd love to see you and I bet they would know where Juliet and the girls went."

Mike shook his head. "A month ago, I finally got the nerve to drive by my parents' house, but there was a new family living there." He hung his head. "They're gone, too."

Brittany laid her hand on his arm. "Someday you'll find them and they'll forgive you."

"I don't think so."

Brittany searched for a way to make him hear. "Has God forgiven you?"

"Of course," he responded at once.

"Then why can't you forgive yourself?" She squeezed his hand. "You were a different person then. I know they'll forgive you. I feel it right here." She pointed to her heart.

Later, as her plane took off, she wondered if perhaps Nick could find Mike's family.

Within minutes of arriving at her grandparents' house, she was sorry she'd come. Carissa came running down the stairs, a big smile on her face. Brittany couldn't remember when she'd seen her so happy.

"I'm so glad you're home." Carissa grabbed her by the hands and spun her around. "It's going to be a wonderful Christmas." She hugged her. "I think it's time we started being friends again."

"Really?" She stared in awe at Carissa. "What brought this on?'

Carissa giggled. "Love, my dear cousin." She lifted her arms in victory. "Love."

"You're in love?" She barely dared to ask. "Who's the lucky guy?"

"Nicky, of course."

Brittany grabbed her chest. *Breathe, Brittany, breathe. You know she's lying.*

Carissa rambled on about how wonderful he was. She pointed to the abalone shell barrette in her hair. "Isn't it just divine? He sent this to me just yesterday."

"It's beautiful." Brittany forced herself to keep smiling. *Please give me strength.* This was the season of love, not hate. She refused to let Carissa steal her joy. "I'm so happy you're happy," she said, hugging her cousin for an element of surprise. Then, she ran up the stairs to her room. *It can't be true.* Had Nick sent Carissa a gift? No. She tossed her purse on her bed. She refused to believe it. But what if... Her heart felt like it was about to explode.

She only had to make it through until New Year's Day. Ten days. She groaned and threw herself on her bed. Ten days of Carissa. *Lord, please give me strength!*

"Pull yourself together," she said aloud. "You know it's a lie." Christmas at home was always a joyous occasion and she refused to let Carissa steal that from her.

She got up and went in search of her grandparents, running into Frederick outside the library.

"Brittany," he threw his arms around her waist. "You're back." He looked around before whispering, "Can I tell you something?"

She knelt down beside him. "Of course," she answered conspiratorially.

"Carissa stole Mr. Nick's card."

"What card?"

"The one he gave me that had his home number on it." Frederick looked ready to cry. "How can I call Nick for help if she tries to turn me into a cat?"

Brittany bit her cheeks, trying hard not to laugh. "Frederick, you know she can't really do that, don't you?" She ruffled his hair. "You do know that, don't you?"

He looked at his shoes. "Yes, I guess."

"Didn't Nick give you a stone to remind you that God was always with you?"

Frederick pulled the rock out of his pocket.

"I'll write down Nick's number for you, but don't forget God is there to protect you always."

She stood just as her grandfather rounded the corner. "There you are," James said. "We're about ready to go cut down the tree."

Brittany stepped up into the sled. Noticeably missing were Carissa and Aunt Constance, for which she said a silent, *Thank you.* She sat between her grandmother and Veronica. Pulling the blanket up over their legs, Lillian patted Brittany. "So glad you made it in time."

"I wouldn't miss this for the world," she said.

It was one of the family traditions Brittany loved most. Once everyone was settled, Jerome, the stable master, took his seat behind the horses and said, "Giddy-up."

The snow didn't dampen their spirits as they sang Christmas carols and drank hot chocolate. Once they had all agreed on the tree, Jerome cut it down and while he tied it to the sled, they had a snowball fight. Brittany thought about Nick and wondered what he was doing. *Please keep him safe.*

Christmas Eve arrived with a flurry of activities. After breakfast, they all gathered in the great hallway for the tree decorating. Once again, her nemesis was absent. Brittany whispered to Veronica, "Where's Carissa?"

"Sick in bed," her younger cousin answered.

"What's wrong with her?" she asked, almost concerned.

"She's been throwing up a lot. Just like the last time she went into withdrawal."

Brittany considered checking in on Carissa. If it was true, then she'd need a friend standing by. "Who's with her?"

"No one. She locked the door and won't let anyone in."

Thoughts of Carissa were quickly pushed to the back of her mind as the family gathered around the tree to decorate. Huge, it reached almost to the cathedral ceiling. With ladders placed around the tree, they all took turns climbing to place their decorations.

Carissa snuck to the top of the stairs. Laughter filled the hallway below. She hated missing out on the fun, but it had to be this way. Well, Brittany was smiling now, but come New Year's Eve, Carissa's little surprise would knock that smile off her face once and for all. She silently laughed at her new plan. After all, this year's revenge was close at hand.

Chapter 15

The Hathaway New Year's party was in full swing. With a ballroom full of family and friends, the Christmas tree in the corner looked dull compared to all the glittery dresses and jewelry.

Carissa seemed fully recovered from whatever was bothering her. Carissa and Chadwick were on the dance floor, both kept glancing Brittany's way. She could tell they were up to something. Brittany smiled at them. A proper lady always smiles, even when she doesn't feel like it.

"Why are you hiding out in the corner?" Veronica asked.

"About to make my escape," she answered.

"Skipping out on the traditional midnight kissing again?"

Brittany grinned. "You know me too well."

Veronica linked her arm through Brittany's. "Don't know if I told you, but I love your dress."

Brittany ran a hand down the front of her gold sequin dress. "Thanks." She glanced across the room at Carissa. "Do you think she minds they're the same color?"

Veronica giggled. "Color's the only thing they have in common. Yours is so elegant, while Carissa's is trashy chic. How do you think that skimpy dress even stays up?"

"Duct tape," she joked.

Veronica covered her mouth, trying to contain her laughter. Veronica pointed to her mother. "Mom's definitely in her element." They watched as Constance glided from guest to guest, like the queen of the party.

The noise in the room rose as the excitement of the New Year drew near. She whispered to Veronica. "I'm getting out of here while I still can."

Brittany pulled her shawl tight around her as she stepped out into the garden. The only person she wanted to be kissing at midnight was a country away. She looked up at the stars. Maybe Nick was outside looking up at the stars, too. "Star light, star bright. Carry my love to a star far away. Twinkle brightly so he knows I am thinking of him."

Horns blasted and lights flashed in the distance. Fireworks signaled the entry of another year. She heard the French door open behind and turned. Her heart sank.

"Oh, Brittany dear, you're just the person I wanted to see." Carissa grabbed her hand. "Come inside. I have some wonderful news to tell you."

She slipped her hand from Carissa. "You can't tell me out here?"

Carissa shivered. "It's cold." Hugging her arms to herself, she said sweetly, "And you know I've been sick."

Brittany hesitated. She had a premonition something awful was about to happen. She glanced at the stars, *Please give me strength.*

Carissa grabbed her by the hand again, "Come on." She pulled her along the path to the parlor. "Let's go in here where we can be alone." She closed the door behind them. Crossing over to the mahogany bar in the corner, Carissa lifted a bottle of champagne from a bucket of ice. "I know you don't drink," she said pouring two glasses. "But once you hear my news, you'll definitely want to celebrate with me." Carissa handed her a glass before making herself comfortable on the loveseat. She patted the cushion beside her. "Come on. Join me."

Brittany cautiously sat in the Victorian chair across from Carissa and set the glass of champagne on the mahogany coffee table between them. "What's this all about?"

Carissa could barely contain herself. "I want you to be the first to know." She put her hands over her mouth, as if trying to suppress a grin.

"Know what?"

Carissa jumped to her feet and spun around in a circle. "I'm pregnant!"

Brittany gripped the chair beneath her. She barely managed a whisper, "What?"

"I'm pregnant." Carissa's face glowed with joy. She grabbed both of Brittany's hands, pulling her from the chair and forcing her to twirl around the room. "I want to keep this between us, at least until I can tell Nicky."

Brittany jerked away from Carissa and grabbed her stomach. This couldn't be happening. She backed toward the door. Carissa had lied about being pregnant before. She must be lying now. Brittany hugged her arms around herself. But how could she claim to be pregnant with Nick's child if they had never had sex. Brittany felt her world spinning out of control. *It's not true. It's not true.* kept running though her mind.

"I'm so happy." Carissa wrapped Brittany in a bear hug and then whispered in her ear, "A baby, life's sweetest gift of love."

Brittany was suffocating. She tried to pull away, but Carissa just held tighter.

"I don't understand." Her voice trembled. "How did this happen?"

"How?" Carissa released her hold. Stepping back, she started to laugh. "Silly girl." She threw her hands over her mouth. "Oh right, I forgot you're a virgin and don't know about these things."

"I'm not stupid," she fumed. "I meant how could you be pregnant? Nick's been in Mexico for three weeks."

"He stopped here on his way out of the country." Carissa danced around the room. "I guess a white wedding dress is out. Thank you for bringing him back into my life. Who would have ever thought it would be Nicky and me, instead of you?"

"It's not true."

"Oh, yes it is. Would you like to see the test results?"

Brittany didn't hear anything else over the pounding of her heart. Her head was swimming and she couldn't breathe. She sunk into the nearest chair. *Why God, why?* She put her head in her hands.

She never heard Carissa leave.

"Darling, I've been looking everywhere for you," Chadwick said, shutting the door after himself. "I have something important to ask you."

She stared blankly at him, then started to rise from her chair. He put his hand on her shoulder to stop her, but she removed his hand. "I need to go."

"Just give me a minute." In astonishment, she watched him kneel before her. "I promise you it will be worth it." He reached inside his purple dinner jacket and pulled out a small box. "Brittany, will you marry me?"

Her mouth fell open. The four-karat diamond was set in gold with rows of diamonds circling the band. It was the gaudiest ring she had ever seen.

Chadwick removed it from the box and started to place it on her finger. She jerked her hand free. Jumping up, she accidently knocked Chadwick to the floor. The ring stuck in the plush carpet, as if mocking her.

"No!" *Could this night get any worse?*

Chadwick picked up the ring. He held it out to her again. "Brittany, I love you," he said, his lips puckering as he moved in for a kiss.

She sidestepped away. She had to escape this madness.

"Brittany, darling, come here." He held his arms open.

She retreated once more, but backed into the bar. "I need to leave," she said, hating that he was so close.

"Not until you say *yes*." Chadwick put his arms around her, blocking her exit.

She ducked underneath, but he grabbed her before she could take a step. She glanced at his hand. "Chadwick, please let me go."

"I love you, Brittany," He lowered his face to hers once more.

She quickly turned. "You're acting crazy." She twisted out of his grasp. Her heel caught in the plush white carpet and she tumbled onto the loveseat. Chadwick sat down beside her and she began to shake. "Chadwick, please."

"Stop playing games and take the ring," he seethed. "Can't you see this is the best possible thing for both of us?"

"Never." She tried to stand, but he put his hand firmly on her leg. "You're hurting me," she cried.

"Hurting you?" He gripped harder, his eyes turning steely and cold.

She writhed, trying to free her leg. "Let. Me. Go."

"Never." He grabbed her by the back of the neck with his other hand and pushed her face toward his.

She latched onto his hand, trying to pull it from her hair. Bile rose in her throat. Out of the corner of her eye, she saw the untouched glass of champagne. She lifted it and tossed it into his face.

He jumped up in shock and Brittany dashed from the room. Her whole body shaking, she stumbled up the stairs, slammed her bedroom door, and locked it before collapsing to the floor. Rage tore through her. First, Carissa's news and then Chadwick's unwanted advance. *Why is this happening?* Carissa's pregnant with Nick's baby? She threw her shoes across the room. *Tell me it's a lie!*

Carissa watched Brittany flee up the stairs and heard her slam the door. She snickered. That did not look like a happy woman. She grinned and opened the parlor door. Taking one look at a wet Chadwick, she ran to him. "What happened?"

"She threw champagne on me," he sniveled.

She rushed to the bar for a towel. "Why?"

"She said *no*, Carissa. Let's leave it at that."

"I don't believe it." She stared at the door. How had this not worked? It was a foolproof plan.

"Well, believe it," he said.

"We set her up perfectly." She stared at the door, "I spent the whole holiday break playing sick." She stomped her feet. "What did you say to her?"

"I asked her to marry me, just like you said."

"I thought for sure she would have been so devastated by my news that she would jump at your marriage proposal," Carissa rubbed her forehead. "For no other reason than revenge on Nick!"

"I told you it wouldn't work." He wiped the front of his shirt.

She dropped down onto the loveseat and put her head in her hands. Six years ago, she had run into another man's arms out of revenge. She'd been so sure Brittany would do the same.

"Maybe she isn't in love with this guy after all," Chadwick said. "I, for one, have never seen her so much as hint at liking anyone."

"Oh, she's in love with him. He's the reason she's never fallen for anyone else all these years."

Chadwick walked over to the bar and poured himself a drink. "Now what?" He pointed his finger at her. "You assured me if I went along with your scheme, she would marry me." He slammed his glass on the bar. "You know I need her money. My father is cutting me off."

"You could always get a job," she said haughtily.

He glared at her, then suddenly smiled. "I could always marry you."

She threw her head back and laughed. "Dream on." She snapped her fingers. "Relax, there's another way to get her."

"How?" he pouted.

"I have some ecstasy in my room. Slip some in her drink and in the morning, when she wakes up naked beside you, goody two-shoes will have no choice but to marry you."

"Perfect!" He followed Carissa upstairs.

She opened the door to the sitting room beside her bedroom. "Make yourself comfortable." In the bathroom, she gathered the drug and caught her reflection in the mirror. Only it was a twenty-two-year-old version of herself looking back at her.

For a moment, she was back in Cancun. Jealous rage had sent her to Pierce's villa that morning. *She would show Alex and Brittany.* She banged her fist on the vanity. Only it was her who was punished, not them. Pierce had slipped something into her drink and she'd woken up next to him with a ring on her finger, a prisoner of a loveless marriage.

The fear, the pain, and the rage all flooded back. Carissa's hands started to shake. She dropped the pill back into the drawer and slammed it shut. *No one deserves that. Not even Brittany.*

Carissa slunk back into her sitting room. "Sorry, I thought I had some, but I don't." She handed him a vial of cocaine instead. "But I have this. We should party."

Brittany curled up in a ball on her bed, unable to sleep. The noise from the party drifted up until the wee hours of the morning. *Why, God? Why? I trusted you. I*

trusted him. Her head throbbed as her thoughts and Carissa's words collided. *Pregnant! I know she's lying.* She choked on her tears. *But you can't accuse someone of being the father if they have never had...* Her heart shattered into a thousand pieces.

The stars twinkled in the sky, mocking her. She jumped up. "It was a stupid wish." She pulled the curtains closed. "Just a stupid wish." Brittany returned to bed. How long she lay there, she didn't know. Minutes seemed like hours, hours an eternity.

There was a soft knock on the door. She watched Nannie enter the room. "It's a beauti... Good gracious, child. What's wrong?

"I'm fine, Nannie," she lied.

"You don't look fine." Nannie felt her forehead. "Are you sick? Maybe you have what Carissa has?"

"I don't think so," she said, barely containing her anger.

"No, I don't think so either. If I didn't know better, I'd think that girl was pregnant. Throwing up in the morning and fine in the evening."

Brittany started crying all over again.

"Child, what is it?"

She sobbed harder. Her cell phone rang.

Nannie picked it up off the bed. "Oh look, it's that nice gentleman, Nick."

Brittany snatched the phone from her hand and answered. "What do you want?"

With a startled expression, Nannie backed out of the room.

"Happy New Year to you, too," Nick said.

Her heart skipped at the sound of his voice, but then anger took over. She would not allow her heart to take her on this fool's journey again. Her hands shook. Her stomach felt queasy. How dare he call her? "I will ask again. What do you want?"

"I called because I'm in Colorado and I want to see you."

"Really?"

"Brittany, what's wrong?" Nick asked. "You got my text, didn't you? I had a job in Mexico."

"Yes, but I have one question for you. Did you make any stops along the way to Mexico?"

Nick didn't say anything right away. "Just a quick one in Denver, but—"

She couldn't control the words that tore from her gut. "I hate you!" she screamed and hung up on him.

So Carissa wasn't lying. He really had come here.

The phone rang again, but she sent it straight to voicemail. He called a third time and still she ignored it. Before he could call a fourth time, she dialed her pilot. "Are you available to fly me out of here today? Okay, I'll be at the airport at noon." She turned off her phone, dumped it into her purse, and in a moment of rage, threw the purse across the room. "I hate you!" she screamed again. Quickly tossing her things into a suitcase, she knew she couldn't stay under the same roof as Carissa for one more moment. She would rather sit at the airport alone than breathe the same air as her traitorous cousin.

Carissa was coming down the stairs when the butler answered a ring at the front door. "Nicky, darling!" She ran down the stairs to greet him. "How nice of you to come all this way just to see me." Running a hand across his now full beard, she added, "You could have taken the time to shave first. I must say, this look isn't very attractive."

"I'm here to see Brittany," he said.

"Well, how rude. You have a real woman in front of you and you want the Ice Maiden." She ran her hand down his chest.

Nick grabbed it and held it up, forcing her to raise her eyes to meet his. "I told you before, don't touch me."

Carissa only laughed. "Maybe you and the Ice Maiden are made for each other."

"Are you going to get her or do I have to go find her?"

"I can't," she said lightly.

"You can't or you won't?" Nick countered.

"I can't. She isn't here."

"I know she's here. I talked to her just this morning."

Carissa laughed hysterically. "So that's why the Ice Maiden flew out of here so fast."

"Where did she go?" he asked, now concerned not only for her safety, but for what it meant about their relationship.

"I don't know," she snapped. "It's not like she confides in me." Carissa made one more attempt. "You know, I'm much more fun than she could ever be."

"Not even in your wildest dreams is that possible." Nick's cold black stare made her step back. "I'll find out what you've done and when I do... I promise you will pay."

She inched her way toward the stairs. "Your threats don't frighten me."

"If you think I'm only threatening, that's your second mistake."

She laughed. "What was the first?"

"Trying to come between me and Brittany."

The noise of the airport lobby couldn't dim the sound of Carissa's laugh floating around his head. *What has she done?* Nick sat staring at his phone. Brittany's picture flashed as he started to call her. He shoved the phone back in his pocket. There was no point. She wouldn't pick up.

He held his head in his hands. How was he going to fix this mess? The same way he fixed all his problems. Get to know the enemy. He pulled his phone back out. He called Lisa at PSA. "I need two favors," he said. "I'll be arriving at BWI at about two o'clock. Will you send someone to pick me up?"

"Of course," Lisa answered.

"Have you sent the Carissa Hathaway file to my house yet?"

"It will be there by the time you arrive home."

"Great." As an afterthought, he added, "Could you check on her activities in Cancun, about six years ago?"

Lisa's response was immediate. "Already on it."

"What do you mean?"

"Carl already has me searching for anything I can find on Carissa and Brittany in Cancun," she said matter-of-factly.

"Why is he doing that?"

"Because Judge Hathaway asked him to."

"*Hmm.*" He rubbed the back of his neck. "Wonder why after all this time?"

"I can email the files now."

"No. I don't have my laptop with me and you know I work better if I have everything laid out in front of me."

"One of these days," Lisa teased, "you're going to need to go green, you know."

"I tell you what." He grabbed his duffel bag and headed to the boarding line. "The day Carl does, I'll consider it. Oh, and one more thing—put a flag on Carissa Hathaway. Just something to cause her a little inconvenience. And a tail on her, too. And make sure she sees it. I want her to know she's being followed."

"You know I just can't do that because…"

"She is a known associate of Vito Capri's. Isn't that reason enough?" Nick relished the idea of a little payback. "If she so much as jay walks, I want her picked up."

On the plane, he closed his eyes and pretended to be asleep. He reached into his jacket pocket, feeling the ring box. He had been so eager to return home and tell Brittany he loved her. But the risk he took to get back to her had proved to be in vain.

Driving out of Mexico had been impossible. Mendez's brothers had people looking for Max and Nick everywhere. It would have only been a matter of time before they were discovered. In a moment of brilliance, he determined the only thing to do was to smuggle themselves out right under their noses.

In one of the Mendez's routine shipments of cocaine to the U.S., he and Max had hitched a ride home. The only problem was that it meant hiding inside a coffin in the hot Mexican heat for almost a full day.

But the thought of seeing Brittany made the journey bearable. Now he was home but the joy he'd felt at the sound of her voice, now weighed like a ton of bricks on his heart. Her last words echoed in his mind: "*I hate you.*"

Chapter 16

Nick dropped his backpack at the foot of the stairs and picked up the manila envelope sitting on the side table. He could hear his mother in the kitchen. The file in his hand would have to wait.

Before he was halfway down the hall, she came out of the kitchen, wiping her hands on her apron. "You're home." Giving him a big hug, she linked her arm in his and herded him into the kitchen. "Sit. I'll fix you something to eat. You look horrible."

Nick ran a hand through his thick beard and attempted a laugh. "That bad, huh?"

She handed him a glass of ice tea. "Are you hungry?" She gently pushed him into a chair.

"I don't have time." He started to rise. "I'll be in my office if you need me."

"What's so important that it can't wait?"

He waved the folder. "This."

"Work, work, work. You need something better to keep you occupied." She patted his arm, "Have you been to see Brittany yet?"

Nick slumped back in the chair. Just hearing her name hurt. "No."

"Why not? I thought the two of you—"

"There is no *two of us*." He put his head in his hands.

Lucy sighed. "I was afraid of that... after that awful woman called here claiming to be your girlfriend."

He jerked his head up. "What woman?"

"She said her name was Carissa."

Nick jumped, knocking his chair to the floor. "My girlfriend? Over my dead body."

Lucy touched her chest. "Oh, thank heavens." She shook her head. "You don't know how relived I am to hear that."

"Next time she calls, hang up."

"I already do. Did you meet her in Mexico?"

"No, she's Brittany's cousin." He righted the chair he'd knocked over, his knuckles turned white as he gripped the back of it. "And while I was away she did something to make Brittany hate me."

Lucy rubbed Nick's back. "If Brittany truly loves you, she'll come around."

"I hope so." He waved the folder in the air. "I'm hoping this info will help me figure out how to speed that along."

Nick sat at his desk and opened the file. He scowled at Carissa's picture. He turned the photograph over. He couldn't stand to see her face for one more second. Other than the death of Brittany's parents, their files read alike. Same private schools, same college, one studied art while the other interior design. It wasn't until college graduation that their files went in opposite directions. For the last six years, Carissa had been in and out of rehab.

There was a list of known boyfriends—Vito Capri was one of them. Carissa had turned state's evidence in order to avoid jail time, sending Vito and his brother Dmitry there instead. But there was no mention of Cancun.

He opened the second folder and let out a low whistle. The top page was a marriage license for Carissa Hathaway and Pierce Dubra. The second contained a death certificate for Pierce. *Now we're onto something.* He skimmed the pages quickly before returning to the first page and reading every word.

His heart sank as he read the police reports. The first report stated that Pierce Dubra had shot Alexander Rolands. The second was the murder of Pierce Dubra. The prime suspect, *Brittany Fitzpatrick.*

Nick wasted no time calling Lisa. "Get me everything you can on Pierce Dubra and Alexander Rolands."

"Way ahead of you. The courier should be there any minute."

In the meantime, he read and reread the crime report. The night of the shooting, Brittany brought Alexander there. What was Rolands to Brittany? Nick rubbed his head. He knew she had to have had relationships over the years. Was this Rolands person one of them?

The files on Dubra and Rolands arrived. Dubra's was a thick one. Though suspected of being a jewel thief, he had never been caught. Resorts like Cancun had been the stomping grounds for this thrill-seeking son of a billionaire. The more he read, the more he wondered how Brittany could have become involved with someone like him. Carissa, he could understand. She would have been captivated by the thrill and his money. But Brittany? He thought she'd have stayed clear of him.

Rolands' file, on the other hand, was short. His family ran a luxury hotel in Cancun. It looked like he had just been at the wrong place at the wrong time.

The phone rang—Lisa. "I thought you'd like to know that Brittany is about to land in Cancun."

He jumped up. "What?"

"Seems she goes there four or five times a year."

"Get me a ticket."

"Isn't there a bounty on your head?" Lisa paused. "Carl will not like you going back to Mexico."

"Let me worry about that. Just get the ticket."

"By the time you get there, she'll be on her way home. She only ever stays one night."

"Doesn't matter, I want to see for myself what goes on in Cancun."

He hung up, ran upstairs, emptied his bag on the floor, and repacked it with clean clothes. He dropped it by the front door and went back into his office. He picked up the man's picture from the file. *Are you Brittany's lover?* He'd gone looking for dirt on Carissa and instead found Brittany's secret. He was a fool.

He pulled the pictures of himself and Brittany from his wallet. *Why are you flying off to be with someone else when we have things to work out?* Nick ran a finger down across her face. *Why, Brittany? Why?*

His phone rang and caller ID said it was Lisa again. "Sorry Nick, the first flight I can get you is tomorrow morning."

"Book it, please." He put down the phone and picked up the police report. No matter how many times he went through it, he couldn't understand why they suspected Brittany. There was no evidence. So what did they know that wasn't in the report?

Nick spent a sleepless night tossing and turning. His dreams alternated between making love to Brittany and sending her to jail. He was grateful when the alarm went off. He caught his reflection in the bathroom mirror. He hadn't shaved in over a week. His mother was right—he did look awful. He ran a hand though the full beard. If Brittany was still there, she would not be impressed. He picked up the razor and shaved down to his normal stubble.

As the plane landed in Cancun, he wondered what he was about to find. Before disembarking, he put on sunglasses and pulled a Baltimore Orioles cap down on his forehead. He casually walked through the airport, stopping at the gift shop for a postcard. He hadn't see any of Mendez's henchmen, but it paid to be cautious. Nick didn't relax until his cab pulled up to the Rolands resort.

At the front desk, he asked, "Has Brittany Fitzpatrick checked out yet?"

The gentleman eyed Nick suspiciously. "I'm sorry. I cannot give out that information."

Nick flashed his PSA badge. The clerk waved the badge away.

"I'm not asking for her room number. I just need to know if she is still here."

"One moment," the clerk replied. He pressed a button and within seconds, the office door behind him opened.

"Is there a problem, Francisco?"

Nick was shocked to see Alexander Rolands in a wheelchair. He took one look at Nick and stopped. "You have some nerve, coming here," Rolands declared, making a fist.

Nick stepped back. "You know who I am?"

"Brittany's description was pretty accurate." He leaned back in his chair, glaring up at Nick. "Why are you here?"

"I'm looking for Brittany. Is she still here?"

"No. She isn't." Rolands grinned. "So you came all this way for nothing."

Nick stared at Rolands. The man's hatred was unmistakable. "Listen." He stood ramrod straight. "I don't know what you think I did, but you're wrong."

Rolands pointed a finger at him. "I know you hurt her."

Nick looked Rolands straight in the eyes, "And how did I do that?"

A guest walked up to the front desk. Rolands nodded toward his office. "We can talk in there." They entered and Rolands pushed a button to close the door behind them.

He motioned for Nick to sit on one of the leather chairs in front of the large oak desk.

Still standing, Nick asked, "What does Brittany think I did?"

Rolands looked at him in disgust. "Like you don't know."

"Honestly, I don't." He rubbed the back of his neck. "All I know is everything was great between us before I left for my last assignment."

"So great," Rolands snorted, "that you got Carissa pregnant."

"What?" He stared in disbelief. "Are you crazy?"

Rolands struggled to stand. With wobbly legs, he took a step toward Nick. "I ought to wring your sorry neck."

Nick collapsed into the leather chair. "I never touched her." He couldn't stop shaking. How could Brittany believe that lie? "I swear," his voice cracked with grief, "I never touched her."

Rolands lowered himself back into his chair. "Carissa says otherwise."

"Carissa is a liar."

Nick's phone rang. Caller ID indicated Carl. "Excuse me. I have to take this," he said and moved across the room to stand in front of French doors that led out to a landscaped patio.

Carl didn't wait for Nick to say hello. He shouted, "What are you doing in Mexico?" Nick didn't have to see him to know that the blood vessels in Carl's forehead were about to explode. "You know full well there's a bounty on your head."

"I'm far enough away from Mendez—"

"You know full well he has people everywhere." Nick had to hold the phone away from his ear. "I want you on the next plane out of there."

He knew his boss was right. It wasn't safe for him anywhere in Mexico. He ran a hand through his hair. "My plane leaves in the morning."

"Let's hope that isn't too late. You'll be the death of me yet." The line went dead.

Nick put his phone back in his pocket. He wanted to pound his head on the glass door. Instead, he took a deep breath and turned toward Rolands.

"He was yelling so loud, I couldn't help but hear your conversation," Rolands began. "Why did the Mendez family put a bounty on you?"

"I killed their brother." Nick sat back down.

With a whistle, Rolands spoke. "I heard about that on the news." Rolling behind his desk, he picked up the phone. "With just one phone call, I won't ever have to worry about you hurting Brittany again."

Nick stood to leave. "Do what you must. I know how to fight Mendez's henchmen and I'll be long gone before they arrive." He shook his head. "What I don't know is how to fight Carissa's kind of evil," he muttered.

Rolands studied Nick before taking his hand off the phone. He rolled over to the oak bar in the corner. "It's a little early for drinking, but some days you just need to bite the bullet." He grinned. "I have a feeling this is one of those days, don't you?" He poured them each a shot of tequila. "I have no love for Mendez and his kind, but there's no way I can know if any of them are staying here." He handed Nick a drink. "Hopefully not, because you'd be hard to miss."

"Best thing to do is hide in plain sight." Nick downed his drink and set the glass on the coffee table. "Does this hotel have a barber?"

After the haircut, Nick looked in the mirror and rubbed his head. He hadn't had such short hair since his Army days. He hardly recognized himself. He hoped Mendez's henchmen wouldn't either.

Nick hurried back to the front desk where Rolands was speaking to Francisco. "Can we talk?"

Rolands looked at him blankly. Finally, recognition hit and he slapped the arm of his wheelchair. "Man, who needs plastic surgery when a haircut will do the trick?" To the clerk, he said, "Check Mr. McFadden into the VIP suite. He will be my guest. And have the bell hop take his bag to his room."

"Your guest?" Nick handed the bellman his backpack and followed Rolands into the office again.

"Brittany is very important to me. I don't want to have to explain how I put you out on the streets for Mendez to find you." Rolands held out his hand. "We got off to a rocky start. Let's amend that." Nick accepted the proffered handshake. "For some reason, Brittany loves you. So that makes you a friend." He smiled. "And my friends call me Alex."

"I don't understand it. Ten years ago, Brittany and Carissa were the best of friends." Nick rubbed the back of his neck. "What exactly happened here six years ago?"

"Let's go out on the patio," Alex said, grabbing a bottle of tequila and putting it in his lap. "It's a long story." Nick held the door and followed him out. "I will tell you, but only because I love Brittany."

Nick downed his drink in one gulp. Anger started to boil. *Had this man been holding Brittany just last night?* He clenched his jaw.

"Not like I see you love her. Brittany's my best friend." Alex poured Nick another shot. "Maybe you can convince her that me being in this chair isn't her fault. I know I've tried and failed miserably." Alex shook his head. "As crazy as it may seem, it's Carissa that I'm in love with."

Nick sputtered. "Really?"

"I know it's hard to believe, but she wasn't always like she is now." Alex glanced out at the ocean. "The drugs changed her."

"But Brittany visits you," Nick insisted.

"Because Carissa believes I'm dead."

He wondered just how many lies Brittany was hiding.

In a faraway voice, Alex said, "I always thought that if you could combine them, you'd have the perfect woman." He laughed. "People think that Carissa is the dominant one, but that's not true."

"I don't see that," Nick said.

"You haven't spent enough time with the two of them together. For four years, I was with them almost twenty-four/seven. Carissa has no boundaries, so Brittany reins her in, keeping her in line. Carissa, on the other hand, makes Brittany stretch hers." Alex downed a third shot of tequila and smacked his glass on the table. "And that brings us to the horrid summer six years ago."

Alex recounted how he'd talked the two of them into coming to Cancun the summer after graduation. He'd planned to propose to Carissa on her birthday. But two weeks beforehand, at a party, Pierce Dubra took one look at Brittany and would stop at nothing until he had her. At first, she seemed flattered by the attention, but there was something about him she didn't like. Carissa was always trying to push Brittany into someone's arms. That summer, it happened to be Pierce. Alex looked apologetically at Nick. "Carissa hated you even back then. She couldn't understand why Brittany couldn't get over you."

"Why? I never did anything to Carissa."

Mocking Carissa's voice, Alex said, "That horrid man didn't even have the common decency to visit after you took not one, but multiple bullets for him. It's time to trade him in for a new one."

Nick lowered his head. "I thought Brittany was dead."

Alex nodded and continued. "On Carissa's twenty-second birthday, we went to a party aboard Pierce's yacht. She ended up losing twenty thousand dollars at the poker table and in a foolish moment, made one last bet with Pierce—with herself and Brittany as the stakes." Alex poured himself another shot and downed it, slamming the glass on the table again. "I'm sure the game was rigged, so she lost."

Nick's back stiffened. His eyes narrowed.

Alex closed his eyes. "I will never forget the smug look on Pierce's face as he threw his cards on the table. The chill of his voice claiming my girlfriend and Brittany as his. He put his arms around Carissa and Brittany. I knocked his arms away. He just laughed at me and said I could have one last night with her, but tomorrow they were his."

"I offered to pay Pierce to forgive the debt, but he laughed and refused. Brittany was beside herself. I think if she could have, she would've jumped overboard and swam all the way back to the States. The whole way back to the resort, Brittany and Carissa screamed at each other. Before I could even park the car, Brittany jumped out of it and ran to her room." Alex rubbed his head. "I remember tossing Carissa's engagement ring in her lap and leaving her in the car. The rest of that evening is sort of a blur.

"When I finally got back to our room, Carissa was passed out across the bed. Every time I thought I had succeeded in moving her, she would sprawl back out." He shook his head. "I can truly say it was frustration and poor judgment on my part that sent me to Brittany's adjoining room. So, idiot that I was, I convinced Brittany to let me sleep on the corner of her bed."

Nick stiffened.

Alex held up his hands. "Sometime after I fell asleep, Brittany slipped down on the floor. Even if she hadn't, we were fully clothed. But before the sun even rose, Carissa found me in Brittany's bed. She screamed, 'I'll make you pay' and ran off to Pierce. Three days later, a note arrived that she'd married him."

"Did Pierce force Brittany to move into the villa?" Nick said.

Alex shook his head, "She went willingly." Seeing the shocked look on Nick's face, Alex looked away and softly added, "Brittany went to protect Carissa."

"From what?"

Alex's voice quavered, "Pierce got Carissa hooked on heroin."

"Was Brittany doing drugs, too?"

"If you have to ask that question," Alex said, "you don't know Brittany very well. She wouldn't even smoke marijuana. At the end of the summer, Brittany and I went back to school."

"I thought you said you had graduated."

"I was starting medical school and Brittany was in a Master's program. Two days before Christmas, Brittany received a video of Carissa having sex with multiple partners. You could tell she was so strung out she didn't even know what was going on. The note attached just said, '*help me.*' We flew there to rescue her. We thought the note was from Carissa, but I'm pretty sure now that it was just a trick of Pierce's to get Brittany back in Cancun. Because the minute Carissa saw the two of us together, she flipped out and ran upstairs. We followed. Carissa and Brittany started yelling at each other. Carissa accused Brittany of trying to steal Pierce from her, just like she thought Brittany had stolen me. Carissa flew across the room, pulling a gun from her nightstand. From out of nowhere, Pierce entered the room and threw a vase at Carissa, knocking the gun out of her hand. Everyone but Brittany dove for the gun. Pierce came up first and aimed it at Carissa. I jumped in front, taking the bullet meant for her."

Alex looked at the near empty bottle of tequila. "Good thing the story is almost over. Or we might need another bottle." His voice wavered. "When Pierce turned up dead the next morning, Carissa pointed the finger at Brittany, saying her cousin was jealous and wanted to destroy her. The police couldn't prove anything. My parents had been with Brittany in the hospital waiting room all night."

"Why didn't they suspect Carissa? Isn't it always the spouse?"

"Coast Guard cleared her. They had fished her out of the ocean." Alex clenched his fist. "They'd called Pierce to notify him. Since he answered, there was no way Carissa could have done it." He banged his fist on his chair. "If you ask me, Pierce pushed Carissa overboard."

Nick rubbed the back of his neck and shook his head. "What a mess." Nick glanced at Alex's pale face and drooping shoulders. "If you still love Carissa, why let her believe you're dead?"

Alex stared straight ahead. "Never once has she asked Brittany if I survived the shooting." His voice broke. "And I forbade Brittany to tell her."

Nick twisted his hands together. "From my reports, it looks like Brittany comes here often. Why is that?"

"She comes to check on Carissa's house."

"Her house?" Nick stammered.

"When Pierce died, Carissa inherited the villa and everything else he owned. Brittany pays to keep the grounds looking good and the yacht out of the water, so she comes to make sure everything is okay."

"Doesn't make sense. She could easily hire a property manager."

"She could." Alex grinned. "But you know Brittany."

Nick leaned his head on the back of the chair. A soft smile touched his lips "An angel even to her enemy."

Chapter 17

Vincent sat with his feet propped on the desk, twirling a dart in his hand. He was getting tired of this game. It was time to finish it. Before Sonny could even close the door, Vincent screamed, "Where is she?"

Sonny shrugged. "No one knows. It's a little hard to keep track when she has her own jet."

"I don't want to hear your excuses." He gave Sonny a death stare, then glanced at the photograph of McFadden hanging on the dartboard just behind Sonny's head. Laughing, Vincent threw the dart. As it whizzed by Sonny's head, he yelled, "Find her!"

Sonny jumped out of the way, screaming. The dart hit dead center.

"This cockroach has evaded me for the last time." Vincent banged his hand on the desk. The girl was the key to getting McFadden. He felt it in his bones. Pointing another dart at Sonny's head, he added, "Find her or suffer my wrath."

Sonny backed toward the door. "I thought we were looking for Maria's murderer? Why are you worried about McFadden and the girl?"

Vincent crossed the room in two seconds. "It's been over a month. Are we any closer to finding the killer?" He grabbed Sonny by the shirt.

Sonny shook his head.

Vincent let go of Sonny, "It's time to get back to business."

"Why not grab his mother?" Sonny asked.

Vincent hit him soundly on the head, nearly knocking him to the floor.

"What am I, a barbarian? I don't grab mothers. We wait for the girl. She has to come home soon." He shoved Sonny out of the door. "And when she does, you had better be there to grab her."

Vincent started to shut his office door when he heard his brother Vito's voice in the other room. He didn't sound happy. Vincent stormed into the kitchen. Whoever was messing with Vito was going to pay.

"No!" Vito yelled and slammed the phone on the counter. "She must think I'm a fool."

"Who?" Vincent asked.

"Carissa Hathaway."

The hair on the back of Vincent's neck rose. "What did she want?"

Vito scoffed. "Cocaine."

"You've got to be kidding?"

"I told her it takes some kind of nerve to rat me out and then call me for drugs."

Vincent paused with his hand on the refrigerator. "Is she in New York?"

"Yup, for the weekend. Something about a big family get together."

Vincent's heart skipped a beat. "The entire family?"

"Yeah, seems like they celebrate Judge Hathaway's birthday here every year."

So there is a God and he just dropped the golden goose in my lap. "Where and when is this party?"

"Tonight at the Fitzpatrick Hotel."

"Call Carissa back and tell her you'll bring her whatever she wants."

"You're as crazy as she is." Vito tossed the phone to Vincent. "You want to hook her up? Go ahead. I'm not going to jail again."

He called Carissa and said someone would be dropping off her package shortly. For the first time in months, he smiled. All the waiting was about to pay off.

Nick was surprised to see Miles at the airport. "Since when do you play chauffeur?" he asked.

Miles stepped back, staring at him in amazement. "Man, what happened to your hair? I didn't even recognize you." Miles slapped him on the back.

"That's the idea. So what are you doing here?"

"Since you played renegade and went off the reservation, Carl sent the big guns. Boy, are you in hot water. He's furious."

Nick grimaced. "I got that impression."

In the car, Miles said, "I know she's 'the one,' but it was really stupid of you to go back to Mexico with a million-dollar bounty on your head."

Nick stopped midway fastening his seatbelt. "A million dollars?"

"Yeah, the price went up." Miles gave him a sly glance. "I could always use more money..."

"And what would you do with a million dollars? Other than work. You have no life."

Miles laughed, "You are so right."

"Anyway, you can't take me down."

Miles sucker punched him in the arm. "Meet me in the gym and we'll see."

"Last time I won three out of three," he countered.

"So was it worth it?" Miles asked.

"What?"

"The trip to Mexico. Did you meet up with her?"

Nick shook his head.

"Sorry, man."

"Yeah, me too."

As they pulled up to PSA headquarters, Miles said, "You were right about Capri and your girlfriend. I've been checking on her house like you asked and more than once I saw Capri's henchmen in the area."

Nick punched the air. "I knew it."

"It's not Capri I would be worried about, though. She has some guy living with her."

"They're just friends. He's watching her for me."

Miles shook his head. "Darned if I'd let a good-looking guy like that watch my girl."

"Not all guys are like you."

Soon they arrived at headquarters. After a reaming out by Carl and orders not to leave the state, he was finally able to head home.

Miles dropped him off at his house. "I know you think you're going straight to Brittany's house, but she isn't there. Hasn't been since before Christmas."

Nick thanked him for the heads up and jumped in his own car.

At the Arts Center, Mike opened the door. "Can I help you?"

"Hey man, it's me."

Mike stepped back, giving him the once over. "Sweet mother of pearl, don't you clean up nice?" He opened the door wider, letting Nick in, and slapped him on the back. "Glad to see you. I thought for sure we'd have to send a search party after you."

"Where's Brittany?"

"You don't waste any time, do you?"

"Wasted too many years as it is. I need to set things right before this day is done."

"You oughta know Carissa told Brittany she's pregnant."

He took the cup of coffee Mike offered. "It's not true. I swear I never touched Carissa."

"Good luck convincing Brittany of that."

"I don't understand how she can believe it."

"Honestly, I think she's allowing the pain from the past to cloud her judgment." Mike leaned on the counter. "You need to give her time to think it through, to pray about it. She'll come to the right answer. Just give her time."

"In my line of work, time could run out in a flash of a second." Nick sipped the hot coffee. "You know Capri is watching her house."

Mike nodded.

"So where is she?"

"New York."

"Doesn't she ever stay home?"

"If you had your own jet, would you?" Mike answered. They both laughed.

"Where's she staying?"

"Her family's hotel, The Fitzpatrick, in New York."

Nick looked at his watch. He could be in New York in a little over three hours if traffic was good.

Nick turned to leave, but Mike grabbed his arm. "Just one bit of advice to give you before you confront her... *pray*." He pointed up. "You'll need all the help you can get on this one."

In the car, Nick called Lisa on his cell phone. "Get me a reservation at the Fitzpatrick in NYC."

She hesitated. "Didn't Carl tell you not to leave the state?"

Nick chuckled. "I distinctly heard him say 'The States'."

Lisa gave a heavy sigh. "You know you aren't the only one on the hot seat."

"Yeah, sorry about that. I'll make it up to you somehow."

"Get me a date with Miles and we'll call it even."

"Miles!" He laughed. "I'll see what I can do."

"You know I'll have to inform Carl about this call."

"I know. Tell him not to worry. I'm just going after a girl."

"Tell him yourself. He's staying at the Fitzpatrick for the same party you're planning to crash."

Nick groaned. "I should have known. The judge and he are old school chums." He laughed. "Guess I won't be sneaking under the radar this time."

His knuckles turned white as he gripped the wheel. He was no stranger to risk, but somehow this one felt bigger than any he had ever taken.

Chapter 18

Nick arrived at the Fitzpatrick Hotel a few hours before the party for James Hathaway was to start. He checked in before realizing he hadn't thought things totally through. He couldn't go to the party dressed in jeans and a t-shirt. He would have to go shopping. Before leaving the hotel, he made a stop in the kitchen.

Vincent met Carissa in the bar, slipping a tiny packet of heroin into her purse. "I know you asked for coke, but wouldn't you rather have the really good stuff?" He smiled. "You just need to do a little something for me."

Carissa leaned away from him. "What's that?"

"Get Brittany outside." He suppressed a grin. Victory was within his grasp. "Alone."

"And how am I supposed to do that?"

"That's your problem, not mine." He nodded toward her purse. "That's just a sample. If you want more, you'll figure it out."

"Wh-what are you going to do to her?"

"Talk, just talk. What else can I do on a busy New York street?" He threw some money on the table for their drinks and left. Now he just had to wait.

It was easy for Nick to slip into the crowd during cocktail hour. The Hathaways knew how to throw a party. It looked like half of New York was here.

Carissa's red sequin dress made her easy to find. But where was Brittany?

He watched the door and ran his fingers around his collar. The tie was choking him. His heart nearly leaped from his chest when Brittany walked in. A black dress hugged her figure gracefully. Its sheer material around the shoulders made it modest, but sexy. He wondered if the day would ever arrive when her beauty wouldn't take his breath away.

It took all his strength not to run up and throw his arms around her. Before he could do that though, he had to set things straight.

Toying with the ring box in his pocket, he knew that before the night was over she would say either yes or... he didn't want to think about the other option.

One server brought Brittany a glass of water and another offered *hors d'oeuvres*. Nick smiled. The future heir of the empire was being well taken care of. She walked over to an elderly couple and kissed them both on the cheek. He assumed they were her other grandparents, the Fitzpatricks. Though she acted happy, the smile didn't reach her eyes.

Carissa let out a laugh, causing heads to turn. Brittany visibly tightened.

He hung back, watching, until all the attendees were seated and the main course was being served.

"What's this?" Carissa screeched.

"Your meal." The waiter looked puzzled. "Is there a problem?"

"Of course, there's a problem. Everyone else has filet mignon..." she waved her hand in disgust, "...and you bring me *chicken*?"

"It's what you ordered, miss," he protested.

"I did no such thing," she said haughtily. "I detest chicken."

"I took the liberty of ordering it for you," Nick said, pulling a chair up beside Carissa. He felt all eyes on him, but forbid himself to look across the table at Brittany.

"And who do you think you are?" she asked, not recognizing him.

Brittany gasped. "Nick!"

"Nicky!" Carissa looked him over fully. "My, my," she purred, "don't you clean up nicely?" For a second, she seemed to forget about her food. Then, anger flashed in her eyes. "What gives you the right to order for me?"

"Once we're married, you'll have to get used to dining on chicken." He heard Brittany's sudden intake of breath. "I make good money, but nothing compared to what you're used to." Brittany started to rise, but without looking, Nick firmly said, "Sit down, Brittany."

Surprisingly, she obeyed.

He put his arm around Carissa, pulling her to him. Carissa leaned into him.

"What's the meaning of this, young man?" James asked.

Nick glanced in his direction. "Sorry to crash your party, sir, but in a few minutes, everything will be explained." He kissed Carissa on the cheek. "Won't it, darling?"

"I have no idea what you are up to." She gave a sideward glance at Brittany. "But I love it."

"You surprise me, Carissa. Surely, you would have known that I'd live up to my responsibilities. I firmly believe if you can't pay the price, you shouldn't play the game." He patted her stomach almost lovingly.

Her eyes grew wide as if she suddenly realized he knew about her lie. She pushed his hand from her stomach. "Don't touch me!"

"Marriage is the only answer." He picked up the frozen drink in front of her and handed it to the waiter. "Take this away and bring her some milk."

Carissa grabbed for her glass. "You'll do no such thing." Instead, she handed the waiter her plate. "Take this back and bring me the steak like I ordered." The waiter all but ran back to the kitchen.

James looked from Carissa to Nick. "You're getting married?" The judge glanced at Brittany, taking in her pale face and stiff body.

"Of course not, Grandfather. Nick is obviously drunk and—"

"I assure you, I'm not drunk." He smiled at Carissa. "Am I to assume the only person you told about your pregnancy is Brittany?"

Constance spit her drink across the table. "You're pregnant?"

"I guess that means your friends and family don't know either. I think we should remedy that immediately." He started to rise, ready to propose a toast.

"Don't you dare," Carissa hissed. She scratched her arm and picked at the skin.

"Why not? I would have thought you'd be proud of our baby," he taunted.

"Carissa, if this is true..." Constance said, venom in her voice.

Carissa flipped her hair over her shoulder and rolled her eyes at her mother. "There's no need to get hysterical," she said. "I'm not pregnant and he knows it."

"But you told Brittany you were having my baby," he countered.

"It was a joke!" she laughed, but then grew quiet when no one else joined her. "Doesn't anyone have a sense of humor? I really didn't think she was gullible enough to believe it." She glanced across the table at Constance. "Mother, you can breathe. I haven't brought shame to the family name. There's no baby. I never slept with him." She glared across the table at Brittany. "The fool is so taken with the Ice Maiden he wouldn't even touch me." She glanced around the table, a sly smile on her face. "It was just a joke."

Nick stood and leaned across the table, looking Brittany in the eyes. "Did you hear that? I never touched her. Now I have one question for you. Did you have sex with Alex?"

Brittany's lips quivered as she whispered, "No."

"See how easy that was? I asked you a question, you answered it, and I believed you. Imagine that! I believed you. Why?" He swallowed hard. "Because I love and trust you." He slowly shook his head. "You, of all people, know that things aren't always the way they seem. You should have trusted me. Love without trust is nothing." He couldn't look in her misty eyes and say what he had to say. "If this is how love is, then this fool is leaving. Goodbye, Brittany." He turned and walked out the door.

He didn't stop walking until he was in Central Park where he sat down on a bench. There were couples everywhere walking hand in hand. A horse-drawn carriage trotted by with a couple inside looking so full of love. He placed his elbows on his knees and hung his head on his hands. Love was truly a word for fools.

"...this fool is leaving." Nick's words swirled around her like a tidal wave. Brittany felt like she was drowning. What had just happened? She was the fool, not him. She wanted to jump up and run after him, only she was frozen in place.

Carissa sat smugly across the table. "He's leaving. You better go after him."

Like a bursting dam, everything lashed out of Brittany. "How could you?"

"Girls, take this to your rooms," James ordered. "Carissa, we will be discussing this later."

Both of them stood, facing off like two boxers before leaving the party.

Carissa saw the waiter coming from the kitchen and waved him over. "Be a dear and have my dinner sent to room 321. And be sure to bring it in. I hate my food sitting in the hallway." He nodded and hurried back into the kitchen.

Brittany waited for her, still seething in the lobby. "How could you?"

"It was too easy. You should have known better, but sweet trusting Brittany fell for it hook, line, and sinker." Carissa laughed in her face. "I guess he didn't wait around for you to come running after him." She smiled. "Let's call this even for you ruining my life."

"You did that all on your own, Carissa." Brittany poked her in the chest. "It was you who gambled our lives away, you who married Pierce, and you who took drugs."

"And it was you who hooked me on heroin," Carissa snapped.

"I didn't give you heroin."

Carissa grabbed Brittany's finger from her chest. "No, but you allowed them to give it to me."

"I did no such thing." Brittany glared back.

Carissa grabbed Brittany and started to shake her. "You slept with Alex, then got him killed."

"You live in a world of make believe." She pushed Carissa back, hard. "Maybe you've forgotten that it was *you* who pulled the gun on *me*. If Pierce hadn't stopped you, I'd be dead."

"It should have been you that died, not Alex."

"Not that you ever cared enough about him to ask, but..." she hesitated. "Alex isn't dead. That bullet he took saving your worthless life put him in a wheelchair."

Carissa gasped, her eyes wide. A second later, she smacked Brittany. "How could you keep that from me?"

Brittany put a hand to her stinging cheek. "Why?" She leaned close to Carissa's face. "You acted like he never existed."

Carissa's nostrils flared. "Tonight, I got my revenge. The love of your life has turned his back on you." She smiled smugly. "Just like Alex did to me. But you're too self-righteous to go after him." She turned her head and nodded at the door. "For all you know, he could be standing right outside the hotel waiting for you."

Brittany turned and ran for the door.

Before getting up from the sofa, Vincent laid a package on the coffee table and nodded at Carissa. He laughed to himself as he watched her pick it up. She wanted the good stuff and he had given it to her—almost pure heroin. Oh, tonight was going to be a good night. Revenge was being served all around.

Brittany raced out into the night looking left then right. Her heart sank. Nick was gone.

Not willing to waste any more time, she pulled her cell phone from her purse and dialed his number. It rang once and went straight to voicemail. Tears welled up. She was such a fool. She started to leave a message, "Nick, I'm so..." The hard tip of a gun pushed against her ribs.

"Hello, darling. Start walking."

She stiffened. She'd only seen Vincent Capri briefly, but she knew without a doubt it was him.

"If you scream or bring any attention to us at all, I will pull this trigger." He pressed the gun even harder into her ribs. "Do you understand?"

She nodded.

"Start walking." He glanced down and noticed the open phone. "Who are you talking to?"

"No one." He squeezed her arm. "It's Nick's voicemail," she whispered.

He snatched the phone. "Hello, Nick. I'll be in touch." He tossed it behind them. "Get moving."

When she hesitated, he put his arm around her back, drawing her close to shield the gun from the prying eyes of passersby. She did as she was told.

They had barely taken two steps when the doorman called after them. "Ms. Fitzpatrick, you dropped your phone."

"Ignore him," Vincent commanded.

"Ms. Fitzpatrick!" The doorman picked up the phone and started after them.

"If he gets any closer, I'll shoot him," Vincent warned.

She turned slightly to the diligent hotel employee. "Please, just give it to my grandfather," she said. "Tell him I'm with Chester."

The doorman bowed slightly and turned toward the hotel.

"Do I look like a Chester to you?"

"It was the first name I could think of." She only prayed that the door attendant would give her grandfather the message quickly. Chester was their code name for help.

Chapter 19

Nick's phone rang—Brittany. He pushed it straight to voicemail. He couldn't handle talking to her right now, so he shoved the phone in his pocket and watched black clouds slowly steal the stars away. It was the perfect end to an imperfect day. Darkness.

He leaned his head back, trying to find one particular star. All he could see was a vision of the pain in Brittany's eyes. He had wanted to punish her for believing Carissa, but he'd gone about this all wrong. Instead of letting his anger rule, he should have used his head. His fingers tightened around the phone in his pocket.

He sensed someone sit on the bench beside him. He didn't look up. The smell told him it was someone who hadn't bathed in a while.

"Hey man, you look like you could use a swig." A hand held out a bottle in a brown paper bag.

Nick waved it off.

"Woman trouble?"

He looked up at the man and was surprised at the warmth in the stranger's eyes. "How can you tell?" he asked.

"Seen that look too many times not to recognize it." He chuckled before putting the bottle to his lips. After a long pull, he wiped his mouth with the back of his hand. "Let me give you a little advice. There's nothing on earth that can't be fixed, but death." He eyed Nick. "She isn't dead, is she?"

Nick smiled. "No."

"Then get off this bench and go get her. Kiss her like it's the last time and do that every day, and I promise you everything will work out."

"You think so?"

"The Bible says, 'Love is patient and kind; love does not envy or boast; it is not arrogant or rude. It does not insist on its own way; it is not irritable or resentful; it does not rejoice at wrongdoing, but rejoices with the truth. Love bears all things, believes all things, hopes all things, endures all things.' Do you love her like that?"

"You believe in the Bible?" Nick's eyebrows drew together.

"Of course, I do." A troubled look came over the man. "You believe in Jesus, don't you?"

He shrugged.

"Man, you have worse problems than a fight with the little woman. You need to get right with Jesus before anything else can be fixed."

Nick looked at the homeless man. His clothes were beyond dirty, his face hadn't been washed since the last time it rained, and all his belongings fit in a small cart. "How can *you* believe in Jesus?"

"How can I not?"

Nick couldn't help himself. "If this Jesus is such a loving God who takes care of you, what are you doing living on the street?"

"Jesus didn't put me here. I did that," he replied calmly. "Jesus didn't tell me to get drunk and put my wife and kids in the car and drive them to their death." He took another swig.

Nick stared at him, appalled at his story.

"Satan got a hold of me and wouldn't let go until everything I had was gone." The old man wiped a tear from his eyes. "What are you still doing sitting here? There's a woman out there crying for you. Go tell her you're sorry."

"Who says it's my fault?" he asked defensively.

"Doesn't matter. I dare say it was both of you. You need to apologize for making her cry. Life's too short to be going to bed angry." He slapped Nick on the leg. "Or alone."

Nick stood up and held his hand out. "Thanks for setting me straight."

The man wiped his hand on his dirty pants before taking Nick's hand. "My pleasure."

"I'm Nick. And you are?"

"David," he said, turning to lay across the bench as if camping out for the night. Looking up at the sky, he added, "Don't forget to pray before you get there. God will give you the right words."

Nick pulled out his wallet and handed him all the cash he had. "Go buy yourself something to eat."

David waved it off.

"I promise you, nothing would make my woman happier. Please take this."

David sat up grinning and closed his hand around the money.

Nick started to walk away, but turned back. "Thank you."

David rose and pushed his cart. As he walked away, one star emerged from the clouds. Nick heard him say, "I'll be praying for you."

He looked at the lone star. "Was he one of your angels?"

The star twinkled in response.

"I'm beginning to think you are real." His heart swelled with warmth. He grinned. Time to go tell Brittany he loved her. And this time he was going to pray before knocking on her door.

The hostess whispered in Constance's ear. "Madame, could you come with me?"

She looked with annoyance at the young girl. "What is it that can't wait?"

"You're needed in your daughter's room."

Constance threw her napkin on the chair. "I'll be right back," she said, faking a smile. "Carissa needs something."

As she crossed the lobby to the elevators, the doorman hurried over. "Ms. Hathaway, your niece dropped her phone."

"Then why are you giving it to me?" she said, pushing him away.

"I thought you could give it to Mr. Hathaway."

The young girl was holding the elevator. "Madame, you need to hurry."

Constance looked from the girl to the doorman. This was not turning out to be the grand evening she had expected. "Just leave it at the front desk. I'm sure she'll be back for it."

"No, ma'am. She left with someone called Chester."

For a second, Constance's heart stopped. *Chester?* Was Brittany in trouble? "What did this Chester look like?"

"Tall with dark hair. I didn't really see his face."

"Oh, that was Nick. Just leave it at the desk." Constance hurried to the elevator. *Chester, indeed.* Brittany was obviously trying to cause more drama.

She entered the elevator and then exited on her floor. As she stepped from the elevator, the hotel manager came running. "Thank heavens. Room service found..."

Constance stood in the doorway, astonished to see paramedics working to resuscitate her daughter.

"Carissa!" she gasped. "What's going on here?"

"Mrs. Hathaway, your daughter has overdosed."

It was then Constance noticed the needle lying on the floor beside Carissa. The paramedic looked up. "We've already given her two doses of naloxone. We need to get her to the hospital, immediately."

Constance stared at the pale form on the rug. "Is she breathing?"

"Barely." The EMTs loaded Carissa on a gurney with practiced ease.

Constance nodded and then turned to the hotel manager. "This will be kept quiet, will it not?"

"Yes, ma'am. I've already spoken with my staff."

"Who found her?"

"A young server. She's in the other room talking to the police."

"The police?" Constance balked. "Why are they here?"

"Ma'am, it was a drug overdose. The police had to be called." Constance stared at Carissa with rage, wanting to scream at her still form. After a long slow breath, she turned back to the manager. "Take her down the freight elevator and out the back door."

"Madame, if that's what you wish."

"It is," she confirmed.

A sigh of relief escaped his lips. Apparently, he didn't want bad publicity either.

A uniformed officer approached. "We'll need to file a report. Do you know her dealer?"

"I most certainly do not," Constance huffed and walked over to the bed.

"Will you be following us to the hospital?" the paramedic asked her as the EMTs maneuvered the gurney into the corridor.

"No," Constance said, picking up Carissa's purse from the mattress and laying it on the stretcher. "Any information you'll need is in there." Then, she stormed out.

From the hallway, she watched her daughter being whisked away, wishing she really did have the power to turn Carissa into a cat. Now she would have to clean this mess up just like all the other times.

She turned back to the hotel staff, pretending to wipe tears from her eyes. Waving the manager and room service over, she reached into her purse and pulled out six one-hundred-dollar bills.

They each waved their hands in the air in refusal.

But she tucked the bills in each of their hands. "You saved my daughter. If you hadn't found her..." She let her voice trail off and then sniffled loudly. "Please, take the money, and remember. This is between us. No one else needs to know."

"Yes, ma'am."

In the elevator, Constance checked her hair and re-did her lipstick. As the door opened, she put on a smile.

"Everything okay?" her husband asked as she returned to the party.

"Yes, Carissa just wanted to let me know she was going out for the night." She took one look at her cold plate and waved for the waiter. "Please fix me another. This is cold."

"Did you see Brittany?" Veronica asked.

Constance rolled her eyes. "No."

"I'm going to go check on her," the younger girl said, looking worried.

"No need. The doorman said she left with Nick."

Chapter 20

"Nick, I—" Brittany's voicemail to him was interrupted by a deep male voice that made Nick's heart constrict. *"Hello, darling. Start walking,"* it had said.

Vincent! He began to run. He had to find Brittany. Why hadn't he answered the phone? His foolish pride might have gotten her killed.

No. He knew Vincent. Brittany wasn't dead. Yet. It had already been hours since the call. He had to find her. He dodged people on the street. Someone yelled, "Hey!" He was still five blocks from the hotel. Time was of the essence. Without pausing, he pushed the speed-dial number for Carl.

Nick burst through the hotel door where Carl and Brittany's grandparents were waiting for him in the lobby.

"How do you know Vincent has her?" James asked.

He put his phone on speaker and replayed the message.

"Mr. Hathaway," the doorman approached them, "did you get your granddaughter's phone?"

The group turned as one to look at the doorman. "Her phone?" James repeated.

"She dropped it when she left."

Nick immediately stepped toward him. "You saw her leave?"

"Yes. She dropped her phone and when I tried to return it she asked me to give it to Mr. Hathaway."

James cleared his throat. "And why didn't you?"

The doorman's eyes darted from one person to the next. "I told your daughter-in-law and she said to just leave it at the front desk."

"Was anyone with her?" Nick tried to keep his voice calm.

"Yes. Like I told Mrs. Hathaway, she left with Chester."

A loud gasp came from the group. Lillian grabbed her husband's hand with tears welling in her eyes. "He told Constance she said 'Chester' and that woman just sat there this evening like nothing was wrong!" Lillian turned toward the ballroom.

James stopped his wife. "We'll deal with that later. For now, let's focus on getting our granddaughter back."

Nick paced the lobby like a caged animal.

"The last thing we want to do is panic," Carl said.

"How did Vincent even know she was here?" Nick asked, more to himself than anyone else. "Did he just happen to be here, too?"

Brittany's other grandfather, Mitchell Fitzpatrick, signaled for the hotel manager to join them. "We need to see the hotel's security tapes."

"This way, sir."

They all squeezed into the security room. It was lined with computer monitors, each showing four different camera feeds. Nick pointed to the display of the front entrance, requesting the security guard start the replays a few minutes before Brittany had placed her call to him. They watched as the security guard rewound the footage.

"Look. There's Vincent coming out of the hotel behind her," Nick said.

"Can we see the lobby tape next?" Carl asked. They watched the images rewind in slow motion.

"Stop! He just laid a package on that table and it looks like he's nodding at Carissa." Nick wrung his hands together.

"She wouldn't have done this." Lillian moved in close to her husband, looking at him with pleading eyes. "Would she?"

"I hope not." James patted her arm. "Let's see when he arrived."

The guard rewound the tape further. Nick leaned down, watching every frame. "There!" he said. "Look, there's Vincent coming into the hotel." They watched him cross the lobby and head into the bar. "We need to see that tape."

The security guard spun his chair around and rolled to another screen. They all stared speechless as Vincent took a seat with Carissa.

"Where is she?" Nick all but shouted.

The manager looked from Nick to James. "Don't you know?"

"Know what?" James asked.

"I was sure Mrs. Hathaway would have told you."

James leaned into the manager's face. "Told me what?"

"She OD'd earlier this evening." A gasp rose from the group. "EMTs transported her to the hospital."

Lillian grabbed her chest. "Is she alive?"

"Yes, ma'am. She was alive when she left here."

"And her mother knew this all along?" The tremor in James' voice belied his calm exterior. Tiny beads of sweat appeared on the manager's forehead. With one hand on the doorknob, he nodded. "Send someone for her immediately. And bring my son, too."

When Constance was escorted into the security room, she didn't look happy to have been pulled from the party for a second time that evening. Seeing her in-laws, plus Nick and Carl and the Fitzpatricks, she took a step back, right into her husband. She crossed her arms. "What's going on?"

James stepped forward. "That's what we would like to know. Where is Carissa?"

Constance's body stiffened. "I told you. She left."

Lillian moved toward her. "How exactly did she leave?"

Constance looked from the manager to her in-laws, fear beginning to show in her eyes. It was quickly replaced with hatred as she glared at the manager.

Before she could utter a word, Lillian grabbed her by the arm. "Your daughter is lying in a hospital bed, maybe dying, while you sit at the table like nothing is wrong. What kind of a mother are you?"

Constance's mouth flew open. Her hand clutched her throat. She looked at her husband. He stood with arms across his chest, glaring at her. She touched Jim Jr.'s arm, almost begging. "It's not like this is the first time it's happened." She flashed a fake smile at Lillian. "What was I supposed to do? Sit all night in a dirty hospital waiting room?"

Lillian's body went rigid. "Yes. You are." She pointed a finger in Constance's face, the pink nail mere inches from her nose. "That's what loving mothers do!"

James pulled Lillian away from Constance. Jim Jr. grabbed his wife by the arm and spun her around to face him. "Do you even know which hospital?"

Constance knocked his hand off her arm. "No!"

Carl pulled out his phone, "I'll find out." Then, he left the room.

James looked at Constance like he was staring down a criminal. "Were you told that Brittany left with Chester?" he questioned.

She took a step back, fear fully shining in her eyes now. "Yes."

James clenched his jaw. He took a deep breath before shouting, "And why didn't you inform anyone?"

Constance was visibly shaking, "She's with..." She pointed to Nick. "Isn't she?"

"She said *Chester,*" a sob broke from Lillian. "How could you not tell us?"

Constance raised her hand to her forehead. "Those girls have been nothing but drama for too many years. I figured it was just more of the same."

Nick crossed the room in two strides and lowered his face to hers. "You call this drama? If Vincent hurts Brittany in any way, trust me, you'll see drama. You better pray we get her back unharmed. If not, the second person I'm coming for is you."

Constance backed away, looking around the room for help. Angry eyes stared back at her.

"Get out of my sight!" Lillian screamed.

Constance slowly backed out of the room, slamming the door behind her.

Carl returned with details about Carissa's whereabouts. Jim Jr. asked the manager to arrange for a ride to the hospital.

"I'm going with you," Lillian said. She turned to look at her husband. "Two granddaughters are in trouble. There's nothing I can do for the one right now." Then she looked at Nick. "Find her."

"Yes, ma'am. I will," he replied solemnly.

"Then, I need to go to the one I can help now." Lillian hugged her husband tightly. "Keep me informed." He nodded. Turning to Nick, she added, "Please hurry."

Nick followed them out of the room, but instead of waiting for the elevator, he took the stairs to the tenth floor two at a time. In his room, he emptied his duffel on the bed. It was always packed in case of trouble. He laid his guns and knife on the bed before quickly changing clothes, then shoved his new five-hundred-dollar suit into the bottom of the bag, and double checked that the Glock was loaded before slipping it into the holster behind his back. Strapping the second gun to his ankle, he tucked the knife in its case on his belt. Ready for battle.

Before he could reach the lobby, Carl called. "We're heading to the PSA office. Did you drive?"

"Yes. I'll meet you in the lobby. I already called for the car."

"Good. In the meantime, I have PSA looking at all the traffic cameras around the hotel to see which way they went."

It took them twenty minutes to make it to the New York office. By then, IT had been able to follow Vincent's trail out of New York, heading south.

"I'm going after them," Nick said.

Carl shook his head. "You aren't going to be able to catch up to them. I have all available resources looking for them right now. It's a little hard to hide on the Jersey turnpike."

Nick punched the air. "We both know he won't stay on the turnpike. If he does, he'll be changing cars soon." He started toward the door. "I have to be as close as possible when you find them."

"Our team's already checking every exit and rest stop along the way. If they change cars or leave the turnpike, we'll know." He nodded toward a chair. "It won't do any good for you to just take off without a plan. You know that."

He couldn't sit. Every nerve in his body wanted to pounce. His mind raced. He had to save her.

"We'll leave here shortly." Carl pointed to the chair again. "Now sit."

Nick paced.

"Don't make me have to pull you from this."

He stopped dead in his tracks. "No. You can't."

"Then, take a deep breath and sit! We need a plan of action."

For the first time in his life, he knew the turmoil families felt when their loved ones were missing. A wave of hopelessness washed over him. He hung his head.

"We'll get her back," Carl promised.

Fifteen minutes later, they received a call—Vincent had switched cars and was still heading south on the turnpike. Nick jumped up. "Can we go now?"

Carl nodded.

Nick wasted no time getting into the vehicle and started to pull away before Carl had even shut the passenger door.

"Nick!" Carl grabbed the door, slamming it shut. "If you can't control yourself, I'll have no choice but to pull you from this case."

Nick's hand hit the wheel. "You can't do that, sir."

"With the state you're in, you're either going to get her killed or us." He patted Nick's arm. "I know she's important to you. She is to me, too. But we won't be able to help her if we don't make it there alive."

Nick nodded and took a couple deep breaths. Carl was right. He would be no help to Brittany dead. Never in his life had he felt so helpless. *Jesus, if you are there, please... I beg of you... don't let him hurt her.* He felt a calming spirit come over him. *Okay, show me what to do.*

Chapter 21

Brittany's head throbbed. Her mouth was dry. *Where am I?* She tried focusing in on the strange room. The sun streaming through the lace curtains hurt her eyes and she had a hard time keeping them open. Suddenly, it all came back. Vincent Capri had kidnapped her. Her body started to tremble.

When she tried to sit up, her head burst with a blinding light. Moaning, she fell back onto the bed. What had they done to her? She was still dressed, but her heels had been tossed on a chair across the room. She wasn't tied up and briefly wondered if the door was locked when it opened. A tall Italian man entered.

"So, sleeping beauty has awakened and here I thought I would get the honor of waking you with a kiss." She didn't like the glint in his eyes. She forced herself up, quickly praying for help. He pointed to an unopened door. "Bathroom is there. Let me know if you need help."

"I don't." She tried to push herself off the bed, but fell back down.

"Looks to me like you do." He grinned. "I told Vincent he was using too much chloroform." He took a step toward her. "I can help you clean up."

"*No,*" she said more forcefully.

"Suit yourself. I'll be back in five minutes. Be ready. Vincent hates to be kept waiting."

"Ready for what?"

"Breakfast, of course."

"Breakfast? I want to go home."

He pointed to the bathroom door. "Wash your face and fix your hair. You're a mess." He left the room and shut the door behind him. Brittany listened, but didn't hear him lock it.

Why would Vincent kidnap her now? She shivered as she thought about the things she'd heard that the Capris were capable of. She had to get out of here. Forcing herself to forget the pain flashing through her head, she struggled to the window. The yard backed up to woods. If she could climb out the window, she'd be able to hide in the woods until Nick found her. And find her he would. She knew it without a doubt. She just had to give him the time to do it.

To her surprise, the window opened with ease. The fresh air helped clear her head.

"Get away from that window."

Her heart nearly leapt from her chest. She hadn't heard the door open. She spun around, but in just three steps, the henchman was beside her.

"Get in there and wash your face before I do it for you." He slammed the window shut and pushed her toward the bathroom. "If you were thinking about jumping, I would advise against it. One foot on the ground and we won't have to feed the wolves tonight."

She slammed the bathroom door behind her. *Wolves?* She hadn't heard any wolves. Brittany looked in the mirror and realized the reason for her throbbing head. There was a knot the size of a goose egg on her forehead and dried blood caked to her hair. She didn't remember being hit. The cold water felt so good, she cupped her hands and drank some. On the vanity was a basket of toiletries. After brushing her hair and teeth, she felt better. The effect of the chloroform must be wearing off. Good, she needed a clear mind to get out of this in one piece.

A banging on the bathroom door made her jump. "Hurry up. Breakfast is getting cold," the man bellowed.

"I'm ready. Stop pounding," she said, opening the door. He grabbed her arm.

She jerked it away. "Don't touch me." With her head held high, she walked to the door.

Handing her the shoes, he laughed. "Miss high and mighty. Let's see how long before you're nothing but a bawling baby begging for me to help you." He shoved her out the door into the hallway. "Down the stairs to the right is the dining room. Vincent is waiting." He followed behind her, pushing her to move faster.

"Stop pushing." She hurried down the stairs, her heels clinking on the Italian marble tile. As she turned down the hall, she glanced at the solid oak front door.

"Don't even think about it." He grinned. "Wolves, remember?"

Vincent rose as they entered the dining room. He pulled out a chair beside him. "Welcome to my home."

Brittany stared in surprise. It was the first time she noticed how much he looked like Vito, only more striking. No one with a face like that could be all bad. Could he? *Brittany, don't be an idiot.* Behind that face hides a madman who has no qualms about killing. Which is why he isn't hiding his identity. She froze. He must be planning to kill her.

Her jailer pushed her into the chair. Vincent patted her arm. "So, we finally get that date we were supposed to have ten years ago."

"Do you kidnap all your dates?" she spat.

Vincent ignored her and kept talking. "I hope the room is to your liking. There are clothes in the closet that will fit you. And if you need anything..." He nodded toward her jailer. "...ask Sonny. He'll be more than happy to get it for you."

She looked at Sonny. "I need to go home now!"

"I don't think so." Vincent grinned. "What's your hurry? We haven't even started to get to know each other yet."

"The moment you kidnapped me told me all I needed to know about you."

"I didn't kidnap you. You came willingly."

"I did no—"

"That isn't what the doorman will be telling anyone who asked. You calmly walked down the street with me and got into my car." He smiled, showing perfectly white teeth. She could almost see the glint of venom. "Like I said. This is a second chance at our date." He banged his fist on the table. "The one you stood me up for to date that treasonous snake, McFadden." He dished out some eggs and bacon and put it on her plate.

She pushed the food away. "This isn't a date. I'm your prisoner."

"Suit yourself." Vincent grabbed her plate and threw it across the room. The china shattered. Eggs and bacon flew everywhere. Then, he grabbed her face. "You will do as I tell you," he sneered, "or you'll end up just like that plate. Do you understand?"

She nodded.

Sonny brought another plate and Vincent filled it in front of her. "Now eat."

He watched her take a bite. Brittany shoved the food to the corner of her mouth and pretended to swallow. There was no way she would be swallowing this food until she saw Vincent and Sonny eat out of the same bowl. He had drugged her once and she knew he'd do it again.

Vincent and Sonny ate the rest of their meal in silence while she moved food around on her plate with a fork. When they were finished, Vincent leaned back, "Time to call your boyfriend."

"What?" She dropped her fork. "I don't have a boyfriend."

He grabbed her by the arm and pulled her from the chair into his lap. She tried to pull away, but he tightened his grip. "No wonder McFadden likes you so much. You're a feisty little thing. After I've taken care of your boyfriend, I think I'll take care of you."

"Not even in your dreams." Ice met steel as they stared into each other's eyes. Vincent put his hand behind her neck and pulled her toward him. "What you need is a man to show you your place." He leaned in to kiss her. She turned her head. Vincent laughed. He released his hold and she scrambled off his lap and stepped back, right into Sonny. Seizing her by both arms, Sonny dragged her down the hall. Vincent followed.

Brittany could feel her mouth trembling, so she bit her bottom lip. Sonny opened a door and shoved her into the room. Stumbling, her heel caught on the Oriental rug. Somehow, she managed not to fall.

Vincent took a seat at a Brazilian cherry desk. "Now we'll get this business over with." He pointed to a leather chair in front of him. She noticed it didn't match the one beside it. "Sit down."

She stood unmoving until Sonny pushed her into the chair. She glared at her captors.

Vincent pulled a cell phone from his desk and held it out. "Call your boyfriend."

She wrapped her hands around the wooden armrest. "I told you. I don't have a boyfriend."

Sonny hit her on the back of the head. "We know all about you and McFadden." He took the phone from Vincent and forced it into her hand. "Call him now or the next hit won't be so easy."

She rubbed the back of her head. "I'm afraid you've been misinformed. Nicholas McFadden is not my boyfriend." She looked from Vincent to Sonny.

Vincent rose slightly, leaning across the desk to stare into her eyes. "You think I haven't seen the two of you running around together or that little picnic in the park? Stop stalling and call him, before I get angry."

She wanted to scream that she wouldn't be the instrument used to kill Nick. Maybe he wouldn't come... he had stormed out last night. Maybe he would still be too mad to come for her. No. She knew without any doubt he would come. She had to warn him. *Please help us both,* she prayed.

She glanced at the phone. Hope filled her. "I don't know his number."

"I'm supposed to believe you don't know his number?"

"It's programmed into my phone." She glared at him. "The phone you tossed on the ground."

"No matter," Vincent said, handing Sonny a slip of paper. "I have his number. For your sake, you better hope he's home."

She watched Sonny push the numbers. "Wait!" she yelled, pulling Sonny's finger from the dial pad. "What am I supposed to say?"

"Tell him you won't be home for dinner?" Sonny's chuckle stopped midway at Vincent's glare.

"Say hello. Then, I'll do the rest." He motioned for Sonny to finish dialing. Sonny put the phone on speaker before holding it in front of Brittany.

Please don't be there, she kept repeating to herself. It wasn't until Nick's mother answered the phone that she realized she'd been holding her breath. She couldn't keep her voice from trembling. "Is Nick there?" She was grateful when his mother answered no. She bowed her head. *Thank you.*

Obscenities flew from Vincent's mouth. "You tell that cockroach he'd better be there when I call again or the girl dies." He threw the phone across the room, breaking it into pieces. Brittany looked at the parts on the floor and said a prayer of thanks. Now she wouldn't have to make another call.

"Don't worry," Vincent laughed. "I have more where that came from." He walked around the desk and stopped in front of her. Running his fingers through her hair, he smiled. "Now it's time for our date."

She pulled her head away from him. "I will never date you."

A dark shadow crossed his face, taking the smile with it. "Have it your way." He glared at Sonny. "Get her out of my sight."

Sonny clutched her by the arm and dragged her from the room, closing the office door behind him. Brittany glanced around. There was a sitting room to her right and another closed door to her left. Sonny hurried her up the stairs back to her room. He slammed the door shut. Once again, she listened but didn't hear the door being locked. *Why not?* She paced the room trying to figure a way out. The woods weren't that far—she could easily make it before they knew she was gone. Looking at the long drop from the window, she glanced back over her shoulder to the door.

The front door was near the bottom of the stairs. Could she sneak out without them seeing her? She tiptoed back across the room and slowly opened the door. The hall was empty. Quickly, she made her way to the stairs. Her heart was pounding. She had to calm her breathing or they would hear her. Still no one. Could she possibly make it out the front door? She had to try.

Quietly, she slipped down the stairs, hugging the wall. She ran for the door and it opened with ease. *Freedom!* But just one step off the porch, she heard a low angry growl. Her heart froze as three ferocious wolves came racing toward her. She leapt backward onto the porch and lunged for the door. Her heart sank. It was locked!

Praying with all her might, Brittany pressed her back against the door. The wolves sat snarling at the foot of the porch steps, their teeth wet with saliva. Time stood still. She dared not move.

Suddenly, the door opened and she fell backward right into Vincent's arms. "Going somewhere?" He smirked, spinning her around. "I thought for sure Sonny warned you about leaving the house."

"I did," Sonny said smugly, "but you know those pretty ones. They aren't always the smartest."

She tried to squeeze by Vincent, but he grabbed her by the hair. "Next time you think about escaping, remember the wolves. You were lucky this time. I had the sensors on slow, but next time they will be on fast." He shoved her face into an alarm pad. She watched him punch numbers in. "I just changed the speed in which the gates holding the wolves will open. You see how fast they got here this time... well, next time will be quicker. And once they taste that pretty little flesh of yours, I won't be able to call them off." He opened the door. The wolves still sat growling. Sonny handed him some meat. Vincent tossed it to the wolves. He grinned at Brittany. "See how quickly they devoured that steak? Remember that. One step off the porch and that will be you."

She tried to get away. Vincent pressed her up against the door with his body. He leaned in, smelling her hair. "I just might have the same problem." He nibbled her neck.

Brittany struggled to get away. "Get off me."

"You surprise me," he said, running his fingers down her face. "You look like an angel, but inside you're a she-devil." He whispered in her ear. "I like a girl who fights. We're going to have such fun."

"I don't think so." She tried to push him away, but he pressed into her harder. "Maybe McFadden wasn't man enough to tame you," he purred, then lowered his mouth to hers. Brittany jerked away. "But I am." He grabbed her face, forcing his tongue into her mouth.

She bit down. Hard.

Screaming, Vincent's fist landed on her cheek, the force knocking her to her knees. He spit blood on her. "You're going to pay for that."

The room was spinning, but she couldn't allow herself to feel the pain. She started to crawl toward the stairs. Vincent grabbed her legs and pulled her back across the cold marble. "You want to fight?" He rolled her over, straddling her and pinning both of her arms to the floor with his knees. "Then we'll fight... and when the fight is all out of you, we'll finish what we started."

She closed her eyes when he ripped the front of her dress. His hands cupped her breasts. *Please God, help me.*

"McFadden has good taste. Remind me to thank him."

Brittany again turned her face when he tried to kiss her. Being hit was better than the repulsive feel of his lips on her.

Vincent forced her to look at him. "You are powerless against me and the sooner you understand that, the easier this will be."

She refused to look away. "You'll have to kill me first."

He laughed. "There is another way."

A chill ran down her. Bending forward, he ran his tongue across her lips and down her neck. She whimpered. "There it is," he said, lifting himself off her. "Fear." He pulled her up from the floor. "You think you're afraid now?" He grabbed her neck and squeezed hard. "The best is yet to come." He turned her face toward the corner of the ceiling. "Smile for the camera."

With every ounce of strength she had, Brittany yanked free of his gasp. She stumbled backward until she hit the oak banister. Pain ripped through her back. Fear propelled her up the stairs and to her room.

Sonny followed. "Good girl." This time he locked the door.

Shaking, she ran to the bathroom and scrubbed until her skin turned red. Escaping had been a stupid idea. She pulled her ripped dress back up into place. In the basket on the vanity was a pack of safety pins. As she tried to salvage her clothing, the tears started to fall. *God, where are you?*

Chapter 22

Lucy had no idea where her son was. She tried Nick's cell phone, but it went right to voicemail. Without another thought, she called Carl. If he didn't know where to find Nick, he would at least know what to do.

Her voice trembled as she asked to speak with Carl.

"I'm sorry, he's in a meeting," Lisa said.

"This is an emergency. I demand to talk to him right now."

"I'm sorry, but he can't be disturbed."

"Listen. To. Me." Lucy emphasized each word, trying hard not to scream into the phone. "I don't care if he's with the President of the United States, I'm not hanging up." With each word, her voice rose until she was on the verge of hysterics. "Tell him this is Nick's mother and I need to talk to him now."

"I'm sorry. I have orders not to disturb him."

"Not even for a kidnapping?" Lucy yelled.

"Hold, please."

Lisa opened the door to Carl's office. "I'm sorry, sir, but there's a woman on the phone claiming to be Nick's mother. She said something about a kidnapping."

Nick jumped from his chair and lunged for the phone, but Carl picked it up first.

"She's on line one." Lisa shut the door.

Carl put the call on speaker. "Lucy."

Her words spilled out all over each other until Nick said, "Mom, calm down. I'm here. Take a deep breath and start over."

"I think he has Brittany," she gasped. Nick's heart skipped a beat. "When I told her you weren't here, this horrible man got on the phone and said if you weren't home the next time he called, he would kill her."

Nick flew from the office, bursting through the garage to his car. The Porsche had never moved so fast around the curves of the parking garage. He blew his horn and cursed the D.C. traffic. Within minutes, flashing lights pulled up beside him. He groaned. He wasn't pulling over.

His phone rang and Carl's name flashed across the screen. Nick pushed the answer button on his steering wheel.

"I've arranged a police escort."

"I appreciate that." He waved at the officer. At the Maryland line, State Police took over. He made it home to Columbia in record time.

Running through the door, he yelled, "Mom, did he call again?"

"No," Lucy said.

He looked at his mother's tear-streaked face. With a confidence he wasn't sure he felt, he said, "She'll be all right."

Lucy twisted the tissue in her hand. "How can you be so sure?"

He hugged his mother and looked up at the ceiling. "Because she loves Jesus and He loves her. I know she'll be alright." Suddenly, without a doubt, he knew it was true.

Within minutes, the house was overflowing with PSA and FBI agents. Carl and James Hathaway arrived shortly thereafter. Time dragged by. Minutes seemed like hours.

Brittany huddled on the Queen Victoria chair watching the door. The sun was shining into the room. The alarm clock read twelve forty-five.

The door opened and Sonny motioned for her to follow him. She hesitated, but Sonny stepped toward her with an angry scowl. She jumped up and followed him.

Vincent took one look at the safety pins on her dress and laughed. "What? The princess is too good to wear the clothes I offered her?"

She stood tall. "I prefer my own."

In two steps, he'd grabbed her by the front of the dress. A gasp stuck in Brittany's throat as he pulled her to him. "You'll learn that you have no power here. You'll do what I say." He ripped the dress further, pulling the pins out. With one hand, he reached inside his trouser pocket, pulled out a switchblade, flipped it open, and held the tip to her throat.

She tried not to breathe. Her heart pounded so loud she was sure Vincent could hear it.

He lightly ran the knife down her neck to the front of her dress, slicing it from the bodice to the hem. She grabbed the shreds and pulled them close.

He nodded to Sonny, who came up behind her and pinned her arms behind her back. She struggled to get free. Vincent stepped back, his eyes running over her body. She'd never felt so dirty in her life. "Yumm... McFadden has great taste." He ran his hand down her body. "Maybe I will change my mind and not kill you." He winked at Sonny, "She'll make a great gift for those men in the crack house." They both laughed. "Tied up to a bed all naked just waiting for them."

"No," she screamed, fighting to break free of Sonny's grip. "I'm a virgin. You can't do that."

Vincent leaned his face into hers. Looking her straight in the eyes, he said, "You won't be when we are finished with you." He threw his head back and laughed. Bile rose in her stomach.

He put the knife under the strapless bra.

She froze. Her prayer turned into a scream of panic. *God help me.*

He smirked. "No point in rushing the unveiling." He moved the knife down her stomach. "Soon you will be taking it off for me."

"Never."

He grabbed her face. "The drugs I will be giving you will make you beg for me."

She closed her eyes and prayed. *God, please help me.*

"You see, you're helpless. If I want to see your bare skin, I will."

Sonny released his hold on her and she started to back away.

"You aren't too bright, are you?" Vincent grinned. "If I want you to sit..." He shoved her into the chair. "You will." Then, he leaned into her face and rasped, "If I want you to stand..." He yanked her to her feet by her hair. "You will." With a last show of amusement, he tapped the knife on her face. "I have all the power."

Brittany willed herself to be calm. God was with her. No matter what happened, God was with her. *Please God, I could really use your help.*

He pinched her cheeks. "You see, no one's going to save you. Not that cockroach you call a boyfriend. Not your grandfather. No one."

She stared him right in the eye. "God will."

For a second, he was speechless. Then, laughter erupted from him. "God." He looked at Sonny. "This fool thinks God will save her." He returned her gaze. "There is no God and you'll soon discover that."

"There is."

"Hmm." He grinned at Sonny. "Maybe God is who saved her last time." His laugh vibrated through Brittany. Vincent turned her around and completely pulled the dress off her shoulders. She tried to cover herself with her arms. Sonny grabbed her, pinning them by her side. Vincent poked the tip of the knife into the scar on her shoulder. "Is this where I shot you?"

She swallowed hard and whispered, "Yes."

Vincent buried the knife into the scar and twisted it. Brittany screamed.

"I emptied a semi-automatic into that water. You should be dead." He ran his hand down her back. Just before he reached the top of her underwear, he paused. "Aww, I did hit you more than once." Again, he stabbed the knife into the scar.

Pain racked Brittany's body. Tears flowed down her face.

Vincent twisted the knife and the room spun in front of her. "Are there any more?"

Sonny touched his hand. "Not a good idea."

"Don't tell me what's not a good idea," he shouted.

Sonny pointed to the blood flowing down Brittany's leg. "She's about to bleed on your imported rug."

With a quick tug, Vincent jerked the knife out and walked to the bar. Tossing Brittany a towel, he threatened, "If one drop of blood touches my floor, the wolves will be having you for dinner." Then, he returned and leaned into her face. "Is that understood?"

She nodded, pushing the towel to her hip and watching the blood seep through. She pressed harder. And prayed harder, all the while watching Sonny pull out a tarp. He laid the plastic on the chair just before Vincent pushed her into it. "Don't move or you die." He walked to his desk and pulled out a new phone. "It's time to call the boyfriend again."

A few minutes before 1:00 p.m., a white van pulled up in front of the house. FBI agents converged on the vehicle with guns drawn. Nick watched from the front door. It was only a few minutes, but it seemed like an eternity before they returned to the house carrying a package addressed to him. After it was cleared as safe to open, he ripped into it. Inside was a DVD and a note: *Let the fun begin.*

The living room was silent as he, Carl, and James sat on the edge of the couch watching Brittany's failed escape. If there had been a way to reach in and grab Vincent, Nick would have choked the life out of Capri.

The sound of the phone made Nick jump. He started to grab for the receiver, but an FBI agent stopped him. Holding up fingers—one, two, three—he then nodded for Nick to pick up.

"You touch her again and I'll kill you," he yelled into the receiver.

Vincent's laugh could be heard across the room. "So you got my message."

"Keep your filthy hands off her."

"Keep your head, son," James said. "No sense in angering him more." He took the phone from Nick. "This is James Hathaway. I want to speak to my granddaughter."

"The honorable Judge Hathaway, what lovely granddaughters you have. This one is so much sweeter than the other one. Sorry about Carissa, but you know traitors need to be dealt with."

"Let me talk to Brittany."

"You aren't the one controlling this situation."

"What do you want?" James gripped the phone, his white knuckles the only sign of stress.

"Two million dollars and I want McFadden to deliver it alone."

Nick gasped at the large amount.

"You'll get the money," James promised, "but not before I talk to Brittany."

"I'll allow that. She's right here."

They heard Vincent mumble something just before Brittany shouted. "He's going to kill Nick."

At the sound of her voice, Nick grabbed the phone from James. "Brittany," he blurted.

"It's a trap," she cried. "Nick, don't come."

There was a loud thump, and then a moan, before Vincent returned on the line. "You have until tomorrow morning. McFadden brings it or the girl dies."

"I'm warning you, if you hurt her, *you* will die," Nick said.

"I'll call back at 7:00 a.m." The phone went dead.

The FBI agent shook his head. Vincent had hung up seconds before they could finish the trace. "He was only on long enough to know they're in West Virginia."

Nick felt the color drain from his face. He looked at Carl's crestfallen expression and knew he too had heard the rumor of Vincent's West Virginia kill house.

Brittany cowered on the floor where Vincent had knocked her down. She turned to inch away from him as he reached down and yanked her up. Sonny righted the chair and Vincent tossed her into it. He and Sonny both zip tied her wrists to the arms of the seat.

She tried to fight the restraint. She heard Nick's words in her head. "*Wait until you are alone to break the ties.*"

With a wave of his hand, Vincent dismissed Sonny. "Now the fun begins." He walked over to the bar and pulled out a tray. Looking at her, he asked, "What should we start with?" He carried it to his desk and set it down in front of her. "Ecstasy, cocaine, or heroin?"

Brittany struggled to get free. "I'm not taking any of that."

He threw his head back and laughed. "How are you going to stop it? Looks to me like you're a little tied up at the moment." He ran a hand down her face. "It doesn't really matter which one we start with because you're getting them all." He walked back to the bar and poured two drinks. "You see, I lost one really good customer in your cousin, but you, my dear, are going to take her place. She had a weakness for all three, as I'm sure you will, too."

Fear gripped her heart. "What do you mean you *lost* her?"

"Carissa's dead," he said matter-of-factly. He pointed to one of the drugs on his tray. "Seems like someone forgot to cut her dose and gave her almost pure heroin."

Brittany's vision blurred, her chin trembled, and tears slipped down her cheek.

"Why are you crying for her?" he taunted. He knelt in front of her. "You know she's the one that turned you over to me."

"*No!*" she screamed. "You're lying."

He shook his head. "Don't worry, I took care of that traitor for you." In one drink, he poured the ecstasy. "Let's get on to happier things. We might as well start with the E, since it will make you more agreeable." He held the glass to her lips, but she refused to open.

Closing her eyes, she prayed, *The Lord will keep you from all harm. He will watch over your life.*

Vincent squeezed her mouth open and poured. She managed to spit it out.

"So you're going to play the hard way? I'll tell you like I told my sister Maria, drinking this will make things easier for you."

He yanked her head back and poured the drink down her throat, not allowing her to spit. When the glass was empty, he let go. She gagged and then vomited. He jumped, but wasn't fast enough. He backhanded

Brittany, sending her and the chair toppling over. "This is a five-hundred-dollar shirt." He screamed for Sonny. "Get back in here."

Sonny hurried into the room, but stopped midway, staring at the vomit covering Vincent.

Vincent waved his hands. "Clean this mess up." Sonny headed toward Brittany. "Not her," Vincent said, pointing to the puke on the floor. "Everything, but her. She made this mess, let her lie in it."

"If we leave her like that, the room's going to smell bad really fast."

Vincent walked over and kicked Brittany's chair, flipping her over to lay face down on the floor. With one last kick, he stormed out of the room. "Keep her like that. I'll be back for her."

When Vincent returned, he righted the chair and pulled her back to the desk with Sonny's help. "Now let's do this again." He poured a line of cocaine on the tray and pushed her head down into it. "Take a deep breath through your nose."

She held her breath until Vincent put his hand over her mouth, holding it tight. "Eventually you'll have to breathe. And when you take that deep breath for air, you're going to forget all about the pain. Your body will be riding high on joy unlike anything you've ever felt."

She could hold her breath for a long time underwater, but this was different. *Please God.* Her ears rang. She no longer heard Vincent's words. Panic rose within her. She needed air. Just as she felt the breath starting, she sneezed, sending the powder flying off the tray. Not one bit was left.

Vincent backhanded her again, sending her and the chair toppling over. "You think you're smart, don't you? Well, there's more where that came from."

She lay on the floor watching him prepare the heroin. Sweat beads dotted her forehead. Her heart felt like it would explode. She struggled to break free of the zip ties. Her waist started to bleed. Panic-filled prayer coursed into her mind. *God, where are you? I know you're watching over me. You've protected me so far.* A sob caught in her throat. *Please don't let him stick that needle in me. Please God, please help me.* She looked up at Vincent, "Please, don't do this."

He put his foot on her chest and pressed. "I like women who beg." He laughed. "Soon you will be begging for more." He righted the chair. Grinning, he walked behind her. With all his might, he pushed the back of the chair, sending it flying into the desk. She groaned as her face hit the wood. Yanking her by the hair, he said, "Let's see you get out of this."

Brittany fought the zip ties as Vincent leaned down to wrap a tourniquet around her arm.

She head-butted him. She saw stars. Vincent dropped the needle, cursing. His face turned red with rage. He smacked her across the face with enough force to topple her over. The jar from the floor racked through her body. The office door flew open with a bang.

One glance at the door and Brittany felt all hope drain from her body. *Vito.* Now there was two of them.

"How could you?" Vito ran into the room screaming, "You know what Carissa meant to me. How could you do that to her?"

Vincent glared at Vito. "She was a traitor not worthy to live."

Vito advanced with his fist ready to do battle.

"Calm down," Vincent said, kicking Brittany before stepping back. He walked over to the bar and poured Vito a drink. "I'm not going to fight you, Vito. I know you're upset. Give it time and you'll realize what a big favor I did for you." He strode to Vito and put an arm around his shoulder. "You know I love you, little brother, and only was thinking of you."

Vito pointed at Brittany tied to the chair. "What's *she* doing here?"

"Unfinished business." Vincent poured a drink over Brittany. She winced with pain as the alcohol hit the knife wound on her shoulder. He stood over her grinning.

"Well, you better do something with her fast. Mother's on her way."

Vincent spun around. "What do you mean 'on her way'?"

"Like, she'll be here in ten minutes."

Vincent banged his fist on the bar. "She never comes here." He threw his hands up. "No one ever comes here."

"She said she couldn't stand being in New York while her daughter's killer was roaming the streets."

"So, she decides to come here? Now?" Vincent looked at Vito. "And how did you know I was here?"

Vito shrugged his shoulders, "A hunch."

Vincent kicked Brittany's chair. She couldn't see Vito, but she could hear him moving closer. A sob escaped her. *God, where are you? I can't fight two of them.*

Vito grabbed the back of her chair. "Unless you want Mother to find a half-naked woman tied to a chair in your office, I'd advise you to help me get her out of here."

Vincent leaned down, putting his face inches from hers. "You may have a reprieve for the moment, but we aren't finished yet." He waved his hand at Vito. "Take her to the guesthouse. I don't want to see her face 'til morning." Then, he stormed out of the room.

Vito removed his jacket and draped it over her before kneeling to cut the ties on her wrists, whispering, "God sent me."

"What?" She stared at him in surprise. The ties fell off and she was free. She hugged Vito's coat to her. Her arms hurt too much to put it on.

"Don't quite understand it myself, but I clearly heard a voice in my head telling me to come here." He shook his head. "Had to have been God, right?"

She bit her bottom lip, doubtfully. "You know God?"

He nodded. "While I was in jail, I met this chaplain—Pastor Rousey. We had some really long talks about Jesus. For the first time in my life, I found something worth believing in."

She struggled to stand, but her legs collapsed.

Vito caught her. "Just sit here a minute." He glanced at the blood running down her leg. "What did he do to you?"

A sob caught in Brittany's throat. "He stabbed me where he shot me before."

Vito grabbed another towel from the bar. "Put pressure on it." He helped her stand and then tucked her arms into his coat. "You're okay now."

She took a single step and the pain in her hip screamed.

"I know it hurts. Just lean on me and I'll get you out of here."

She hugged him. "Thank you." Then, she looked upward and whispered softer still, "*Thank you.*"

Vito took her by the arm and guided her out of the house.

Brittany hesitated when they reached the front door.

"The wolves are put away," he assured.

"How do you know he won't release them?"

"Who, Vincent? He wouldn't do anything to hurt me." She faltered, then he added, "I promise you, the wolves are locked up."

She leaned on Vito as they walked to the guesthouse. Halfway there, Brittany looked up at Vito. She couldn't keep the tears from falling. "He said he killed Carissa."

Careful of her wounds, he gave her a sideways hug. "She isn't dead, just in really bad shape."

Brittany threw her hand over her mouth. "Not dead?"

He shook his head. "No."

When Vito shut the guesthouse door behind them, she let out a huge sigh of relief.

"As long as my mother's in the house, Vincent won't bother you." He patted her arm. "Don't be afraid. The Lord's looking out for you."

She took his hand. "Will you pray with me?"

He nodded.

Brittany prayed. "Please, dear Heavenly Father, I come to you in awe and thanksgiving that you sent Vito to shield me from danger. Please take the fear from my heart. I know you are watching over me, but I'm still afraid, not only for myself, but for Nick. Please, don't let Vincent kill him. I ask you also to protect Vito as he watches over me. Amen." She opened her eyes and turned to Vito. "So how are you going to get me out of here?"

"I'm not."

She stepped back. "But..."

"I was told to come here. Nothing else." He patted her arm. "I'm sure He has something else in mind." Vito walked into the kitchen and returned with a first aid kit. "Do you trust me to bandage you up?"

Brittany hugged his coat around her.

He raised his hands. "I promise I'll only touch where you're bleeding."

She turned her back to him and dropped the coat to just below the shoulder wound. She winced as he poured peroxide on it. "Hey, warn a girl next time."

He laughed. "Then, you would have tensed up." He gently rubbed her shoulder. "Looks like you need stitches. I'm going to try to butterfly this together with the bandage. He patted her arm. "I can't promise it won't hurt."

Brittany suppressed a scream as he started to work on her shoulder. She sighed. To keep her mind off the pain she asked, "Why don't you tell me about how you came to know Jesus?"

Vito laughed, "It was crazy. I've been to church most of my life—it was an hour to sleep off Saturday's hangover. I don't recall ever hearing a word the priest said. And here I was in jail, and to get out of my cell for a while, I signed up for Bible study. First person I saw was this big burly guy, who looked more like Santa Claus than a Pastor. He greeted us like we were old friends, not criminals. And when he talked about Jesus, his face just lit up. You believed every word he said because you knew he believed it. Pastor Rousey talked about forgiveness." Vito finished bandaging her shoulder. He stepped back. "Imagine that. Jesus forgiving me."

Brittany nodded. "He does."

"It wasn't long before I was having long talks with him." Vito smiled. "And the rest, as they say, is history." He nodded at her hip. "How about the hip?"

She turned to glance behind her. "Maybe I could do it."

Vito shook his head. "You know I've seen you in a bathing suit." He laughed. "Actually, what you have on now covers more than that string bikini you used to wear."

She grimaced and nodded. Vito kept talking as he worked on her hip. When he was done, he said, "My sister has some clothes in the first bedroom on the right. I think they're your size."

She hugged him. "Thank you."

He went to the refrigerator and pulled out a soda, "Would you like something?" She shook her head. "Guess I'm going to have to find a whole new line of work." Then, he raised the soda bottle in a mock toast. "Here's to a new beginning."

She smiled. "How about here's to getting out of this place?"

Chapter 23

For the first time in forever, Brittany didn't welcome the rising sun. A sob caught in her throat. She had prayed all night and still her mind was racing with turmoil. Her heart would not accept the fact that she would be the cause of Nick's death. She crawled onto her knees and prayed. *Save him, please.*

She lay her head on the edge of the bed. That was where she was when Vito knocked on the door to tell her he was leaving to go up to the main house for breakfast. She ran to the door and pleaded with him. "Please, give me the keys to your car."

He shook his head. "Sorry. I can't."

"Why? You said God sent you to help me."

"Yes. He did." Vito looked her in the eyes. "If I helped you get out of here, Vincent would just come after you and his anger would be ten times worse." Vito gave her a gentle hug. "I have been praying all night... as I'm sure you have, and I still don't have any answer." He stepped back. "I'm new at this, but somehow I get the feeling today will be okay."

"He's going to kill Nick." Brittany grabbed Vito's arm. "Help us."

"I'll do what I can." Vito started to turn away. "As long as my mother stays in the main house, Vincent will not hurt you here. I know he plans to take you someplace else today, so I'll try to find out where and call PSA and let them know. That's all I can do."

Brittany squared her shoulders and looked him straight in the eyes. "Are you afraid of your brother?"

Vito looked at her in surprise. "No. He would never hurt family."

"That isn't true. He killed your sister."

Vito took a step back. "Why would you say that?"

"He said he—"

Vito held up his hands, "You had to have misunderstood."

"No. He said—"

"Enough." He turned to leave. Brittany grabbed his arm.

"Please, get me out of here?"

"I can't." He took a deep breath. "When he finds you, and he will..." Vito closed his eyes. "...I'm afraid of what he'll do to you."

Brittany blinked back the tears, refusing to let them fall. "What about what he is going to do to me if I stay?"

Vito touched her cheek. "As hard as this is, we have to trust God to show us what to do."

"I just wish He would hurry," Brittany said.

Vito nodded. "I'll bring you back something to eat."

When Vito returned, he was not alone. Vincent and Sonny were with him. Vincent strode directly to her and held out a phone. "The number's already programmed. Just hit call."

She glanced at Vito, sending him one last plea for help. But he said nothing. Brittany gathered her courage. "And if I say no?"

Vincent raised his hand, as if to hit her, Vito stepped between them. "Give me the phone," he demanded.

Vito hit the call button, waited a moment, and then handed her the phone. "Be smart," he warned.

This was her last chance to save Nick. She drew a deep breath and said, "Vincent wants me to tell you where to drop the money, but..." She stiffened, knowing the punishment Vincent would swiftly mete out. "...But don't do it. He'll kill you."

Vincent pushed Vito out of the way, snatched the phone from her hands, and slapped her so hard that her body tumbled across the room.

A loud smack sounded through to the other end of the line, and then a scream. Brittany's cry vibrated through Nick, filling him with anguish. "Brittany!"

"McFadden—" Vincent began. His voice came loud and clear over the speakerphone.

"Put Brittany back on," Nick said.

"She's been a bad girl."

"If you hurt her—"

"Now you listen to me. If you do not bring the money, I promise, her body will never be found. Of course, I'll have my fun with her first."

"You touch her and—"

Carl was listening in and signaled for Nick to be quiet.

James stepped nearer to the phone in Nick's hand and said loud enough for Vincent to hear, "I have your money."

Nick began pacing the room. Rage flowed through every ounce of his being. Vincent was going to be the one to pay.

When he heard Vincent say, "Here's how this is going down," Nick stood rigid. "You have one hour to arrive at the Harper's Ferry visitor's center on Route 340. There's a picnic area near the parking lot with a phone taped to the seat of the first bench. Use it to call me at the programmed number." Nick's mind was already whirring with possible capture scenarios. "And if I see any PSA, FBI, or any other initials," Vincent threatened, "she's dead. Is that clear?"

"An hour," Nick yelled. "It will take longer than that just to get there."

"The clock is ticking." Vincent hung up.

Nick spun toward the door. James was there with the satchel of money. "Bring her back alive."

Carl said, "I'll arrange for a police escort to the West Virginia line. From there you'll be on your own."

Nick nodded and rushed to his car. He couldn't be late.

The drive to Harper's Ferry was the worst hour of his life. Over and over, he remembered the sound of Brittany's scream. When traffic slowed near his destination, he slammed his fist on the steering wheel. He finally parked the car with only minutes to spare.

At the picnic area, he raced to the first table, where a family was seated. Nick flashed his badge. "I'm sorry. I need to see that bench."

The kids jumped up excited. Nick flipped the bench over and grabbed the phone to make the call.

Vincent picked up on the first ring. "Too bad you made it," he said. "I was hoping to start the fun early."

"Let me talk to her."

"That isn't part of the game."

"This isn't a game." Nick looked around the area. Other than the family staring at him, there was no one else nearby. "Where is she?" he demanded.

"You'll find out soon enough."

It took every bit of strength for Nick to keep his head. Until he had Brittany back, Vincent was in control.

Nick was given instructions for the next stop. Three stops later, Nick snapped, "I've had enough of this. Where is she?"

Vincent chuckled. "Next stop is the diner off of Route 79. There you will get your final instructions."

Nick pulled up to the vending machine at the diner. He was surprised to find detailed directions taped to the back this time, instead of a phone. He programmed the address into his GPS and took off. Hands gripping the wheel, his knuckles turned white as he drove farther up the mountain. Five miles up the road, he lost the GPS signal on his phone. He hit the steering wheel. There was no way PSA could track him here. He glanced upward. *God, it looks like it's just going to be You and me.* He picked up the printed directions.

Fifteen miles later, Nick turned off the main road onto an overgrown side road. Dread filled him when he drove under the hanging sign of a deserted coal mine. He parked his car by a large fallen oak near the entrance, as instructed. Patting his gun holster under his jacket, he said a quick prayer for his angel, and then grabbed the bag of money before exiting the safety of his vehicle.

Nick squinted against the glare of the noon sun. *Where are they?*

He'd only gone a few feet before Vincent stepped out from behind a large tree. "Well, well, well. Here we are." Vincent pointed a gun at Nick. "The girl isn't going to save you this time."

Panic filled him. Where was Brittany? His heart sunk. Had Vincent already killed her? "Where is she?" he yelled.

Vincent pulled Brittany out from behind the tree. Relief flooded his soul. *She's alive.*

His relief was short-lived. Her mouth was duct taped and her face was covered in bruises. Her hands were behind her back, most likely tied. The terror in her eyes was his undoing. "Brittany." He took a step forward.

Vincent pointed his gun at Nick. "Stay there."

His hand tightened around the bag of money. "Take the tape off her mouth."

Vincent shook his head. "She talks too much."

"You want the money and me. She has nothing to do with this."

Vincent grinned. "But she does," he sneered. "You wouldn't have been such a thorn in my side for the last ten years if not for her."

"Listen," Nick bargained. "All the money is here. Let me give her my car keys. Once she drives away, I'll do whatever you say." Nick dropped the satchel of money on the ground. Holding his hand out to Brittany, he said, "Come here."

Vincent tightened his grip on her arm. "I'm in charge here. Not you." Pointing the gun at Brittany with his other hand, he said, "Toss the money over here."

"Then, un-tape her mouth."

Vincent gave Nick a long, hard stare. "I'll let you have this one." With an evil laugh, he ripped the tape off.

Brittany yelped in pain, then cried, "Run, Nick. Run!"

Vincent grabbed her by the hair. He gritted his teeth and rasped, "Shut up or he dies now." Pressing the gun to her chest, he turned back to Nick. "Now reach inside your jacket and slowly pull out your gun." He nodded his head to his right. "Toss it. Or else."

Nick obeyed.

Vincent yanked Brittany's hair and said, "I'll deal with you later." He violently shoved her away. She stumbled and fell to the ground. Nick made a move toward her, but Vincent pointed the gun at him. "Stay there."

Nick watched helplessly as Brittany rolled toward what looked like an old mineshaft. When she stopped and sat up, he breathed a sigh of relief. The quick glance she sent his way stabbed at his heart. Never again did he want to see such sheer terror in her eyes.

"That's more like it," Vincent said. "You see, I win this round. Your back-up won't arrive—"

"What back-up?" Nick snorted.

"Don't play stupid. I know all about the dozen or more PSA and FBI agents two minutes behind you. By the time they get away from my men, I'll be long gone with your girl and the money." Vincent laughed. "And best of all, the infamous Nicholas McFadden will be dead."

Brittany said a silent prayer, thanking Nick for teaching her how to get out of zip ties. While Vincent gloated, she slipped her hands out of their binding and slowly inched closer to where Nick's gun lay on the ground. She watched as Vincent fingered the trigger on his own gun, goading Nick about the horrible things he was going to do with her once he'd shot Nick.

She kept her eyes on Vincent, who was so focused on Nick, he hadn't even noticed her scooting backward. She said another quick prayer when her hand felt the cold metal. Holding it firmly in her hands, she scrambled to her feet. "Drop the gun," she ordered.

Vincent gaped at her, then glanced down at her trembling hands and laughed. "Little girls oughtn't to play with guns. Someone might get hurt."

"Drop it or I'll shoot," she repeated.

The horror of pointing a gun at a man had her stomach twisted in knots. Her ears roared with the beating of her heart. She tried to still the shaking in her hands. Brittany didn't want to pull the trigger, but she didn't have a choice. This evil man in front of her was the devil incarnate. He would kill Nick and her, of that she had no doubt. It was him or them. *If there's another way,* she prayed, *please show me.*

Vincent smiled as he raised his gun and pointed it at her.

Brittany didn't hesitate any longer. She fired. The recoil of the Glock knocked her backward. She fell, crashing through the rotting boards of the abandoned mineshaft. She screamed and flailed her arms, desperately searching for something to hold onto.

The jagged edge of a board tore through her forearm, and then she was falling, plunging into darkness. Above her, she barely registered the sound of another shot.

Burning pain exploded in Nick's back. He fell to the ground. Brittany's scream pierced his heart. Even worse, was the ensuing silence. His angel was dead. Despair filled the dark chambers of his soul. Emptiness like he'd never known filled him. He'd loved Brittany and now she was gone.

He'd failed to save her. Again.

Without Brittany, life wasn't worth living. Nick welcomed the cold darkness with open arms. Maybe death would unite them, as life never had.

Brittany clawed at the wall of the shaft, trying to latch onto any object to break her fall. She called out to God for help. Seconds later, she hit something hard. Her hands wrapped around what felt like wood. She clung to it. *"Thank you, Lord,"* she breathed. Her fingers explored the wall of the shaft and she determined it was a large tree root that had blocked her descent.

She looked below her.

Nothing but darkness. *Please God, show me the way out of here.*

Her eyes adjusted and she discovered a rope hanging just out of reach. She had two choices: make a jump for it and pull herself out, or wait until Nick found her. Where was he?

She'd seen Vincent fall to the ground, but she'd also heard another shot before toppling into darkness. Had he killed Nick?

A moan racked her body. He couldn't be dead. *Please God, don't let him be dead.* But if he wasn't, where was he? Hopelessness consumed her. "*The Lord will keep you from all harm He will watch over your life,*" she reminded herself.

The words calmed her troubled heart and hope filled her anew. She looked at the rope, and then down into the black hole. Shivering, she wondered what the rope was connected to. What if she jumped and missed? *Okay, God. This is really going to be a leap of faith.*

She leapt for the rope, her fingers closing around it. "*Thank you, God,*" she whispered.

But the sudden weight on the rope dislodged it, and she was falling again. She hung on for dear life. The rope burned her hands until at last it came to an abrupt halt.

Fear gripped her and the pounding of her heart drowned out all thought. After a long moment, she caught her breath. *Okay, Brittany. You can do this.* She looked up into the sunlight at the shaft's opening, and then down into the darkness. She could hang here and pray for someone to rescue her. Or she could trust that God was beside her, guiding her up the rope.

God is my strength. I can do this

Her decision was made. Inch by inch, Brittany raised herself up the rope, keeping her eyes on the sunlight above. Her arms began to ache. The wound in her shoulder burned like acid. Brittany stopped and glanced down. In that moment of weakness, her hands loosened their grip and she slid several feet back down the rope.

Okay, God, I get it. I have to keep my eyes on you.

Looking up, she began the exhausting climb once more. Like a mantra, she kept repeating, "*Eyes on Jesus.*"

It seemed like an eternity, but at last, Brittany pulled herself onto solid ground. Her eyes immediately went to the spot she had last seen Nick. He lay motionless. Her heart screamed.

A soothing hand stroked his forehead. *Your job here is not done.* The voice was gentle, but strong.

Nick opened his eyes. Frank was standing a few paces away over a motionless Vincent. Thank God, the cavalry had arrived. Was it too late? He twisted his body in the direction of the mineshaft.

He could see Brittany just crawling out of the pit. His heart leapt with joy. She was still alive. Love filled him. He tried to push himself up, but his right arm wouldn't move. He glanced down and noticed a pool of blood near his torso.

Brittany stumbled toward him, half crawling her way over. "Please God, don't let him be dead," he heard her repeat until she knelt by his side.

Nick reached for her. "You're alive."

Brittany bent over him, tenderly stroking his face.

He tried to rise. "Help me up."

She wiped blood from his mouth. "You're bleeding. You need to stay down," she said.

He pushed himself up using his left arm, "I'm okay."

She helped him to his knees. His right leg refused to hold him though, so he started to fall. Brittany caught him.

Putting his left arm around her, he pulled her close to his chest. "I love you," he whispered, lowering his mouth to hers. The sweet surrender of her lips said more than words ever could.

"Oh, how sweet," Frank hissed. "The lovebirds are having their final goodbye kiss."

Nick broke away and looked up. Frank stood a few feet away, his gun drawn and pointed at them. He kept his voice calm, trying to mask the panic. "Frank, what are you doing? Put the gun down."

"Sorry. I can't do that."

Brittany moved closer to Nick.

"What's going on? Why are you doing this?" he asked.

"If I'd known the little princess was going to kill Vincent, I wouldn't have had to shoot you in the back."

"You shot me?" Nick sputtered in surprise. "Why?"

"It was either shoot you or..." he spit toward Vincent's body, "...he was going after my daughter." Frank paced, waving the gun and ranting wildly. "Now I have to kill you both." He tucked his gun in his jacket and bent over Vincent's body. "Yes, that's the thing. I'll use Vincent's gun. That way everyone will think he's the killer."

A hiccupping sob escaped Brittany. Nick pulled her into his side. She winced in pain. "Frank, you don't have to do this," Nick said.

Frank glared at him. "Oh, yes I do." He waved the gun at them. "If you live, my life is destroyed."

Brittany slumped against Nick.

"Brittany, look at me," Nick said. "*Look at me.*" She slowly focused her eyes on his. "I need you to slowly get behind me." He lowered his mouth to her ear, whispering, "I have a gun strapped to my right leg. Get it and put it in my left hand." He kissed her. "Don't worry, angel. Jesus is right here with us."

Brittany wrapped her arms around his neck, hugging him tightly.

"Get behind me now," he repeated.

Frank laughed as Brittany crawled behind him. "You think that will save her? Sorry, bud. She's still going to die." He shook his head in apparent disgust. "But of course, Nicholas McFadden has to be the hero, even in death."

Nick felt the cold steel as Brittany put the gun in his hand.

Again, Frank pointed his weapon and said, "Sorry, man. I wish there was another way." Frank's finger tightened on the trigger.

Now! Nick pulled out his gun and fired. He hit Frank dead center. Frank put his hand to his chest. A look of shock crossed his face. He hit the ground with a thud.

Nick squeezed Brittany's hand. "It's over, angel. You're safe."

A rushing darkness swirled in his brain, and then his body collapsed.

"Nick!" Brittany screamed. After all they'd been through, he couldn't die.

She hugged his motionless body to her. Suddenly, the woods were bursting with men. Someone touched her shoulder, trying to separate her from Nick. She turned, kicking and screaming.

"Brittany, it's okay." Carl's voice broke through her panic.

"Uncle Carl!" He dragged her to her feet and she tried to twist from his grasp. "Let me go. Nick needs me."

Carl held tight. "Right now, he needs the paramedics."

A blue-uniformed EMT knelt by Nick's body.

"Is he... dead?" she asked, her heart hammering.

"No, but he's lost a lot of blood," the paramedic said, continuing to work over Nick.

She bowed her head and prayed like she had never prayed before.

Carl interrupted. "You need a paramedic, too. You're covered in blood." He stepped back aghast, and lightly touched her face. "What did Vincent do to you?"

"I'm fine," she said. "Help Nick."

"Don't you think he would want you to get help?"

"I'm not hurt," she protested, her gaze focused on Nick.

Carl picked up her hands and she stared at them, surprised at the blood and raw skin. Carl ran his fingers down her left arm and she saw that it was bleeding as well. The ground tilted and a whistling sounded in her ears.

She felt Carl scoop her up in his arms and carry her to an ambulance. Medics washed and bandaged the wound on her arm before working on her hands. All the while she felt numb, her gaze locked outside on the ground where Nick lay.

Voices swirled around her and she barely picked out a few words. "...Stitches... stab wounds... concussion... shock."

Carl's face was suddenly inches from her own. "They need to get you to the hospital immediately."

"Not without Nick," she pleaded.

"Brittany."

She glared back. "No."

Carl shook his head and let her be. Finally, paramedics lifted Nick from the ground on a stretcher. Brittany tried to run to him, but her legs wouldn't cooperate. She limped unsteadily toward them. They'd cut off his shirt and a bulletproof vest lay on top of his legs.

"He had on a vest?" She turned to Carl. "Why didn't it stop the bullet?"

Carl picked up the jacket and his jaw tightened. Anger flashed in his eyes. He put his finger through the hole. "Kevlar can't stop hollow-point bullets. Cop-killer bullets."

Grief like she'd never known gripped her heart. She held on to Nick's hand. "Please, don't let him die. Please, don't let him die. God, please, I beg you." Uncontrollable sobs racked her body.

The Lord will keep you from all harm. He'll watch over your life. Nick's, too.

"Thank you, Jesus." She wiped her tears and kissed the top of his head. "I love you."

The paramedics lifted him in and she started to climb in the ambulance with him.

Carl stopped her. "I'm sorry, but you can't go with him."

Her voice broke, "Why not?"

"You need to be looked at yourself. Those EMTs won't be able to give Nick their full attention if they're looking after you." Carl put his arm around her and held her back. "You'll see him at the hospital."

Brittany's heart felt the slam of the ambulance door. They might have shut her out, but her heart was inside with Nick.

Chapter 24

Brittany barely noticed the doctor stitching her up. All her thoughts were on Nick in the operating room. If only she could see his face or hear her name on his lips one more time. *Please God, let me hear him say 'I love you' one more time. Please, don't let him die.*

The nurse opened the curtain of her examining room and Brittany saw Carl keeping guard. She followed him to the waiting room where Nick's family had gathered. A woman rose and walked toward her. Brittany knew at once she was Nick's mother. The tears she'd held back flowed freely. His mother wrapped her arms around her and they sobbed together.

Two strong arms engulfed them and she recognized Mike's voice as he prayed, "Dear Heavenly Father, we lift these two women up to You. You know their grief. Please, I ask You to give them comfort. We pray for Nick and claim this verse for him, *I will not die but live, and will proclaim what the Lord has done.* We know he's in Your hands. He's been asking many questions about You. I pray You show him Your way. Your will be done. Amen."

Mike kissed them on the top of their heads and Brittany wiped her eyes.

"I came as soon as your grandmother called me," he said.

"I'm so glad you are here."

Nick's mother, who asked Brittany to call her Lucy, introduced her to Nick's brother and his family. Surprisingly, everyone already knew Mike. It took her a moment to remember he'd spent Thanksgiving with them.

They sat around talking, each telling a story about Nick. Mike held her hand, offering comfort, while Carl stood guard by the door. An hour later, her grandparents arrived. Brittany rushed to them, her tears starting again.

"Would you like to go to the chapel?" Lillian asked.

"No. I don't want to miss the doctor when he comes." She squeezed her grandmother's hand. "Besides, '*Where two or three are gathered together unto My name, there am I in their midst.*' This is our chapel for now."

Mike, along with Nick's brother, made a coffee run for everyone. When they returned, Mike cocked his head where Carl still stood. "What's with the two guys at the door?"

Carl gave him a look that said, *Quiet.* Then, he whispered, "*Guards.*"

Brittany stared out the window. The view of the setting sun gave her soul a calmness she hadn't felt all day.

At the sound of the door opening, she spun away from the window. A doctor entered, smiling. "He's a very lucky man. A previous bullet wound saved his life. Incredible, but that's what happened." Removing his green surgical hat, the doctor ran a hand through his thick white hair. "Lucky, lucky guy. The bullet entered his back at the exact spot where he'd previously been injured. The scar tissue changed the path of the bullet ever so slightly. Another inch and there would have been nothing I could've done. As it is, the bullet lodged in his spine, causing paralysis on his right side." He smiled reassuringly. "I believe that's temporary. We'll know more in the next twenty-four hours."

"Can we see him?" Lucy asked.

"He's still in recovery. We'll move him to ICU in about an hour. One of you can visit him then, but only for a few minutes."

Brittany noticed Carl following the doctor as he exited the room, so she left the group and slipped into the hallway. As she walked up behind them, Brittany heard Carl say, "He needs to be put into a private room as quickly as possible." Carl touched the doctor's arm. "His life and my niece's are still in danger. A mob family, the Capris, will be seeking revenge for the death of their son."

"We're still in danger?" Brittany blurted. She grabbed her chest, fear bubbling up. A hiccupping sob escaped her. "It's not over?" Carl's face started to blur and the hall grew dim. Her legs collapsed underneath her. Strong arms caught her, and then she was vaguely aware of being put on a stretcher.

When she came to, the doctor was standing beside the bed. Her grandparents and Carl were behind him.

She started to move her arm, but it was strapped to an IV board. She stared at the needle, flashing back to the syringe in Vincent's hand. Brittany gripped the bed railing with her other hand. She was safe. He could never hurt her again. He was dead. She had killed him. *She killed him.*

Beads of sweat dotted her forehead. She started to shake uncontrollably. Tears streamed down her face. She reached toward her grandmother. "I killed him."

Lillian rushed to her. Sitting on the bed, she hugged Brittany tightly and said, "You had no choice."

James quickly moved to their side. He rubbed Brittany's hair. "You did what you had to do. All that matters is that you're safe and Nick is alive."

Her grandfather's words penetrated the darkness swirling around her. She took a deep breath, pulled back from her grandmother, and wiped her tears. "I'm sorry." She hiccupped a laugh. "I'm being such a baby."

Carl patted her leg. "After all you have been through, I would have been surprised if you didn't break down."

The doctor stepped up to the bed. "Would you like something for the anxiety?"

"No." Brittany shook her head. "I'm okay," she smiled. Nick would need her and she had to have a clear head. She took a deep breath. Vincent Capri was dead. He would never hurt anyone again.

The doctor handed Brittany's chart to the nurse, then smiled. "I want you to lie here and rest. When Nick is ready for a visitor, I will send Carrie back to remove the IV."

When the curtain closed behind them, she squared her shoulders and looked at Carl. "So, we really are still in danger?"

"Unfortunately, yes." He nodded at the curtain. "I have two men, plus myself here for you, and two on Nick. No one will get to you. I promise."

She held her grandmother's hand. "What about Carissa?"

Carl shook his head. "She's in a drug rehab center that has tight security."

"Do you think she's going to be okay?"

"Yes, thank goodness," Lillian scowled, "no thanks to her mother." She rung her hands together. "If I never see that woman again, it will be too soon. Thank goodness Jim has finally seen her true colors and left her."

Brittany squeezed her grandmother's hand. "I know it's going to be difficult, but when I get home, the first thing I'm going to do is mend this rift between Carissa and me. If nothing else, this whole mess has taught me how fragile life can be. It's too short to waste it fighting with anyone."

Lillian and James smiled.

An hour later, Carrie came to remove her IV and announced, "We're about to take Nick to his room. The doctor said you and his mother may escort him." Carrie glanced at Carl who stood by Brittany's bedside. "They told me there would be a bodyguard. You may come, too. But no one else."

"Thank you, God," Brittany whispered as she and Lucy entered Nick's room. She rushed toward his bed, but stopped abruptly. Nick was propped up on his left side. A tube ran down his throat and a line of oxygen was attached to his nose. His right arm was strapped to a board with an IV attached near his wrist. Her valiant knight lay broken and her own heart felt broken as well.

Lucy put an arm around her. "He'll be all right."

Carrie gave them an encouraging smile. "It's okay. You can come closer."

Brittany took the few steps to his side. Her heart was breaking. His pain was her pain. "Nick." Her voice was mixed with love and agony. Suddenly, she felt weak and grabbed the bed railing. *Please don't let me faint again. I need to be with him. I need to be strong for him.*

"We'll be removing the tube from his throat before we move him. The doctor will be in shortly to do that." Carrie checked Nick's blood pressure. "You're good for him. His pressure's come down quite a bit since you came in."

They sat quietly beside Nick's bed. Brittany held his hand while Lucy held hers. Carl remained at the door. Within a few minutes, the doctor arrived and Brittany and Lucy stood in the corner, huddled together. Nick gasped for air when they pulled the tube out. Within seconds, he was trying to talk.

"Brittany," he whispered. He tried to reach for her hand, but couldn't move his arm.

She hurried to his side.

Nick tried to smile. "I love you." He started to cough.

"Shhh. No more talking. They're taking you to your room and we'll be right here beside you the whole time." She leaned down and kissed his forehead.

The nurse talked to them as the orderly wheeled Nick out of recovery. "Normally, we'd be taking you to ICU, but I understand you're a VIP, so you get a private room." She patted Nick's leg. "Don't worry. You'll have the same round the clock care."

Nick watched the door as the nurse and orderly transferred him into his bed. On their way out of the room, they informed the others it was okay to come in.

When Brittany entered, his heart fluttered. Never again would he lose her.

Carl pulled up two chairs, one for Brittany and one for his mom, then he stood at the foot of the bed. "You look great, by the way."

"Not by the look on their faces," Nick joked. He frowned at Brittany's bruises and noticed for the first time the bandages on her hands and arm. "What happened?"

"That Glock of yours has a powerful kick. I fell down a mineshaft." She held up her hands. "Rope burns."

"And the arm?"

"Cut on a jagged board."

"Aww, Brittany. I'm sorry."

Carl put his hand on Brittany's shoulder and nodded to Nick. "She saved your life."

"I thought you didn't know how to shoot?" Nick said to Brittany.

"I said I didn't like guns. I never said I didn't know how to use one. Grandfather insisted we all learn."

Carrie returned and put a shot of something in the IV. Nick's lids grew heavy and he clasped Brittany's hand. "I love you," he whispered before surrendering to the pleasant lethargy spreading through his body.

Sometime during the night, he awoke. In the dim lighting, he saw Brittany curled up in the recliner. Tiny sobs wracked her small body and beads of sweat formed on her forehead. "Brittany," he whispered.

"Nick!" She jumped up and stumbled to his bed. "Do you need the nurse?"

"No, angel. You were having a nightmare."

"I'm sorry I woke you." She knelt down beside the bed so he could see her face without trying to move.

"You didn't." He tried to move his hand, but it wouldn't move. He sighed in frustration. "Can you do me a favor?"

"Anything."

"Will you pull your chair over here as close as you can and hold my hand?"

She hurried to do just that.

He smiled as she settled in her chair and took his hand in hers. "Thanks." He grinned. "This isn't how I pictured us spending the night together."

She giggled. "Me either, but at least it's God-approved."

"G'night, angel." He watched Brittany close her eyes and prayed that holding his hand would keep her from having more nightmares.

On the third day, there was a commotion at the door. Brittany went to investigate. One of the guards yelled to her, "Get back in the room."

Brittany started to shut the door when she realized the man they held against the wall at gunpoint was Vito Capri. "Let him go," she said, stepping into the hallway.

The first guard shook his head. "Do you realize who this is?"

"Yes. Vito's a friend. Please, let him go."

They frisked Vito before releasing him. Neither man holstered their weapons though.

She linked her arm in his. "Vito, why are you here?"

"I need to talk to you and Nick."

She nodded and held the door open for him to enter. Nick instinctively reached for his gun that wasn't there. He glanced at the two guards who had followed them in.

"Brittany?" He swung his legs over the side of the bed, ready to pounce on Vito if necessary.

"He's okay," she affirmed.

Vito handed Brittany her purse. "I believe this is yours."

She nodded, grimacing at the reminder of being held captive by Vincent.

Vito laid a box on the foot of Nick's bed, just as Carl burst through the door, gun in hand. "Who let him in here?" He flew across the room toward Brittany and pulled her behind him. To one of the guards he yelled, "Get her out of here."

"No." Brittany put her hands on her hips. "Put the guns away," she said firmly. "Vito is a friend."

"Have you forgotten the Capris want you dead?" Carl shouted.

"And have you forgotten if it wasn't for Vito, Vincent would have succeeded in drugging me?" She went to Vito and hugged him before sitting beside Nick on the bed. "He's not going to harm us." She glanced at Vito. "Are you?"

"No. I came to give you something and let you both know you have nothing to fear from my family."

Nick and Carl looked doubtful.

"You were right," Vito said, looking at Brittany. "Vincent did kill my sister. Well, I guess he paid someone to do it." He picked up the box and handed it to Carl. "Inside there are videos of Vincent killing my father and many others, including young girls." He choked up, selected one of the videos, and broke it in half. "What he did to Maria is unspeakable. My family will not be seeking revenge for his death. You have my assurance on that."

Carl opened the box and looked up in surprise. "There must be thirty or more discs in here."

Vito nodded. "A lot of cases will be solved." He glanced at Brittany. "You actually did the family a huge favor by killing him. No one knew he was that evil." He wiped a tear from his eye. "He killed my father with my mother lying in bed beside him." He glared at the box. "Narcissistic fool that he was, Vincent videotaped everything. He even recorded where he disposed of the bodies."

Brittany closed her eyes. There was no doubt she would have been the next video. A tremor ran through her body. Nick pulled her closer to him, giving her a sideways hug.

Vito took a deep breath. "I have a feeling God was looking after you both for a long time."

"Why do you say that?" Brittany asked.

"Do you remember the date of the night you two first met?" Vito asked, looking at Nick.

Nick quickly answered, "June sixteenth."

Brittany turned to him, astonished. "You remember the date?"

"Of course, don't you?"

She nodded, unable to keep the grin off her face.

Vito pointed toward the box. "Inside is a ledger with the name and kill dates of every murder. One of the first entries was June sixteenth. He raped and killed a young woman that night." He looked at Brittany apologetically. "If I had known what he was capable of, I never would have tried to fix you up with my brother." He glanced from Brittany to Nick. "And if you two hadn't met that night," his voice broke, "your name might have been in that book, too."

She threw her hands over her mouth. Nick wrapped both arms around her, holding her tight.

Vito ran a hand through his hair. "Once, a long time ago, we were all friends. I hope that someday soon we can be friends again."

"Of course," Brittany said without hesitating. Nick said nothing.

"Something else I wanted to tell you," Vito continued. "I'm leaving the family business."

"Great." Brittany smiled at him. "So, what are you going to do?"

"I'm going to Colorado to join Rev Rousey's prison ministry. I want to learn from the best." He chuckled at the shocked look on Nick's face. "I'm sure that'll be the same look I get from the inmates."

Brittany clapped her hands. "That's wonderful."

"Thanks. Can you think of anyone better suited to witness to criminals than someone like me?"

She took his hand. "Let's pray together."

The three of them joined hands and prayed before Vito turned to leave. Brittany stood and went to him. Laying her hand on his arm, she said, "I know Vincent wasn't a nice person, but he was still your brother. You must be grieving. I'm really sorry. I didn't mean to kill him."

"I know." Vito stared into her eyes. "And I know taking a life is a hard thing to live with, but you not only saved Nick and yourself, but the lives of who knows how many others." He sighed. "If we'd known what he was capable of, we'd have taken care of him ourselves."

At the door, he turned back at them and smiled. "Once I learn how to witness to people, the first person I'm going to save is Carissa."

Brittany gasped in surprise. "Really?"

"I can't help but wonder if I hadn't gotten her high ten years ago, maybe her life would be different now."

Brittany shook her head. "What? I never saw Carissa smoke marijuana back then."

"You were so wrapped up in Nick, you didn't see anything else." Vito grinned.

She glanced over her shoulder at Nick. "Imagine that."

"That's a regret I've had for years," Vito said. "Maybe God will allow me to correct it."

Nurse Katina opened the door. Her mouth dropped at the sight of two guards with their guns drawn. She started to back out of the room.

"It's okay. I'm leaving," Vito said, waving as he exited the room.

Katina stood with her hand on the door handle, looking ready to run.

Nick motioned for her to come in.

Katina smiled at Nick. "Well, you look a lot better. You're even sitting up on your own."

For the first time, Brittany realized that Nick had moved both his leg and arm. She wrapped him in a hug.

"Guess panic overrides everything else." He laughed. "When I saw Vito walk in, my body must have decided it was time for action."

Katina paged the doctor before taking his vitals. She looked at Brittany. "I don't know how you do it..."

"Do what?" she asked.

"It must be hard knowing that any day a bullet might take his life." She started counting the bullet holes in Nick's back. "One, two, three..."

Brittany grabbed the foot of the bed as the nurse continued to count. "Seven times?"

"Eight, counting this one," Nick answered. "Doc said it went in the same hole as one of the earlier ones."

Brittany felt her face go pale.

Nick grabbed for her hand. "If you count by incidents, it was only twice though, and they all involved Vincent."

"Why would someone shoot you in the back?" the nurse asked.

Carl chuckled. "Because you don't draw a gun on Nicholas McFadden and live to tell about it."

Brittany felt sick to her stomach. Nick had been shot eight times. *Eight times!*

She squeezed his leg. "I need some air," she said, and hurried out the door.

Chapter 25

Brittany rushed to the elevator and pushed the button for the lobby. Her heart was pounding so loud she couldn't hear herself think. When the elevator doors opened, she hurried outside. The cold winter air hit her in the face and she shivered.

She rubbed her forehead. How many other enemies out there were still gunning for Nick? Was this what her life would be like loving a cop? Never knowing when the next bullet would shatter their love for good? Her heart skipped a beat. Could she handle waking up each day, kissing him goodbye, and knowing that it could be the last time?

She looked at the mountains. Their white caps painted a beautiful picture against the sky. She smiled. God was absolutely the best artist. *God, can I do this?*

She needed to pray. She went back inside and found the chapel.

The room was empty and she walked down to the second row of pews. A view of the mountains was framed by a round window. Beneath it was a beautiful stained glass window of Jesus. She felt a peace calming her soul. She closed her eyes to pray. Instead of praying, her mind started to drift.

She was floating above water, watching someone fall backwards off the pier. Her heart raced as she recognized her own face. Seconds later, she watched Nick dive in after her. Vincent stood and started spraying the water with bullets. She could see herself floating downward farther and farther away from Nick. Someone had her and put her into Nick's hands. She saw the first bullet hit Nick's shoulder and it went straight through him, into her shoulder. The water turned red. Vincent could no longer see what he was shooting at, but he kept shooting until the gun was empty. Another bullet hit Nick, this one grazing his neck and hers. They were moving away from the bullets, but Nick still got hit again and again. She couldn't see who was in the water with them, but she could feel strong arms holding both her and Nick, moving them under the pier to safety. Nick held onto her and the person behind her held them both. *Who are you?* she started to ask, but then she noticed his hands. Nail-scarred hands. *Jesus.*

She opened her eyes.

Was it real? Had Jesus saved them?

I am with you always. The words resounded deep in her soul. She jumped up and hurried down to the altar. Down on her knees, she prayed. "I'm so sorry God. I forgot to lean on You in my most trying time of all. I allowed my fears to control my thoughts." Tears ran down her face. "Was it real? Were You there? Did You place me into Nick's hands?" She arose, not needing to hear an answer. In her heart, she knew the vision had been real. Jesus had saved them even before either of them knew Him. But He knew them.

Her own words echoed in her mind. Life was too short to waste a moment of it. She rushed back to Nick's room. Right into organized chaos. Nick smiled at her. "Just in time. They're taking me to a real room. One with a view."

She beamed at his enthusiasm.

"Hey, look at this. I can feel my leg again." He took a step toward her and stumbled. She rushed to help him, but the nurse got there first.

"Not so fast," Brittany cautioned, holding his arm.

He pulled her to him. "That means I'm one step closer to being out of here."

She reached up and touched her lips to his. "I love you."

"Hate to break this up," the nurse said, "But your ride is here." She pointed to the wheelchair.

Brittany walked beside him and held his hand the whole way. Her heart was bursting with joy. They were one step closer to their future.

It seemed like forever before the nurses finally left. Lucy and Carl both said their goodbyes, leaving Brittany and Nick alone together.

Nick gazed after them thoughtfully. "Is it just my imagination, or do my mom and your uncle Carl seem to be getting awful chummy?"

She giggled. "I've imagined the same thing. We'll have to keep an eye on those two."

Nick sat on his bed and she sat beside him. "I need to apologize for running out earlier like I did."

"There's no need."

"Yes, there is." She touched his face. "You see, I was afraid." She gently laid her hand on his back. "Afraid of losing you to another bullet." She glanced down. "Your job is so dangerous."

He nodded and squeezed her hand. "Is this where you tell me you're leaving me?"

"No." Brittany tenderly kissed his cheek. "Life without you would be a hundred times worse than the fear I'll have to face every day."

He grinned. "Glad to hear that." He lightly kissed her lips. "What happened to change your mind?"

"I was in the chapel praying and I drifted into a dream." She laid her head on his shoulder. "We were in the water and Vincent was shooting at us, but we weren't alone."

"Jesus was there too, right?"

"How did you know?"

"Because I had the same dream," he replied.

"When? Last night?" Brittany asked, bewildered.

"No. A month ago. That's when I knew Jesus was real."

Tears rolled down her face. "He placed me in your arms. Who am I to take me out of them?"

He held her face between his hands. "I love you, Brittany. I have from the first moment I saw you."

"I love you, too."

When their lips joined, it was a sweet surrender. Nothing could stop a love that Jesus had blessed.

Nick pulled away first, wiping the tears from his own eyes. Grinning, he rose and went to the closet, then pulled something out of his pants pocket. With his hand behind his back, he said, "This isn't how I planned on doing this, but things keep getting in our way." He came to her and took her hand before sitting in the chair beside the bed. "I can't get down on one knee, so this will have to do." He moved his hand from behind his back and pulled out a small velvet box. He opened it. "Will you marry me?"

She gasped in surprise. The ring was a simple solitaire diamond wrapped with tiny diamonds joining the two bands. She threw her arms around his neck. "Yes."

He slipped the ring on her finger.

She held her hand out. "It's beautiful." She looked up at him, "How long has this been in your pocket?"

"Since I got back from Mexico. I was planning on asking you New Year's Day."

"And I had to go—"

"No regrets." He kissed her hand. "Everything worked out the way it was supposed to. All in God's time." He lifted her face so he could see into her eyes. "One other thing. Well, two really. First, we're not having a long engagement. I'd like to get married on June 16. Is that okay with you?" She nodded. "The second thing is, we're honeymooning in Cancun."

"But—"

"No buts. What do you get the woman who has everything money can buy? The only thing I can think of is to clear her name. And that's what we're going to do."

She threw her arms around his neck and he pulled her down onto his lap. They both moaned in pain.

"Aren't we a perfect pair?" Nick grinned. "Bullet hole, stitches, and bruises."

"And loved." Brittany snuggled into his chest. Her heart filled with such joy, she thought it would burst. Joining her lips with his, she whispered, "I love you, Nicholas McFadden."

"I love you back," he said. "Forever and always."

The End

Spiritual hero

Reverend James Rousey

I have been blessed to have many spiritual heroes in my life, people who have impacted my life so profoundly that years after they are gone I can still feel the love of Jesus they carried with them. These are individuals that on first meeting, you know they have something special—people who actually glow with the love of God. I would like to honor them in my writing. In each book, I will have a character named after one of my spiritual heroes. Though they might play a small part in my book, they played a major role in my life.

The first spiritual hero is Reverend James Rousey. Rev Rousey, and his beautiful wife Ruth Ann came into my life when I was sure Jesus did not love me. Someone I worked with told them I was a single mother, struggling to get by. I did not go to their church. For that matter, I was so mad at God, that I had stopped going to church altogether. Nor did they know me personally, and yet they drove miles out of their way to come and help me. I will never forget him hugging me and saying, "Jesus loves you, and so do we." Thirty plus years later, I can still remember that moment as if it were yesterday.

The day Jesus sent a loving couple to remind me, yes, He did love me.

Rev Rousey was a big teddy bear of a man. He always had a smile. When he wrapped you in his arms for a hug, you could feel the love of Jesus radiating from him. When he preached, you listened, for his words were full of truth and love. Rev Rousey exchanged his church ministry for a prison one. So when in my book I needed a prison minster to save my character, Rev Jim Rousey came to mind.

In this world there are few like Reverend Jim Rousey. The spirit of God was definitely upon him, and it was his pleasure to share it. What a wonderful blessing it was to have known him.

Other Books by this Author

"...page after page of inspiring words and photographs showing us how God uses nature to speak to us. A genuine treat for the eyes!"

~Loree Lough, best-selling author of 115 award-winning books

"The photographs and inspiring words of Vickie Fisher's HELLO GOD, ARE YOU THERE? filled my heart with joy and reminded me to look for the blessing of each day."

~Susan Meier, bestselling Harlequin author of A Father for Her Triplets

About the Author

Vickie Fisher lives on nineteen tranquil acres in Westminster, Maryland. She works for Amtrak as a chief entitlement clerk. In her spare time, she enjoys spending time with her children, grandchildren, family, and friends, who she believes are God's greatest gifts. When she isn't writing she is taking photographs of nature. Find more about Vickie at vickiefisher.com.